LILAC MILLS

Sunrise
on the
Coast

First published in the the United Kingdom in 2020 by Canelo

This edition published in the United Kingdom in 2021 by

Canelo
31 Helen Road
Oxford OX2 0DF
United Kingdom

A CIP catalogue record for this book is available from the British Library.

Print ISBN 978 1 80032 225 7
Ebook ISBN 978 1 80032 077 2

This book is a work of fiction. Names, characters, businesses, organizations, places and events are either the product of the author's imagination or are used fictitiously. Any resemblance to actual persons, living or dead, events or locales is entirely coincidental.

Look for more great books at www.canelo.co

Printed and bound in Great Britain by Clays Ltd, Elcograf S.p.A.

Chapter 1

Sophie Lakeland sat on the closed lid of her downstairs loo and contemplated her future. As far as she could see, she didn't have one; yet at the same time, the possibilities were endless. The day stretched out before her, empty and directionless, waiting to be filled with...? She had absolutely no idea what. Which was the reason she was cleaning the downstairs loo for the third time that week when it was only Thursday, and no one had actually used it. Not even her.

She had been giving the washbasin a quick wipe when a wave of desolation and despair had swept over her, followed by a grief so intense it stole her breath and she'd been forced to sit down.

It hadn't mattered that she'd had years to prepare for her mother's demise, weeks and days to face the inevitable, then hours spent holding the increasingly frail hand and waiting for the last hitched breath; the end, when it finally arrived, had still been a terrible shock. Nothing could prepare you for the finality of it, and she wasn't sure whether she'd ever get over it, or if she even wanted to. Her grief was something to cling onto, to make her feel some kind of emotion, however negative. Because without it, all that was left was a terrifying numbness and an awful sense of emptiness.

Oh, dear God, what was she supposed to do now? How was she meant to fill her days with no one to cook for, no one to count out the numerous tablets for, no one to wash, dress, wait on, fuss over, talk to, worry about, cry over…?

The house was as silent as the grave that she wished her mother had been buried in. But, as her mum had wanted to be cremated, Sophie didn't even have the comfort of a graveyard to visit. No headstone, no leafy tree-lined parkland, no carefully chosen flowers. Nowhere to serve as a focus for her grief. Just a scattering of ashes in the impersonal Garden of Remembrance at the crematorium.

Sophie didn't even have an urn.

Her mum had been quite insistent on that front, declaring it morbid. 'I want you to move on, to have a life,' she'd told her. 'How can you do that when you're carting me around with you? And I know you, Sophie – that's exactly what you'll do with my ashes. No, I want them to be scattered as soon as you're given them. No procrastinating, no excuses. If you don't, I'll come back to haunt you.'

Right now, Sophie could think of nothing better than being haunted by her mother. How she longed to hear her voice again, to see her mum's smile despite the awful pain she had been in, and to wrap her arms around those thin shoulders and breathe in the familiar perfume she insisted on being sprayed with every day, despite the fact that the smells of disinfectant and terminal illness were also mixed in with the delicate floral scent towards the end.

Sophie had never felt so alone in her life.

'Stop it,' she muttered, straightening up from her slump and wiping her eyes. They had seemed to leak constantly from the moment her mum passed away, as though up until that point her grief had been contained behind a wall of necessity and chores, which had since been breached by the finality of her mum's death.

Breaking down and giving in to the tidal wave of sorrow was almost an hourly occurrence now, and she was getting mightily fed up with herself and her misery.

Bloody hell, death was an awful business. The only comfort she could glean from it was the knowledge that her mother was finally out of pain and at peace.

The pain belonged to Sophie now – not physical, but emotional. She felt as though her heart had been torn out of her chest and thrown on the floor to shrivel and wither now that there was no one left who loved her. And, in turn, she herself was without anyone else to love or to care for. She'd been doing the latter for such a long time, she now had no idea what else she was supposed to do.

With a deep sigh she clambered to her feet, but before she'd managed to drag herself into the sitting room, the doorbell rang.

'Aunty Anne! Come in.' Sophie stepped back to let the older woman into the hall, giving her a brief hug and a kiss on the cheek as she did so.

Anne patted her on the arm and Sophie saw tears welling up in her eyes. 'How are you bearing up, dear?' she asked, and Sophie's own eyes began to prickle.

'Oh, you know. How about you?' she replied.

'Don't worry about me – losing a sister is bad enough, but losing a mother is a hundred times worse.' Anne should know – she'd lost her own mother, Sophie's gran, a few years back.

Sophie put the kettle on and when the tea was poured she led her aunt into the living room, her eyes welling up again as she glanced around the room.

Memories of her mum were everywhere. For her own sanity she really should remove them, or put them out of sight if she couldn't bear to get rid of them yet. But get rid of them she must.

'Have you decided what you're going to do?' her aunt asked, taking a slurp of tea.

Sophie shrugged, not trusting herself to speak.

'The offer still stands,' her aunt said gently.

'I know, and I appreciate it, I really do; but you've only got a tiny flat, and there's only the one bedroom. Besides' – and here was the major stumbling block – 'you live in a retirement complex. I'm pretty certain that one of the rules is that they don't have anyone under the age of sixty living there.'

Anne scowled. 'They can bend the rules this once. And I'm sure it won't be for long – just until you sort yourself out. I can't believe the council is simply going to turn you out. Surely you can do something? Can you start a petition?'

Sophie let out a slow breath. 'You know it won't do any good.'

'They should be ashamed of themselves. You've lived here nearly all your life, and you've spent the last few years nursing your mum. They need to think how much it would have cost them if she'd been in a nursing home. You've saved that bloody council a fortune, and this is how they repay you!'

It was true. Sooner or later she'd have to move out of this house which she'd lived in for most of her life.

4

The brief foray she'd made into living in her own place hadn't lasted long. The cancer diagnosis had seen to that. She'd sold up, made a tiny profit which was still sitting untouched in her bank account, and had moved back into the family home for the duration.

The problem she now faced was that her mother's home was rented, and Sophie's name wasn't on the tenancy agreement. It belonged to the council and they wanted it back. The fact that it was a three-bedroom property meant it was regarded as being too large for one person to occupy, especially when there was a shortage of council housing. She was under no illusion that she would be asked to vacate it at some point in the not too distant future.

'Denise has offered to have you go and live with them for a couple of weeks,' Anne reminded her.

'That's not going to happen,' Sophie replied firmly. Denise was Anne's daughter and Sophie's cousin. At thirty-eight she was a few years older than Sophie and she'd just been surprised by a definitely unplanned pregnancy. Her twins were due any day now, and there was no way Denise and her husband would cope with having two new babies in the house, along with the two teenagers they already had, plus Sophie. It was very generous and thoughtful of them, but it was totally unrealistic.

She needed to sort out her own place to live, and pretty darned sharpish, but whenever she thought about it a feeling of intense lassitude swept over her. There was so much she should be doing, so many things to organise and arrange, and she didn't seem to have the willpower or the energy to do any of them.

She was worn out, both physically and emotionally.

'You look worn out,' Anne said, echoing her thoughts.

'I am, but there's so much to do, I don't know where to start.'

'What you could do with is a break from everything. Why don't you have a little holiday before you get stuck in?' Anne finished her tea and put the mug on the coffee table. 'I bet you haven't had a proper break since before your mum was diagnosed.'

Sophie thought it was probably considerably longer than that. The last time she'd been away was at least eight years ago, a last-minute splurge with her friends before one of them got married. Not a hen party as such, more like a final fling as a single woman. The fact that her friend had been living with her fiancé for ages didn't seem to matter.

They'd gone to Spain; Ibiza to be exact, and they'd done all the things that a group of women on holiday normally did – stayed up until the dawn brushed the sky, slept until the afternoon when they'd flopped on loungers on the beach to sleep some more, eaten too much, drunk too much, and danced until their feet were sore. It had been so much fun, and she'd been younger and carefree and she'd thought she still had the world at her feet.

Now look at her…

These days, staying up most of the night didn't involve clubs and parties – it had been to nurse her mother. Her feet had still ached, not from dancing but from lifting, fetching and carrying. And any falling asleep she'd done hadn't been on a sun lounger, but in the armchair in the living room where her mother's hospital bed had resided for the last few months. She'd lost touch with her friends, had given up her job, and had gradually faded from the world, as caring for and nursing her beloved mum had taken over her life.

Maybe Aunty Anne was right. Sophie knew she had to make changes, and extremely significant ones, but she simply felt she wasn't ready. And she wondered if she ever would be while she lived in the house that had been at the centre of her very existence for such a long time. Maybe she did need to get away for a while, to give herself the distance, space and time firstly to grieve, and then to decide what she intended to do next. The decisions were big ones, starting with where she was going to live and what job she could possibly do, having been out of work for years. She used to work in admin, but she suspected most employers would take one look at the huge employment gap in her CV and throw her application form in the bin. The only other thing she had experience of was caring for an invalid, but even then employers wanted a Level 2 qualification in this, that or the other before they'd even consider an applicant.

Sophie had nothing that an employer would want, except for a handful of GCSEs and a couple of A levels.

At least she had a small amount of savings, enough for a cheap couple of weeks away – although where she'd go for some sun in October that didn't involve a long-haul flight and lots of expense, she had no idea – and for a deposit plus two or three months' rent on a flat. She only hoped she'd have enough time to find a job before her money ran out.

Perhaps going away wouldn't be such a good idea after all. It would be a waste of money for one thing.

'Look,' Anne said, breaking into her thoughts. 'They're not going to throw you out just yet. The council have to give you a decent amount of notice, and you won't want to take any time off as soon as you start a job, so now is the ideal time.'

Put like that…

'Maybe I could stretch to a few days away in Cornwall or Devon,' she said.

Anne snorted. 'In this weather? You might as well stay at home. No, listen to your aunt and go somewhere nice and hot.'

It would be considerably less hassle (she wasn't sure she actually knew where her passport was) to have a staycation, but one glance out of the window made her think again. It was midway through the morning, but the sky was a sullen, depressing grey and rain was falling in torrents. It was bitterly cold, and the wind was whipping the branches of the trees in the park opposite into a frenzy. Did she really want to spend a few days in a guest house staring at the same rain? Once again, her aunt was right – she could do that far more comfortably from her own living room and with considerably less expense.

No, she decided; if she was going to go anywhere, it would have to be warm and sunny – which meant that most of Europe was out. The only place she could think of that she might be able to afford and would feel comfortable visiting on her own was the Canary Islands.

So with that in mind, when Aunty Anne left, Sophie began the mammoth task of searching for her passport; and if she didn't find it, at least the hunt would have killed a couple of hours.

Chapter 2

As Sophie walked through the sliding doors of Tenerife's airport and stepped into the balmy air, she turned her face up to the sun and sighed with pleasure at the unaccustomed warmth. She was here, really here. In a foreign country. On her own. For two whole weeks.

The thought filled her with a quiet exhilaration which was tinged with apprehension.

The last-minute, remarkably cheap, midweek flight had been uneventful, most of it consisting of reading her book and peering out of the window at the cloud-laden sky. But when the aeroplane drew close to the group of islands, the pilot first pointed out La Palma, then La Gomera on the right of the aircraft, and she craned her neck across the aisle to see better. It was at that point that the conical peak of Tenerife's impressive volcano hoved into view, poking up through a ring of cloud like a pale, shining witch's hat, and she caught glimpses of flatter land beneath before the plane turned and began its final descent.

Now that she was on terra firma, the cloud which she'd spotted from the aircraft's windows seemed to have disappeared and the sky was a bright azure blue, tinged with a silver haze. She'd read that the island could be windy and so she wasn't surprised to feel a stiff breeze,

9

but the wind was a warm one, totally unlike the howling gale back in the UK earlier that morning, and at least the sun was shining.

Sophie took a steadying breath and scanned the throng of people hanging around the doors holding pieces of paper with passengers' names scrawled on them until she found her own. It was her one indulgence this holiday (apart from the holiday itself, of course) – a private transfer to the apartment she was renting. Apparently it was a good half an hour away from the airport and she hadn't trusted herself to be able to find her way there on her own. Not on her very first day, at least. So she'd booked a taxi and, as she sank into the back seat, she still couldn't believe she was here. It felt like a rather odd, yet pleasant dream.

From the second she'd made the decision to book a holiday, the time had passed in a whirl of preparation and guilty excitement. She'd even managed to push her grief to the back of her mind for minutes at a time, as she scrolled endlessly on her rather ancient phone to find an Airbnb to book, then dug out her few summer clothes, washed and dried them, and shopped for some essentials. During those activities the sorrow seemed less sharp, less shocking. Sophie sensed it would always be there, but she also sensed that it would fade and become less painful over time, and part of the healing process was this holiday. She hoped it would serve to draw a line between her life before it and her life after it, and enable her to face her future with a clearer head and more focus.

For now, though, all she wanted to do was to sit back and enjoy the scenery unfolding before her. The bare, dark rock interspersed with cacti surprised her, as did the sheer number of breeze-block-walled fields, topped with cream netting, some of it torn and fluttering in the breeze.

'What's growing in those fields?' she asked, seeing squat palm-like plants behind the netting.

'Banana,' her driver said, glancing in the rear-view mirror.

'There are acres of them!' she exclaimed.

He gave her a wide smile. 'Many bananas. Good to eat.'

She took a closer look as the car slowed to negotiate a steep bend and spotted clumps of the green fruit.

They'd been on the road for a good half-hour and she wondered how much further it was. They were travelling along a coastal road with the sea on their left and every so often she'd catch a glimpse of mountains on the right, with Teide as the pinnacle, still wearing a hat of cloud, only peeping through it now and again.

'La Gomera,' her driver said, pointing to a hazy lump of land out to sea.

Oh, yes, she remembered seeing the island from the plane. It looked miles away and slightly ethereal. Where the sea and the sky met was also hazy, but nearer to shore the water was a turquoise blue, with darker, almost navy patches in places. Little white crests topped the waves, and she guessed it was probably quite choppy out in the open water, although there were plenty of boats bobbing around on it.

'Los Gigantes,' he informed her, pointing straight ahead, and she leaned forward to see the famous cliffs. She had read in her guidebook that they were an impressive 2,500 feet high in places and could be seen for miles. There was a resort of the same name next to them, but she should arrive at the place where she was staying before then. The apartment did boast a view of the cliffs, though, so she hoped it wasn't a case of having to be ten foot tall and standing on a chair to be able to see them from the balcony.

It wasn't.

The apartment block was right on the edge of the sea, with only a broad pedestrian walkway separating the building from a spectacular drop into the pounding waves and jagged rocks below. Looking straight out to sea, she could make out the island of La Gomera; or a part of it anyway, because the bulk of it now appeared to have been swallowed by cloud. To the right, in the distance, were those cliffs rising vertically out of the sea, and to her left were pretty villas and apartment blocks, none of them more than a couple of storeys high.

The apartment itself had a decent-sized bedroom with two single beds, a marble-tiled bathroom, and an open-plan living room and kitchen with a breakfast bar separating the two areas.

This will do nicely, she thought, opening cupboards to see what sort of cooking utensils there were and checking on the condition of the fridge and cooker.

As she unpacked, she made a mental note of the things she'd need. Top of the list were coffee and milk (there was a cafetière in the cupboard next to the sink, she'd noticed), plus bread, butter and jam for the morning. Tonight, she'd treat herself and eat out. She couldn't afford to do that every evening and she was looking forward to exploring what the Spanish supermarkets had to offer, but tonight was special – the first night of the rest of her life – so she intended to make the most of it. She might even have a couple of glasses of wine. No more than two, though, because she hadn't had any alcohol for such a long time that she was scared it might go straight to her head. Many a time over the last few years, and especially in those final months when she didn't think she could bear seeing her mother in pain any more, she'd felt like losing herself in a bottle of Rioja, but she hadn't dared – her mother had needed her almost constantly day and night towards the end...

Stuffing the memories to the back of her mind, Sophie sent her aunt a quick text to let her know she'd arrived safely and that the place she was staying at was lovely. Then she swiftly changed into shorts and a T-shirt, slipped her feet into a cheap pair of flip-flops, grabbed her bag and headed out of the door. She wanted to find the pool, the beach, and the nearest supermarket. And she might even treat herself to a coffee and a sandwich on the way.

She strolled out of the apartment complex and onto the main road, spying a restaurant opposite and deciding to check it out on the way back. A few hundred yards away was a sign for a supermarket and beyond that she could see numerous bars, restaurants and shops. The little town wasn't too busy from what she could see, but there appeared to be enough going on to make life interesting, if that was what she wanted. For the time being, she'd be content to lie by the pool with her book, and maybe find a coastal path or two that she could explore.

Feeling rather decadent (she hadn't enjoyed a coffee out for such a very long time), she picked the nearest café, chose a table outside under a colourful umbrella and watched the world go by as she ate her *bocadillo* (apparently it meant 'snack' in Spanish, but it looked like a baguette to her), which came with fries and a side salad. She wanted to pinch herself; she still couldn't believe she was really here. She kept expecting to snap out of the daydream to hear her mother's feeble voice calling for her, and a wave of sorrow and guilt engulfed her.

The sorrow was to be expected, but the guilt was a whole new feeling; she'd not expected to feel shame for getting on with her life, yet she did. She felt even guiltier when she realised that she hadn't thought of her mum for at least an hour, and that she had actually experienced a sense of contentment for a while as she sat at the pavement café with a view of the sparkling sea and the wonderful warmth of the sun on her face.

It was as though she didn't feel she had the right to be happy, not with her mother's passing so new and raw. Yet she knew that if her mother was here now, she'd tell her not to be so silly. Her mum would never, ever want to hold her back, and she'd said so frequently, especially over the last few months when her health had deteriorated so alarmingly that it was clear the end wasn't far away.

'Put me in a hospice,' she'd said, but Sophie wouldn't dream of it. She wanted her mum to spend the remainder of her life at home, with the one person in the world who loved her more than anything. How could she have lived with herself, knowing that her mother was spending her last few weeks and days surrounded by strangers, no matter how caring and professional they were?

'Sorry, Mum,' she muttered into her coffee cup, well aware that her mother would be horrified if she knew how she was feeling. She should make the most of this holiday and not spend it wallowing in misery, because Lord knows when she'd be able to afford another one.

Gradually she felt the sun, the warm sea air and the relaxed atmosphere soothe her taut muscles and ease some of the tension from her mind, and she sat back and let the island work its magic.

After a while, she paid her bill and took a walk to the supermarket where she picked up a few essentials, then returned to the apartment to change into her bikini and spend the rest of the afternoon by the pool.

She might even go for a dip!

Chapter 3

It was only day four, yet Sophie felt as though she'd been in Tenerife an awful lot longer. Having an apartment all to herself helped, she decided, because it was almost as though she was living there, unlike the temporary feeling you got when staying in a hotel. She had everything she needed, from a washing machine to a comfy sofa. She had some English channels on the TV, a radio station which was aimed at the British (she liked listening to that in the morning while eating her breakfast – the presenter was funny and smart and played some seriously good music) and a decent Wi-Fi signal. She was also enjoying cooking for herself, even if she did miss having someone to share the meal with.

She'd eaten on the spacious balcony every evening, watching the sun sink down over La Gomera. She'd read that there were dolphins and whales in abundance in the stretch of water between that island and Tenerife, but despite squinting at the sea until her eyes watered, she'd not yet spotted any.

Her days so far had been spent reading and napping by the pool. Significantly more napping had taken place than reading, if she was honest, as she hadn't realised how totally and utterly exhausted she was until she'd had the time to relax. Looking after a terminally ill loved one then watching them fade away was bound to leave physical and emotional marks, so for the first couple of days she'd been kind to herself and had simply tried to recharge her batteries. It seemed like Aunty Anne had known what she was talking about after all, and Sophie vowed to buy something nice to take back for her.

Today, though, she'd woken with a sense of purpose. Enjoyable and necessary as the past few days of lounging around had been, she now had itchy feet. She didn't have the funds to hire a car or to go on any organised tours, much to her disappointment, but she did have her legs and there was always the bus service, which appeared to be fairly frequent and quite cheap, so there was nothing stopping her from exploring a little bit of the island if she wished.

Tenerife was considerably larger than she'd first thought and she knew she'd only be able to see a fraction of it, which was a pity because she doubted if she'd visit the place again. But she was determined to see the places she *could* get to, and so with that in mind she took out her guidebook and studied it while she ate a leisurely breakfast of scrambled eggs on toast washed down with hot, strong coffee.

She could walk to Los Gigantes, she realised, and view those massive cliffs up close. The harbour looked pretty too. Or she could walk along the coastal path to Alcalá, a town to the south of where she was staying. Her guide-book informed her it was worth a visit and the walk should take about forty minutes. She really fancied dawdling along by the sea rather than taking the main road, which she'd have to do for some of the way if she went to Los Gigantes, so she decided on the coastal route.

The beginning of the walk was just down the road from her apartment, she discovered. So she grabbed her little rucksack and filled it with a large bottle of water, a towel, a book and sunscreen, then jammed a hat on her head and shoved her feet into a pair of trainers.

Time to go exploring!

It didn't take more than five minutes to reach the start of the coastal path (although she had been tempted to stop for a while to admire the gorgeous seafront homes along the way), and then she was strolling along a wide paved path with dark, rough volcanic rocks on the one side and banana plantations on the other. The surf pounded the rocks, sucking and booming, flinging spray into the air which fell back in sparkling rainbows as the sun caught the droplets. The air had an invigorating ocean smell of salt and seaweed, and the gentle breeze fanned her cheeks, warm and soft on the exposed skin of her arms and legs.

She was developing a tan, she noticed. Her pale, almost translucent colouring was turning a gentle golden brown, and the sun had lightened the front of her hair and brought out a smattering of freckles across her nose and cheeks. She hadn't seen those for such a long time that she'd assumed she'd grown out of them. They made her look more like twelve than thirty-three, she'd giggled to herself when she spied them in the mirror this morning after her shower. The sun used to bring out freckles on her mother's shoulders and arms too, she recalled.

Before she'd ventured out this morning, she'd smeared herself with factor-thirty sunscreen, aware of how deceptive the Tenerife sun could be. The breeze kept the temperature at a comfortable level, but she'd discovered that it could get really hot in sheltered spots, and she guessed she'd burn if she wasn't careful.

As she carried on along the path, she knew she'd made the right decision not to spend the day by the pool. There were a few other people on the path, some jogging, some with dogs, and others, like her, out for a walk; but not so many that she felt crowded. The area was quite wild and rugged, with the waves surging against the rocks and hardly any houses in sight, apart from one villa in the middle of nowhere, sitting on a small rocky outcrop with a pebble beach on either side, and what looked like a farmhouse on the edge of a banana field beyond that. In the distance she could see a couple of low-rise houses clustered together, but this path was a far cry from the built-up area her apartment was in. This was peaceful and serene, despite the waves, and she felt the coil of grief inside her unwind a little bit further. Seeing all this rugged beauty, she understood why so many expats lived here. With views like this and gorgeous weather all year round, she would be happy to live here too.

As she drew closer to the villa, she studied it surreptitiously, not wanting the occupants to see her staring and think her rude. It was a lovely little house, though, perched on its low outcrop just above the waves. It was set far enough back not to be inundated during bad weather, but close enough to feel part of the ocean. At least, that's what she imagined the people who lived in it might feel when they were sitting on the terrace with only a wooden fence separating them from the water below.

I know what would look fantastic instead of the fence, she thought – a toughened glass barrier. She'd seen some on other balconies and terraces as she'd wandered to the shops, and she'd thought at the time that it was a wonderful way of both being secure and making the most of the view.

The villa was painted a faded pale pink, with a terra-cotta tiled roof and a high wall enclosing the gardens. Tall palm trees waved majestically, their fronds towering over the villa, and the tops of other plants peeped over the wall, interspersed with the exotic orange and red colours of bougainvillea, which draped over the coping stones and tumbled down the sides.

The path meandered right alongside the villa, and Sophie was delighted to discover a pair of large, green-painted wrought-iron gates which allowed her to see up the little paved driveway to the front of the villa itself. Up close it was rather more neglected than she'd thought when she'd first seen it, but it was still delightful.

A wide curving path led to a recessed front door, painted green to match the gates, and there were green shutters on all the windows. Unfortunately they were all closed, so she couldn't see inside the villa itself, but she did notice a pergola covering a terrace on the south side of the house, which made sense considering it would be facing the sun for most of the day. More bougainvillea grew up and over it, shading the space underneath, and she was convinced she could see the odd bunch of grapes dangling among the flowers. There was an old table and a set of chairs and she thought she could see a couple of loungers, but she wasn't certain. She might get a better view if she climbed onto the bottom rail, but she already had her nose squashed against the gates, and if anyone saw her they'd be well within their rights to give her a telling off.

Reluctantly, she moved away, still keeping her eye on the sweet little villa. Ooh, look, it had chimneys – two large ones – and she could imagine being snuggled safely inside with a fire in the hearth, on a stormy night with the sea lashing the rocks and the wind howling. Not that she thought Tenerife had many storms, but maybe it got colder towards January and that's why fireplaces were needed.

It wasn't cold now – far from it. The back of her neck was hot and damp, and she fished around in her rucksack for a band to put her hair up with. As she carried on walking, she looked back at the house, seeing it from a different angle. It looked equally as lovely from here, and she envied the people who were lucky enough to live in it.

Continuing her stroll, she rounded a small headland where a handful of surfers were playing in the waves just offshore, and she saw another small bay in front of her. The path led around it, past the farmhouse she'd seen earlier, and on towards the cluster of two or three villas – it was hard to tell the exact number from where she was. She wondered how much further she had to walk until she reached the next village. Although she'd worked her socks off for the past couple of years, looking after her mum and keeping their home running, she hadn't walked this far in ages and her legs were beginning to ache.

When she finally clambered up the rocky path which led around the villas – they were in a great location, but she didn't think they were as nice as the one she'd passed earlier – she saw the start of a lovely promenade with several small black-sand beaches and a seawater pool, and she knew the effort had been worth it.

Sophie was dying to dip her toes in the water, followed by a sprawl on the beach, but she needed a cold drink and something to eat first, so she made her way towards an open-air café, picked a table and sank down thankfully onto a chair.

Tapas, she decided after reading the menu, and as she tucked into a selection of delicious dishes, a rare and unexpected feeling of contentment stole over her. All too soon she knew she'd have to return to reality, but for now she was determined to live in the moment and enjoy every second of this wonderful place.

Chapter 4

If there was one trip she was determined to make, it was a visit to Tenerife's heart – Mount Teide. How could she travel all this way and not see such a spectacular sight? She guessed there must be hundreds, probably thousands, of tourists who never set foot outside their hotels, but she felt it would be a shame not to pay the volcano a visit. The glimpses she'd seen of it had intrigued her, so she'd decided to pop into one of the places advertising excursions, to ask how much it would cost. Although she'd winced a little at the price, she was relieved to be told that lunch was included, as was the ticket for the cable car to the summit, so she'd booked it.

The day of the trip, wearing trainers and carrying a fleece (it could be quite fresh and chilly at the summit, apparently), she settled back in the front seat of the coach to watch the scenery unfold.

As soon as the bus had left the coast, it began to climb up steep, winding roads, where the earth dropped away at an alarming rate and the rugged mountains grew closer and higher. Before long they were a thousand or so feet above sea level, and if she craned her neck and looked behind her, she could see the Los Gigantes cliffs and the harbour below. More twists and turns took them through villages and a small town or two, before they left civilisation behind and were driving up through tall pine trees on either side of the road. For a volcano, and from the pictures and postcards she'd seen, she had been expecting the area to be far more desolate than it was and not so green.

Then abruptly the trees thinned, becoming small, twisted growths, and the coach was trundling along a stretch of tarmac with hardened black lava fields on either side. Wow, she thought, it felt like being on the surface of the moon. The road seemed to her like a long, charcoal ribbon which had been placed precariously on top of the jagged bleak landscape, which might be stark but was also strangely beautiful and compelling. There was something alien and otherworldly about it.

The guide, who was sitting across the aisle from her at the front of the bus, giving his passengers a steady stream of facts and figures, had explained how the island had come into being, and that Teide was also a live volcano. Sophie found it quite disturbing as she'd watched a documentary once about Mount Vesuvius and what had happened to the inhabitants of Pompeii. The fact that this enormous lump of rock was capable of spewing out molten lava whenever the mood took it was rather worrying. As was the information that the island was ancient, yet parts of it were surprisingly new. The last eruption on Teide had occurred just over a hundred years ago, resulting in the blackened mass of tortured rocks to their left. And there was plenty more where that came from, she guessed. Nothing grew on it, not even a blade of grass. Her imagination ran riot as she pictured the slow unstoppable creep of the hot lava down the slope, blanketing everything in its path. It must have been a sight to behold, but she sincerely hoped she wouldn't be around when the next eruption took place.

The road slithered through the relatively flat land of what she learnt was an ancient caldera, with a ring of mountains surrounding the high plateau. The caldera was the remains of an even larger volcano that had blown itself apart at some point in the distant past, the guide informed them, and all that was left was the circle of peaks indicating its circumference. The scale of it was breathtaking.

The major attraction — cone-shaped Teide — was on the left, and as the coach drove towards the cable car, she was amazed to see a hotel in the middle of the plateau. What an impressive and scary place to spend the night, she thought with a shiver. Visiting was one thing, sleeping in such close proximity to this slumbering dragon of a mountain was another thing entirely.

Sophie had never been on a cable car before, and the thought of a glass box swinging on a bit of wire several hundred feet above jagged rocks didn't fill her with confidence. But she was determined to reach the top of the volcano because she'd read that the views were spectacular.

They really were, she discovered, as she stepped out onto the viewing area, pulling her fleece over her head and stuffing her arms in the sleeves. It was several degrees colder up here than at sea level, which wasn't surprising since the volcano was over twelve thousand feet high. The air was thinner up here too, and she'd noticed warning signs advising people with heart conditions and pregnant women not to take the cable car.

Wow, you can see for miles, she thought, gazing at the spectacular view and breathing in the fresh, sharp air. Even in October and at this altitude, the weather and the temperature were still better than what she'd left behind in the UK. No wonder so many people loved this island – she was already falling in love with the little bit of it she'd seen, and the thought of returning home filled her with dread. She wasn't ready to face reality yet, to have to deal with the prospect of finding somewhere else to live, to have to clear out her mum's things, find a job, build a new life.

Giving herself a mental shake, she pushed the negative thoughts out of her mind – there was no place for them up here, high above the world in the shimmering sunshine, where she could almost imagine being able to touch the sky.

There was no place for melancholy or negativity when they descended either, as the coach crossed to the other edge of the caldera and dropped down through spectacular pine forests towards the north-east of the island. The scenery took her breath away, every turn and bend in the road revealing more beautiful vistas, and she couldn't wait to show Aunty Anne the numerous photos she'd taken.

The group were on their way to one of the prettiest towns on the island, La Oratava, where they were to stop for lunch. And as the coach pulled into the car park of a restaurant, Sophie felt a tap on her shoulder.

'I hope you don't mind, dear,' said an elderly lady sitting in the seat immediately behind. 'I hate eating on my own, so would you mind if I sat with you?'

'Of course not. I'd be delighted.' Although she had sat on her own whenever she'd eaten out, she didn't particularly like it, and the thought of having a companion at her table, however new the acquaintance, lifted her already buoyant spirits. 'I'm Sophie.' She poked her hand through the gap between the two seats, and the woman shook it.

'Valerie, but everyone calls me Val,' she offered.

They walked into the restaurant side by side and were shown where to sit. It seemed they were sharing a table with four other people, but she didn't mind – although she realised that she would have minded a whole lot more without her new friend by her side.

Val took her hand and gave it a squeeze.

'I'm OK,' she hastened to reassure the elderly lady, and gave her a smile.

'That wasn't for you, dear, it was for me,' Val said. 'This is my first holiday without my Jim, and it's not been easy. I was determined to do it, though. He wouldn't have wanted me to sit around moping. In fact, he told me as much, more than once. Val, he used to say, there's plenty of life left in you yet, so don't waste it. It's too precious.'

'Oh, I'm so sorry. How long were you married?'

'Over forty years.'

It was Sophie's turn to give Val's hand a squeeze. 'That's a long time.'

'However long it is, you'll find it's never long enough. Time is so precious, and it goes so quickly.' She smiled, her eyes crinkling at the corners. 'You young ones don't realise.'

'I think I do,' Sophie replied. 'I lost my mum less than a month ago.'

'Oh, my dear, I do feel for you. How old was she?'

'Sixty-one.'

'That's far too young. What was it? Cancer?'

Sophie nodded, not trusting herself to speak.

'And you're here all by yourself?' Val asked.

27

She nodded again.

'That's so brave of you.'

Sophie gave her a small smile. 'Not as brave as you.'

'I tell you what, let's be brave together,' Val said, letting go of her hand and reaching for the carafe of red wine which had been placed on the table. 'Will red do you, or do you prefer white?'

'The red will be fine, but only one glass; I don't drink much,' she warned.

The warning fell on deaf ears, because by the time they were called back to the bus, Sophie was feeling decidedly squiffy. The three-course meal had been no match for three glasses of wine, and she hoped she wouldn't fall asleep on the coach and miss the rest of the tour. They were currently on the northern side of the island and would be making their way south to a place called Masca Gorge.

Once again, the coach was heading up into the mountains, and the road was becoming twistier and narrower the higher they climbed. Val was now sitting in the front seat next to her, and every so often she'd reach for Sophie's hand.

'Oh, my word!' the elderly woman exclaimed as the coach appeared to be heading directly for a wall of solid rock, before the road swung abruptly to the left and narrowly missed it. And it wasn't the first time this had happened – it seemed the only way for such a large vehicle to manoeuvre around a narrow hairpin bend was for it to take up all the available space in the road. Sophie felt sorry for anything coming in the other direction, although it was bound to happen sooner or later, and when it did her heart was in her mouth as the two vehicles inched slowly past one another.

Val, she noticed, kept her eyes screwed shut throughout the whole thing.

'The driver must be used to it,' she said to her, but Val, without opening her eyes, shook her head.

'I don't care how used to it he is, accidents happen, and have you seen that drop!'

Sophie had, and wished she hadn't, especially since there was only a low wall of intermittent concrete blocks separating them all from certain death, and—

'Oh...' she breathed as she saw where they were headed, and her soul sang at the beauty of it.

Val risked opening one eye. Then she opened the other and sat up straight.

In front of them, perched on the hillside, with houses tumbling down the steep sides in ordered chaos, was a village, half of its buildings appearing to balance precariously on a knife-edge ridge.

But that wasn't what had taken Sophie's breath – it was the view. A deep V-shaped valley had been gouged into the mountains, the bottom too far down to be able to see, and the sky was a startling blue in between the peaks of the rugged ridges, with the azure sea in the distance.

'So that's Masca Gorge,' she murmured. Then their guide proceeded to give them some interesting facts and figures, before letting his passengers off for a wander around the village and to take some essential photos.

'I can't believe people can actually hike down that,' Val said, as they reached a lookout point (or *mirador*, as it was called in Spanish) where the view down the gorge was spectacular and very definitely worthy of a photo or two.

Both of them got out their phones and took turns taking photos of each other.

'My son thought I'd spend all day lounging by the pool,' Val said. 'This'll show him.' She nudged Sophie with her elbow and laughed. 'Especially when I tell him I walked down it. That nice guide of ours says that it's very popular with walkers, and you can get a speedboat to pick you up from the beach at the end of the gorge that'll take you to Los Gigantes harbour. Fancy that! If I was a few years younger I'd give it a go, but I'm lucky if I can manage a couple of flights of stairs these days without my knees giving me trouble. You ought to do it, though.'

'I don't think so,' Sophie began, but Val interrupted her.

'Why not? You're young and fit, and think of the sights you'd see. I've always wanted to have a ride in a speedboat. If you don't do these things when you're young enough, healthy enough and have still got all your faculties, then when can you?'

'Er... right. I might look into it...'

Sophie liked the idea of hiking down the gorge. You could hike up it too, but the up bit didn't appeal to her half as much as the going down bit, as it would involve considerably more effort and a greater degree of fitness than she possessed, despite Val's misplaced enthusiasm. But she hadn't brought the right footwear and neither did she have a set of those walking poles she'd seen people using. Plus, she didn't want to undertake such a hike on her own, especially since she only had five more days of her holiday left. If she ever came back to Tenerife, she would definitely walk down Masca Gorge, have a celebratory swim from the beach at the end of the valley, then finish off the trip with a ride in a fast boat. For now, though, she'd have to settle for a coffee and a pastry at a little café perched precariously on the side of the gorge where she could admire the spectacular view.

She realised one thing, as she stared out over the steep-sided valley, and that was that Tenerife, with its varied landscapes, friendly people and glorious weather, had most definitely and irrevocably got under her skin.

She'd be very sorry indeed when she had to board the plane for her homeward flight and the real world at the other end.

Chapter 5

This would be the third occasion she took the coastal walk to Alcalá, but Sophie was looking forward to it as much as, if not more than, she'd done the first time. It had quickly become her favourite thing to do in the mornings, as she'd settled down into a routine since the fabulous trip to Teide and Masca. First she'd have breakfast, then pay the supermarket a quick visit to pick up some fresh bread and ingredients for her dinner, followed by the making of sandwiches for when she arrived at one of Alcalá's several beaches, where she'd read her book, do a spot of sunbathing and maybe even dip her toes in the rather refreshing, if not downright chilly, Atlantic ocean. Then there would be the gentle stroll back, past the natural seawater pool, the waves pounding against the rocks, the banana plantations, and her favourite villa.

But today she noticed that something was different.

The first part of her plan went... well, according to plan.

The plan deviated slightly when, as she passed the villa, wondering as usual if anyone actually lived there because she'd yet to see the shutters open or anyone in the garden (although the last time she'd walked this way a chair had been moved, so someone was around), she noticed a piece of card tied to one of the double gates. It had two holes punched in it and was secured to the metal rail by what looked like a shoelace. It also had writing on it, in pen, which had been gone over several times to make the top line stand out. The handwriting itself was neat and quite elegant. But it was also in Spanish, so she couldn't read a single word of it.

Thank goodness for Google Translate, she thought, as she typed the words slowly into her phone, making sure the spelling was correct.

Fully expecting the note to be for a delivery driver, or maybe (and her heart did a flip at the thought) that the house was being put up for sale, she was stunned to read the message her phone revealed.

'Help wanted' it said. Then it went on to detail what kind of assistance was required. It seemed like an elderly gentleman who was due to have a hip operation needed help with home chores (at least, that's what Google told her). Maybe it meant housework?

But the bit that really gave her pause — and began a slow churning excitement in her stomach — was the fact that it was a live-in position. Small payment for services, all food and other living expenses included, according to her phone.

Could she? Maybe…

Should she? Probably not.

Dare she? Yes. No.

Oh dear…

She'd walk to Alcalá and think about it. Now wasn't the time to do anything hasty.

She began walking, her feet seeming rather reluctant to move as the thoughts rolled around in her head like so many loose marbles.

Just making an enquiry wasn't being hasty, was it? In fact, the more enquiries she made, the better informed she'd be to make a decision—

Oh, who was she kidding? Make a decision about *what*? Taking a job she wasn't qualified to do, in a foreign country, where they spoke a language she could neither speak nor understand? She had a life, a family and a home in England, and—

Hang on a sec, what life was this, then? Come to think of it, what home? She'd very shortly be moving out of the one she'd shared with her mum, and she hadn't the foggiest idea where she was going to live. And as for a life – she had no job and not even the prospect of one, no friends, and no social life, unless you counted the online forums and Facebook groups she'd joined to connect with other people in the same situation as her. There was her family to consider, though. Aunty Anne would miss her, and she'd miss her aunt, but with Denise about to give birth any second, her aunt would have her hands full helping her daughter look after the new babies. And that was another thing; Sophie wasn't sure she wanted to miss out on her first cuddle with the little ones.

But it was only for three months… not for ever…

She halted. Maybe she should just go back and reread it. Re-translate it. Just in case she'd got it wrong, and the occupant was redirecting an IKEA delivery or something. Actually, *was* there an IKEA on Tenerife?

For goodness' sake, get a grip, she told herself silently, as she started walking again. She would go to the beach as planned, spread her towel out on the hot, dark sand, eat her sandwich and think it through logically. And if she felt the pros outweighed the cons, then there was nothing to stop her ringing the bell and asking for more details on her way back to her apartment. What was to say she'd get the job anyway? She might take an instant dislike to the man with the hip, or he might not like her. Or, more likely, her lack of Spanish would be a major drawback. Not everyone spoke English on the island, she'd noticed, although many people did have a smattering, usually related to the kind of work they did. And if none of those things proved to be a barrier, then her gender or her age might. The gentleman might not want to share his home with a woman, or he might be looking for someone more matronly.

She decided to keep walking, have a good long think, and take her time – the villa wasn't going anywhere. It would still be there on her way back.

But the job mightn't be.

Someone else might apply for it, someone local. She'd kick herself if she'd been pipped at the post.

Sophie sat on one of the large rocks dotted at intervals along the side of the path and turned to face the way she'd come. From this distance and from this angle, it was impossible to tell if the advert was still attached to the gate.

Oh, it must be, because a woman walking her dog had stopped to read it.

What if *she* decided to apply for it?

Sophie jumped to her feet and marched back along the path.

The woman moved on, towing her dog behind her, but every now and again she glanced over her shoulder at the villa. Sophie increased her pace until she was almost running.

By the time she arrived at the villa's gates, the woman had turned a bend and was out of sight, and Sophie breathed a tentative sigh of relief.

Before she rang the bell, though, which was an old-fashioned pull cord linked to a real brass bell hanging by the side of the front door, she checked and double-checked the notice. Each time, Google gave her the same result, so, without anything further to be gleaned, she took a deep breath, briefly closed her eyes and pulled the cord.

The bell rang. Sophie waited.

And waited.

Nothing. No movement whatsoever that she could see.

Perhaps the occupant, or occupants, were out? There was a phone number written on the card, but she didn't want to call it and risk having an awkward conversation with someone who didn't speak English.

Perhaps she should walk to Alcalá after all, and try again on her return?

She backed away, then turned on her heel, glancing over her shoulder as she did so.

The door opened and a grizzled head poked out. '*Qué pasa?*'

'Er... I... um...'

'*Inglesa?*'

'English? Yes, yes, I am.' She nodded enthusiastically.

'What do you want?' His English was heavily accented, but at least it *was* English.

'The... um... advert?' She stepped closer, until her nose was practically squashed up against the railings of the gate.

'*Sí?*'

'Do you want a carer or a home help?'

'*Qué?*'

She knew what 'qué' meant – her mum used to love watching reruns of *Fawlty Towers*.

'Someone to help you after you have your operation,' she amended.

'*Sí*, yes, I need help with the clothes, the food, the cleaning…' He trailed off, then called out, 'Come in, come in,' beckoning her inside the gates.

Sophie had assumed they were locked because she could clearly see a chain and padlock, but closer inspection revealed the padlock wasn't in fact locked, so she threaded the chain through the railings and pushed the gate open; it wouldn't do to rush off now that she'd disturbed him, she decided, not wanting to be rude.

She tried not to stare at the garden as she walked up the short driveway, but it was even prettier from the inside than it had appeared from the coastal path, with flowering climbing plants growing up the high walls, and the giant palm trees waving in the breeze and casting their shade on the house. There were also the typical cacti which were so prevalent on the island, and in the corner furthest away from the sea was what looked like a vegetable plot.

Dear God, she'd give her right arm to own a place like this.

'Your name?' the elderly man asked her, and she came to a halt on the porch.

'Sophie Lakeland,' she replied.

'Hugo Santana Negrin,' he said. 'You want the job?'

'Er… um…' Surely he wanted to know more about her, give her an interview at least, before he offered her the position?

37

Suddenly she found she didn't care whether he followed the usual protocols or not – she wanted to accept. In all honesty, she didn't want to return to the UK. She wanted to remain in Tenerife, and she wasn't too picky about what she'd have to do to make it happen. He needed an assistant of some kind, and she needed a job and somewhere to live. It was the solution to both of their problems.

'That's wonderful!' she exclaimed. 'Thank you so much. I promise I won't let you down.' Then she saw the confusion on his face and realised she might have been a little premature and that maybe he hadn't been offering her the job after all.

She bit her lip, her heart sinking, disappointment pricking behind her eyes. For a moment there, she'd envisioned herself calling this place home, even if it was only for a few months.

'You are here about the job?' he asked, rather more clearly.

'Yes, I am.'

She lifted her chin and was just about to put forth an argument as to why she should be considered for it, when he said, 'You must come in,' and opened the door wider, jerking his head towards the interior of the villa.

'Oh, OK, thank you.' She stepped past him and into a shaded hallway, her pumps slapping on the marble floor. It was cooler inside, and she realised the reason for the shutters being closed was to keep the midday sun out. Then she wondered if he ever opened them at all, or whether he lived in a permanent state of semi-darkness.

She waited for him to shut the door and show her the way, noticing as he went past her that he was using two sticks to help him walk, and that he was older than she'd

38

first thought. From a distance, and in spite of the salt and pepper hair and whiskers, she had guessed he was in his fifties, but up close she revised her estimate upwards by at least a decade. He appeared robust, though, mobility issues aside, and was quite tall, with broad shoulders which were currently hunched because his walking sticks were too short.

'Please sit down,' he said, leading her through a doorway and into a room which ran the full length of the back of the house.

It was a room that made her heart sing. The shutters were open and light streamed in from two sets of double doors facing the ocean. If it wasn't for the terrace immediately outside the doors, she could almost imagine the house was floating on the sea itself. There was nothing in sight apart from water and sky, and the odd boat in the distance.

When she finally dragged her gaze away from that magnificent view, it was to find Mr Santana (or was that his middle name, and she really should be calling him Mr Negrin? Or maybe it was a double-barrelled name, Santana-Negrin?) staring at her with a knowing expression on his face.

'*La vista*, the view, is beautiful,' he said. 'It hits you, here.' He thumped a hand to his chest, dropping one of his sticks in the process.

Sophie made to retrieve it, but he waved her away.

'I can do this,' he said, doing an awkward sideways bend in order to pick it up. When he was upright again and steady on his legs, although a little redder in the face, he indicated once more that she should sit.

She sank down onto an old sofa, most of it covered by a woollen throw, and Mr Whatshisname took a more upright, high-backed chair, which she guessed was easier for him to get in and out of.

'The job,' he began, 'you want to… er… ask for it?'

'Apply?' she said. 'Yes, please.' She stopped, not knowing where to start.

'Do you live here?'

'On Tenerife? No, but I'd like to.' For a while, at least, until she'd decided what she wanted to do and where she wanted to go.

'You are cleaner?'

Cleaner than what? she wondered, then she understood what he meant. 'Not exactly, although I can clean, and cook, and do the laundry.' She paused. 'I looked after my mother for many years, so when I read the notice saying you needed help to recover from an operation, I thought I would apply. I nursed my mum towards the end.'

'The end?'

'She passed away. Died,' she added, seeing him frown.

'Ah. Your mother, she has not been dead long?'

'Twenty-nine days.'

'I am sorry.'

'So am I, but life moves on,' she added brightly, feeling the familiar sting of tears and blinking them away.

He said nothing more for a while, and although she was desperate to ask him whether she was in with a chance, she remained silent.

'Can you do this?' he asked her. '*Should* you?'

She understood him immediately. 'It's what I know, it's what I'm used to. And it gives me a breathing space. Somewhere new, with new people.'

'But doing what you are comfortable doing?'

He understood her too, it seemed.

She nodded slowly. 'Look, Mr Santana... er, Negrin...'

'Call me Hugo.'

'Hugo.' She nodded. 'I might not have any qualifications, but I can run a house and I've had experience of people recovering from operations, so...'

'Do you like dogs?'

Sophie blinked. 'I guess so. Yes?'

'Paco!'

There was nothing for a second or two, then she heard the click of claws on tiles and the largest dog she'd ever seen padded into view, his tongue lolling out of the side of his mouth, his curved tail waving slowly from side to side.

The animal plodded over to her, the top of his head almost level with her chin, and sat down, then gave her his paw, plonking it in her lap. It weighed as much as a small child and felt solid and heavy.

'He likes you,' Hugo said.

'He does?'

'If he didn't, he would do this.' Hugo put his nose in the air, gave a disdainful sniff and turned his head away.

Sophie giggled and reached out to stroke the dog. To her surprise his abundant black fur was very soft and as fluffy as it looked, and she ran her fingers through it, much to the dog's delight.

'After hospital, I won't be able to walk him. He needs his… er… hair… er…' Hugo mimicked brushing his own hair.

'Ah, he'll need grooming?'

'*Sí*. Every day. The hair, it is everywhere.'

'I'm happy to walk him and groom him,' she said. 'Are there any other duties?'

'Making food, washing clothes, cleaning.'

She nodded again. 'I can do all that. What about you? Will you need any help?'

Hugo grimaced. 'No, I will dress and wash myself. I will not need help for me, just for the house and the dog.'

Sophie took a deep breath and straightened her shoulders. 'I can do that.'

'I can only offer a small wage, and only for two or three months,' he warned.

'That's fine, if accommodation is included.'

'It is. And food.'

'Great!'

Hugo struggled to his feet and Sophie watched him, knowing instinctively that he wouldn't want her help, no matter how much he needed it. If he did take her on, she'd have to be subtle about any attempts to make his life easier for him.

'You still want the job?' he asked.

'Yes, please!' She was shocked at how much she did want it. The wanting was almost a physical thing, a deep need, and it made her heart flutter and pound.

'Take a look around before you say yes. You might want to say no.'

Sophie cocked her head. 'Oh?' Please, please don't tell me there's only one bedroom, she prayed.

'The house, I have only a little TV, and no internet. It is not like a hotel room.'

'I didn't expect it to be,' she said. 'This is a home, *your* home.'

'Go look; then tell me what you decide.'

Sophie looked.

It was perfect; rustic and basic, but perfect. Exactly as she imagined it, even down to the dark wood that was so prevalent in Canarian homes she'd seen on travel programmes on TV. There was an open fireplace in the living room and each of the three bedrooms had a bed, a wardrobe and bedside table. One bedroom was clearly occupied by Hugo and she glanced idly at a photo of him with his arm slung around the shoulders of a younger man. His son, perhaps? Whoever he was, the man was remarkably good-looking.

Feeling as though she was snooping, she had a quick look in the only other room she hadn't explored, and saw that the kitchen held freestanding cabinets, a sink, a cooker and a fridge. It might not be the most modern kitchen she'd seen, but at first glance it had everything she needed.

She had a good feeling about the place, as if it was welcoming her.

When she wandered back into the room with the marvellous view, she felt as though she was coming home.

She made her decision.

Chapter 6

Sophie eyed the couple sitting next to her on the plane as she settled back in her seat and buckled up. They wore resigned expressions along with their tans and summer clothes. Sophie, fearing that the early winter weather in the UK wouldn't be kind, had worn a lightweight, long-sleeved top, jeans, and trainers with warm socks. She currently had a fleece draped around her shoulders – because the inside of the aircraft was cooler than the departure lounge had been, as if the plane was trying to acclimatise its passengers – and she'd placed a coat in the overhead locker.

Once they were airborne, she retrieved a small pad and a pen from her bag and began to make lists. Several of them. It kept her occupied during the four-hour flight and calmed her churning thoughts. She'd always been a list-maker, ever since she was young. It seemed as though the act of putting things down on paper served to tidy things up in her mind and helped her focus, and right now she needed all the focus she could lay her hands on.

Satisfied that she had done as much as she was able to while being jetted through the air at close to six hundred miles an hour, and without the benefit of an internet connection, she put her pad with its invaluable lists away, and went to sleep. The next few days were going to be busy, and she needed all the rest she could get.

However, rest was the last thing on her mind as she collected her little car from the airport car park and drove home.

Home. What an evocative word that was, especially when she technically didn't have one. Although there wasn't a letter from the council waiting on the mat advising her of her need to vacate the property (her home, her mother's home) by a certain date, she knew its arrival was only a matter of time. How much time, she had had no idea.

After dumping her case in her bedroom and shoving a load of dirty clothes in the washing machine, Sophie rooted around in the freezer for something to pop in the oven. The sight of a dish filled with chicken casserole brought a lump to her throat as she realised that her mum had still been alive when she had prepared and frozen it. She used to do that a lot – cook batches of food when she had the chance, then freeze them – because she never knew what might tempt her mum, or whether she'd need to grab a meal quickly and race back to the hospital. Dashing away fresh tears (would this crying never end?), she retrieved the casserole from the freezer and switched the microwave on, making a mental note that she needed to use up as much of the food in the freezer as she could before she left. It seemed a shame to waste it… Maybe Aunty Anne could use some of it?

As she was eating, her phone rang. That was another thing she needed to add to her list – getting the house phone disconnected.

'You're back!' her aunt shrieked, before Sophie had a chance to say hello. 'I hoped you would be.'

'I am. I got in about an hour ago.' She was smiling as she said it – her aunt had clearly missed her. But abruptly her smile faded. Oh dear, Anne wasn't going to like her news very much if this was how she reacted to her being away for only two weeks.

'The twins are here! Sophie, did you hear what I said? Denise has had the babies. They're three weeks early but they're here and they're perfect.'

'That's wonderful news. How is Denise, and what do the boys think of their new sisters?'

'She's good. Sore obviously and tired, but everyone is fine. The boys…? Hmm, you know what teenagers are like. They haven't taken a great deal of notice, if I'm honest. How was your holiday?'

'Great. More than great—'

'They might let her out tomorrow, fingers crossed.' Her aunt clearly had more important things on her mind than hearing about Sophie's holiday.

'Can I pop round in the morning?' Sophie asked, determined to tell her about her plans as soon as possible.

Anne sounded doubtful. 'Denise might not be home until the afternoon, and I don't think she'll be up to visitors for a few days.'

'I meant pop round to see *you*?'

'Of course you can, but it mightn't be for long if Joe fetches her and the babies home, because she'll need me there to help with everything.'

'How about if I come to yours now?' Sophie asked, feeling a stab of pain. She knew her aunty loved her and she knew she was part of the family, but Anne had new

46

commitments and responsibilities now, a new focus (two of them, actually), and Sophie felt a little left out.

–

Sighing, she cleared her solitary plate away and put her coat on. The sooner she told Anne the better, before she changed her mind and backed out of the whole thing.

As soon as she stepped over the threshold of her aunt's compact retirement flat, Anne first enveloped her in a massive hug, then stepped back to scrutinise her.

'You look well,' she said, nodding to herself. 'Better than you've looked for years. I was right – you needed a holiday. The sun agrees with you.'

Sophie smiled. 'Everything about Tenerife agrees with me.'

Anne led her into the kitchen and flipped the switch on the kettle. 'Tell me all about it. Did you have a good time?'

'I did, thanks. It was lovely.'

'Good. I've got some photos of the babies – want to see?'

'Ooh, yes please!' And for the next few minutes the pair of them cooed over tiny noses and starfish hands.

Eventually, Sophie plucked up the courage to tell Anne her news. 'I'm… um… going back to Tenerife,' she said.

'I don't blame you. I went there years ago and it was lovely. You might want to give one of the other islands a go, though. I hear Lanzarote is nice.'

'I've got a job,' she said hesitantly, wondering how her aunt would take the news.

'Already? That was quick. You've only been home five minutes. I knew you'd find something, a smart girl like you. Where is it? What will you be doing?'

'It's in Tenerife, and I'll be looking after an elderly gentleman who's having a hip operation.'

Anne blinked. Then frowned. Then she made them both another cup of tea. Finally she said, 'I wasn't expecting that.'

Sophie continued. 'It's a live-in position. But don't worry, it's only for three months, it's not permanent.'

Her aunt frowned again. 'I don't know if I like the sound of it…' She tapped her fingers against her cheek. 'I just hope you're not doing anything drastic on the rebound.'

Despite Anne's obvious misgivings, Sophie had to smile. 'I'm not on the rebound.'

'No, but you're grieving and sad, and I don't want you to do something you'll regret.'

'And I don't want to regret *not* doing something,' she replied gently. 'I'll be back before you know it.'

'What would your poor mother say?' Anne fretted.

'You know Mum; she'd tell me to go for it.'

Her aunt sighed. 'You're not wrong there.' She got up from her chair and gathered Sophie into an awkward hug. 'Are you sure about this?'

She nodded. 'Just think of it as an extended holiday.'

'Hmm. I'm still not happy, but you're a grown woman and you've got to make your own choices in life. Just be careful, eh?'

'I will,' she promised. 'Now, I've got to dash. There's a lot to sort out.'

She tried not to let the tears pricking the back of her eyes fall as she said goodbye to her aunt. It *was* only for three months, and it wasn't as though she was leaving Anne all alone. Anne had Denise and the babies to keep her occupied, and although she knew her aunt would miss her, the time would fly by and Sophie would be back before she knew it.

Once again, it felt incredibly sad to walk into the empty house. Without her mum there, it was as though the life and heart had been bled out of it, and all that was left was an empty shell. In some ways, she'd be glad to leave, but in others…

Sophie bit back a sob as she got to work. Keeping busy was the best remedy, because if she stopped to think about what she was doing she thought she might freak out. So she began the task of wrapping up her life in the UK (albeit temporarily) by doing some research on storage units and finding one not too far away. Some things she'd take to the charity shop, like her mum's clothes for instance. Other things, very few other things, she'd take with her to Tenerife. The rest would go into storage for when she returned to the UK, because she'd need them in order to furnish whatever place she rented afterwards. Even three months' storage costs added up to less than a hundred pounds and was far, far cheaper than having to buy everything new. She didn't fancy starting from scratch.

She ordered some packing boxes, bubble wrap and tape from Amazon, and did some more research to find a man with a van who'd be prepared to move everything from the house to the storage facility.

It was time to be ruthless.

There was such a great deal to sort out – both her own stuff and her mum's. And she didn't even want to think about what was in the attic. She hadn't been up there since last Christmas, and all she'd done then was grab the tree and the box of decorations, then shove them back up again afterwards. She dreaded having to go up into that gloomy, dusty space which was no doubt full of spiders and other assorted creepy-crawlies. Then there were all those boxes filled with memories; she wasn't sure she was ready to face those either.

In the end she had to, because no one else was going to do it for her, and she didn't intend to leave such personal things for the council to dispose of. The thought of her mother's photos being sent to a landfill site broke her heart, so the following day she steeled herself to clamber up the precarious ladder, making sure to leave the back door unlocked and take her phone with her in case she needed rescuing. After all, she didn't have very many days in which to get everything done before she jetted back to Tenerife, and she couldn't afford to waste any of them being stuck in an attic.

The mere thought of the island filled her with excitement and trepidation in equal amounts. Now that she had returned to England, she wasn't entirely sure she was making the right decision to fly back to Tenerife.

Here everything was familiar; she could speak the language for a start, and she could read the writing on packets and tins in the supermarket and know what they contained. She mightn't have anywhere to live, but that could soon be rectified, as could the lack of a job. She was sure she'd find something, even if it wasn't what she really wanted to do.

Ah, but that was half the problem, wasn't it? She didn't have a clue what she wanted to do.

Then there were the twins to consider. Now they were born they felt more real, and she knew she'd have trouble wrenching herself away once she'd got to cuddle them. She might only be away for three months, but that was a long time in the lives of a pair of tiny babies – they'd change so much during that time and she was going to miss it.

Bloomin' heck, it was freezing up here, she thought, sticking her head into the attic and seeing her breath mist in front of her face.

Suddenly an image of sitting on that lovely terrace, staring out at the sea with the warm sun on her face and a plate of tapas on a table next to her popped into her mind. Not that she'd sat on the terrace, and she'd certainly not had anything to eat at the villa, tapas or otherwise. She had made herself and Hugo a cup of coffee, though, as they'd hashed out the details.

She'd taken some of her things to the villa the following day, but as that was the last day of her holiday she'd not had much time to do anything else other than to change the sheets on the bed in what was to be her room and hang a few clothes in the wardrobe, after clearing out the items that were already in there and putting them in the third and smallest of the bedrooms. It was full of stuff (junk mostly, she guessed from looking at it) and she was looking forward to giving it a good sort out.

Hugo had shown her where things were and how they worked, then she'd taken Paco on a nice long walk before she'd said her goodbyes, promising to be back in a week. Finally she'd returned to the apartment, packed the remainder of her things in her case, and booked a single flight from the UK to Tenerife in exactly one week's time.

Therefore she now had five and a half days in which to pack up her life in England and prepare for a new one in Tenerife.

And she'd hardly scratched the surface of what she needed to do, so she'd better get a move on.

Unfortunately, that was easier said than done. She'd not anticipated just how painful it would be to sift through box after box from both her life and her mother's. It was amazing what had been stuffed up there, from her first pair of tiny shoes to school reports from when she'd started school right up until she was eighteen. She found herself reading each one, a half-smile on her face as she recalled those innocent days filled with childhood worries and carefree joy. How she longed to go back to a time when the only thing she had to concern herself with was that her music teacher wanted her to practise the violin more, or that she was a bit too chatty in class. It had all seemed so very important then.

Maybe what she was fretting about now would seem equally as unimportant in ten years' time but, being realistic, worrying over forgotten homework was hardly in the same league as a complete overhaul of her life.

How she wished her mum was here to talk it over with. Although if she was still alive, then there wouldn't be any need for such upheaval in the first place, would there?

Feeling lost and adrift, Sophie hurried to finish what she needed to do. She couldn't think straight in this house – it still felt as though her mother was just in the other room. And sometimes, as she was going about the business of packing her life away, it was almost as if her mum was standing right next to her.

'Am I doing the right thing, Mum?' she whispered on her last night in the house she'd lived in for nearly all her life. Soon all the things she either couldn't or didn't want to take with her would be packed into the back of a van and locked away in a storage unit until she set foot in England once more.

She took a very long time indeed to drift off to sleep, but as she finally succumbed she could have sworn she felt a cool kiss on her brow and a soft breath of a whispered 'I love you.'

Chapter 7

The odd thing was that on stepping out of the doors of Tenerife's main airport for the second time, Sophie felt as though she was coming home. It was such an unusual feeling that it made her pause for a moment. Technically, she had never been so alone or so adrift in her whole life – despite the temporary job and temporary place to live – and by rights she should be feeling terrified, but she wasn't. She felt liberated and confident as she contemplated making her way up the coast by public transport while carrying so much luggage that she felt like a pack horse.

Before she worked out where to get a bus, she needed to let her aunt know she'd landed safely. Anne had been most insistent yesterday when Sophie had called to say goodbye, and there had been tears on both their faces. She'd found it hard to walk away, to leave her aunt and those two gorgeous little girls behind, but as she'd told Anne more than once, it wasn't for long and three months would soon fly by.

'I've arrived safely,' she said when her aunt answered, and she was immediately treated to a barrage of warnings about eating right, being careful in the sun, not speaking to strangers, and a host of other things that had Sophie trying to stifle her giggles.

She ended the call by promising to take extra care. 'Give those babies a hug and a kiss from me,' she said, a lump in her throat, 'and remind Denise to send me photos. Lots of photos.'

With a deep breath, she pushed thoughts of home to the back of her mind, and approached a holiday company rep to ask her where to catch a bus. The rep pointed her in the general direction and Sophie negotiated the crowds of people and hordes of cars, vans and coaches, and made her way towards the public bus stops. On asking again, a nice gentleman showed her which bus she needed to catch and even asked the driver to let her know when she needed to get off.

As the journey progressed, she began to recognise certain landmarks – and not just the great big volcano in the middle of the island, either – and eventually, after travelling down a straight stretch of road, she spotted the towering cliffs of Los Gigantes in the distance and her heart lifted as she realised she was nearing her destination.

Ooh, look, they were passing through the busy little town of Alcalá, then out the other side and through the familiar banana fields on either side of the road. Finally, the bus rounded a bend and there it was, her home for the next three months. She craned her neck to see through the windscreen and squinted a bit to make sure, but it was definitely the little villa she'd fallen in love with, perched all on its own, on a low rocky outcrop in the middle of the sweeping bay. Its tiled roof glowed terracotta in the mid-afternoon sun and the leaves of the palm trees in its garden fluttered and swayed in the breeze like so many flags set out to welcome her. Beyond the villa, the sea sparkled, the deep blue topped by flecks of white foam as the warm wind whipped up the waves, sending them hurrying for the shore. Even from this distance she could see the spray as the breakers rolled in and crashed against the rocks. The whole scene was exotic and wild, and extremely beautiful.

The driver helped her with her luggage then drove off, leaving her staring at a barrier beyond which a straight narrow track led directly to the villa, with another barrier at the other end, by the coastal path. The track led between fields either side of the road, but on closer inspection she realised they were rather derelict, the plants in them neglected and scruffy, the walls crumbling, and the protective nets either removed or shredded by the wind. As she walked down the road, dragging and carrying various pieces of luggage, she wondered who these abandoned fields belonged to. Were they attached to the villa? And if they were, what did Hugo intend to do with them? Maybe he'd been forced to leave them to their own devices because of his health, but hopefully once he was back on his feet again, he'd be able to restore them to their former glory. It was such a shame to let them fall into disrepair, although she guessed that Mother Nature would claim them back eventually and the bananas would gradually be replaced by the hundreds of varieties of cacti and other native plants.

What was that?

A rustling caught her attention and she stopped, looking around her fearfully, worried that there might be snakes or scorpions hiding in the undergrowth. Did such creatures even exist on Tenerife? She had no idea, but she wasn't prepared to take any chances.

To her relief, she saw it was a lizard. She quite liked lizards, and this one was small and greenish and really rather cute. It had frozen and for a moment she stared at it and it stared back at her, before it found its courage and darted back into the spiky bushes, gone in the blink of an eye.

Embarrassingly, her first comment when Hugo opened the door to the villa after she'd rung the bell wasn't 'How are you?' or 'It's great to be back'. It was 'I just saw a lizard!'

Hugo's eyebrows rose a notch and his lips twitched. 'This is good?'

'Erm… yes?'

'Then I am happy. Come in. Remind me to give you a key.'

He reached out for one of her bags, but Sophie brushed him away. 'Oh, no, you don't. You don't need to be lifting anything heavy. I can manage.' She might be hot, sweaty, and panting a little, but she could definitely manage to carry her bags from the doorstep into her room.

'I'm not old and… what is the word? Weak, that is it. I'm not old and weak yet,' Hugo protested.

Sophie shot him a glance but didn't say anything. In the week since she'd seen him last, Hugo was looking frailer and more gaunt, and she suspected he was in some pain, recognising the signs in the tightness of his mouth and his sunken eyes. The sooner he had the operation, the better.

'I'll just pop this little lot in my room, then I'll make us a nice cup of tea,' she said.

'I don't drink tea.'

'Oh, OK, coffee then?' She made a mental note to buy some teabags when she went to the shop.

'*Bueno.*'

She watched him for a moment as he shuffled off in the direction of the living room, then she picked up her bags, deposited them in her room, and went to the kitchen to make the promised coffee.

'Hello, Paco.' She ruffled the dog's ears as he wandered into the kitchen to greet her, his tongue lolling as he looked at her with big brown eyes. By his sorrowful expression she guessed he probably hadn't been out for a decent walk in a while. She intended to make that her first task after coffee, then she wanted to tackle the kitchen and the bathroom, because Hugo clearly wasn't coping that well with keeping on top of the cleaning, she noticed with a small shudder. On the surface the kitchen didn't look dirty and it was fairly tidy, but closer inspection revealed dried-on stains on the counter top, a rather sticky floor, and – God help her –she almost let out a cry of dismay when she opened the fridge and a decidedly unsavoury smell assaulted her nose.

As she carried the cups into the living room, she was once again taken aback by the astonishing view. She didn't think she'd ever become fed up of looking at it. Although the vista was essentially the same, it was continually different in the way the sun tracked across the sky, the direction the clouds scudded in, the play of light on the water, and the variety of vessels bobbing on the waves. Right now the sea was quite lively, but she knew from her last visit to the island that the water could calm in an instant, and it was this constant change that she particularly loved. It was a bit like British weather but without the rain, and with considerably nicer and more uniform temperatures.

It might be breezy today but it was also warm, verging on hot; a fact that she'd discovered on her trek from the coastal road to the villa. Thankfully, Hugo had opened the large doors, letting the scent of the sea drift through the house, and she breathed in the salty seaweed smell, relishing the freshness.

Hugo was sitting on the terrace and, after placing the coffees on the old wooden table, she took a seat next to him and sat back with a deep sigh, lifting her face to the sun.

'I love it here,' she said. 'The island, this place, your villa.'

He smiled at her. 'As do I. I don't want to have to live anywhere else.'

Sophie reached for her coffee as his words sank in. 'I don't want to', not 'I wouldn't want to', and she would have assumed it was a translation thing if it hadn't been for his tone of voice. He'd sounded sad, regretful, and she wondered why – questions flitting through her head but remaining unasked. She didn't feel she should pry – if he wanted to tell her, then he would. Besides, she might be mistaken, and it hadn't been sadness in his voice that she'd heard but a different emotion altogether.

'Right.' She swallowed the rest of her coffee and stood up. 'I'm going to take Paco out, then have a bit of a potter in the kitchen.' She didn't like to tell him that it needed a darned good scrub from floor to ceiling, in case she hurt his feelings. 'Have you got anything planned for tonight in terms of food?'

'Excuse me?'

'What were you thinking of having for your evening meal?'

Hugo looked out to sea and shrugged. 'There is plenty of pasta and bread.'

When he avoided looking at her, she realised that he probably hadn't had a proper home-cooked meal in a while. She bet that Paco, with his biscuits and tins of dog food, ate better and more regularly than Hugo did.

Well, that was going to change and pretty damned sharpish too. For one thing, the elderly gentleman needed to eat properly to keep his strength up, otherwise he'd be in no fit state to have an operation, and secondly, she didn't intend to live on bread and pasta for the next few months. No matter how ill her mother had been towards the end, Sophie had always made sure to prepare a well-balanced, nutritious meal for the pair of them, and if her mum had only been able to manage a mouthful or two, then so be it. At least Sophie had tried, and sometimes she'd felt that cooking for her mother and persuading her to eat was the only thing she could do to help her in her fight against the inevitable advance of the horrible disease.

There was no way she was going to let Hugo's health deteriorate — not if she could help it — so she added shopping to the list of things she wanted to achieve that afternoon.

Actually, the afternoon was fast turning into the evening, as it was already four o'clock. Thank God she'd managed to get an early morning flight, or they would be dining on little more than fresh air tonight. She could hardly go out to eat and leave Hugo on his own, so she would have had no choice but to eat with him, regardless of how unpalatable the food was.

'Change of plan,' she announced. 'I'll go shopping first.' She knew there was a supermarket in Playa de la

60

Arena and there was undoubtedly one in Alcalá, but with the villa halfway between the two towns, her shopping trip was going to involve a decent walk whichever direction she decided to go in. And she wouldn't be able to carry much either, what with having to haul it all that way. Not only that, but afterwards she wouldn't then feel like taking poor Paco for his walk. It was a pity she couldn't combine the two…

'Will Paco be OK if I tied him up outside a shop?' she asked.

Hugo frowned. 'Why would you want to do that?'

Sophie explained, adding, 'I'll get a taxi tomorrow and do a big shop, but for now we need something more substantial for supper.'

'You're not to take a taxi.'

'Don't worry, I'll pay for it myself – I don't expect you to.'

'Why don't you drive my car?'

'You have a car?' She glanced over her shoulder into the living room as if she expected it to be parked next to the sofa.

'Yes, of course. Didn't I tell you?'

Sophie shook her head. *A car?* Wonderful.

Hang on a sec, did that mean *she* was expected to drive it? Oh, hell, yes, that's exactly what she was expected to do.

'Where is it?' she asked.

'On the main road. You must have walked past it. Juan left it there.'

'Who is Juan?'

'The man who owns the garage. It had to have an ITV.'

'A what?'

61

'*Inspección Técnica de Vehículos*. It's to make sure the car can be allowed on the road. But if you see some of the cars and vans that people drive, I don't think they have it.'

She thought Hugo must be referring to the Canarian equivalent of an MOT. 'I don't have insurance, though,' she pointed out.

'You have a driving licence?'

'Yes...'

'I have insured it for you. I know someone, who knows someone, who fixed it for you to drive my car.'

'OK.' She tried to appear grateful, but to tell the truth she was scared stiff. She'd never driven on the right before, and she didn't know her way around, and all the road signs were in a foreign language, and—

Hugo must have sensed her panic, because he said, 'I will come with you and show you the best supermarket, and we can buy something you like to eat, yes? You'll have to bring the car to me and you'll have to drive, but don't worry, you'll soon be driving like you are Lewis Hamilton.' He chuckled loudly at his own joke.

Sophie wasn't laughing; she was too nervous about the prospect of driving in a foreign country to find it funny. Didn't Hugo realise that she had only ever driven in the UK? And he expected her to get behind the wheel now? *Today?* Eek!

At least she would have the very short reprieve of being able to get used to an unfamiliar car without Hugo sitting in the passenger seat and without being on a public road while she manhandled it down the track to the villa, so she supposed she had to be grateful for small mercies.

With considerable difficulty Hugo struggled to his feet and shuffled back inside, leaving Sophie to gather up the cups, then shut the folding doors and lock them. By the time she'd done that, he'd located his keys and handed them to her.

'This is for the car. This is for the barrier at the top, and this one for the barrier here.'

'Why are the barriers there?' she asked curiously.

'To stop anyone parking on the road. It is my road, and the only way to get onto the main road. Before the barriers, it was always blocked by cars belonging to the surfers. You will need these too.' He dropped another set of keys into her palm. 'A key to the house and to the gate.'

'You don't keep it padlocked all the time, do you?'

'Not when I'm here, but when I go out, I lock it. There are some bad people about.'

Sophie's eyes widened. For some reason she felt that nothing bad could, or would, happen in such a gorgeous part of the world, but she knew he was right.

She had to rein in the feeling that she was on an extended holiday and change her mindset. She lived here now, this was home (for a while), and back in the UK she'd never leave the house without locking it. If she had been fortunate enough to live in the middle of nowhere, she still would have locked her doors. Just because this place was idyllic, it didn't mean there weren't any criminals around, and with so many people using the coastal path which ran between the house and the plantation, all it would take was one thief and an opportunity.

All at once she realised just how isolated and alone she'd be for those few days when Hugo was in hospital, and she was very grateful that she'd have Paco for company. Locked gates, locked doors and a large dog were all the protection she needed.

Chapter 8

Sophie awoke to the boom of waves on rocks and she stretched slowly, letting the sound wash over her. Today was the first day of her adventure in Tenerife, and she intended to savour every minute of it, starting with making some coffee and taking it onto the terrace.

She'd always loved early mornings, when the world was fresh and new, and she sat there for a while, Paco keeping her company, watching the boats bob past. The island of La Gomera was clear this morning, with only a topping of cloud on its highest points and the sun highlighting the folds of the land and a sprinkling of white houses.

Taking a deep breath of fresh salt air, she felt at peace, and a quiet excitement bubbled inside her. Her duties wouldn't be too hard, and she was actually looking forward to cleaning the villa from top to bottom and making it gleam.

'*Buenos días*,' Hugo said, shuffling onto the terrace and easing himself into a chair.

'Morning,' she replied breezily. 'Can I make you a coffee? And some breakfast?'

'Coffee is good. I do not eat breakfast.'

'You don't?' She narrowed her eyes. Was that because he genuinely didn't feel like eating in the mornings or because he couldn't be bothered? 'I'm going to have some pancakes, followed by fruit and yoghurt. Are you sure you wouldn't like some?'

He pretended to think about it, but she noticed the glint in his eyes. 'You can put a little on a plate if you want,' he said, and she knew her instincts were correct.

Sophie switched on the radio and fiddled with it until she found the English station she used to listen to when she was on holiday, humming along to the songs as she set about making the pancake mix and preparing two bowls of chopped fruit topped by generous dollops of creamy yoghurt. It was ages since she'd made pancakes; they used to be her mum's favourite breakfast and she felt a glow in her chest at the thought that her mother would approve of her making them for Hugo. He was too thin for her liking, and she fully intended to build him up before he had his operation.

They ate on the terrace with the soft wind ruffling their hair, and Sophie felt more contented than she had done for a long time. She was beginning to heal, and she knew it would be a slow process, but she understood that she'd made the right decision in coming here.

'Is there anything in particular you'd like me to do today?' she asked, mopping up the last of the syrup with a morsel of fluffy pancake. Hugo, she noticed, had cleared his plate and was diving into the bowl of fruit with gusto.

He shrugged. 'Paco will need a walk.'

'I'll take him after breakfast,' she said. 'Anything else?'

'Maybe you could wash some shirts? I have no more clean ones.' He sounded so apologetic, her heart went out to him.

'Of course, that's what I'm here for. How about if I do what I think needs doing, and you tell me if you're happy with it, or you want me to do something else?' she offered, realising it must be hard for him to have a total stranger sharing his house. She also suspected she wasn't just there for the practical stuff like washing and cleaning; he wanted her company too.

He shrugged again, seeming a bit uncertain.

'Would you like me to fetch you some newspapers? I can walk Paco to the shops and pick you one up?'

'That would be kind,' he replied hesitantly, and she had to tamp down her sudden urge to wrap him in a hug.

'Run me through your normal daily routine,' she suggested. 'I don't want to interfere with it.'

He looked out to sea and pulled a face. 'I make food. I walk Paco a little.' He pulled another face, and she guessed the walking part must be difficult for him. 'I watch the TV. I watch the boats.'

Bless him, it sounded as though he didn't do much at all, and she wondered if he had any family who visited him, or any friends who lived nearby and dropped in to see him. She thought about the ways she used to entertain her mother – doing crosswords together, cross stitching, playing Scrabble and other board games – and she wondered if she could do some of those things with Hugo. Or would the simple fact of having another person in the house be enough for him?

She wanted to ask about his personal life, whether he'd been married or had any children, but she didn't feel she knew him well enough yet, so she told him about her daily routine back home when her mum was still alive and before she became too ill.

'She used to love having me paint her nails,' Sophie said, smiling at the memory, 'and I used to try all kinds of patterns. I wasn't very good at it, but we had fun all the same.'

Hugo held a large, roughened hand out to her and waggled his fingers. 'Red or *rosado* – pink?'

'How about blue, just to be different?' she suggested with a laugh, pleased that she was bringing him out of his shell a little.

There was a hiatus for a few moments, then Hugo said, 'I think I shall like having you here,' and the smile he gave her made her aching heart just that little bit less sore.

She still missed her mother dreadfully, and she always would, but the terrible pain of a few weeks ago had eased a fraction. And if by helping Hugo she also helped heal herself a little more, then it made things easier to bear.

'I think I shall like living here,' she said, and her own smile was as wide as his.

Chapter 9

The speed at which Sophie settled into daily life in the villa astounded her. Hugo was easy to live with, undemanding and uncomplaining, and they muddled along together quite comfortably, each of them content to be in the other's company. They didn't feel the need to chatter all the time either, and Sophie was grateful for that. She'd never been particularly gregarious and the hours and hours when it had just been her and her mum had made her even less talkative. Hugo didn't need entertaining and was perfectly happy to let her potter, and sometimes they'd happily sit for hours without either of them speaking, her with her nose in a book and Hugo attempting a crossword or a Sudoku puzzle.

She quickly became accustomed to going on short runs to the supermarket in the car, often with Hugo accompanying her, which was a help when she was trying to work out what the jar she was holding contained. Sometimes when he couldn't find the right English word, he'd try to describe it or he'd use mime, and she'd fall about in the aisle, giggling at his antics. For a quiet, often reserved man, he had a wicked sense of humour.

When Hugo asked if she would accompany him to the hospital for his pre-operation check she agreed without hesitation, although she had yet to drive any distance on the island, and the thought filled her with trepidation.

'Of course I will. Is there someone you'd like us to pick up on the way?' She knew she wasn't being particularly subtle, but she continued to be curious about whether he had any family. He'd not mentioned anyone and, despite their growing friendship, she still didn't feel it was her place to pry.

'No. No one.'

Should she ask him about the man in the photo? She'd been in his bedroom several times to collect dirty laundry and to put his clean clothes away, and she'd also given the room a clean and changed his sheets since she'd arrived, but she didn't want him to think she'd been snooping, so she bit her tongue.

He'd tell her when he was ready, and she didn't want to delve right now in case there was a heartbreaking story behind the man in the photo. Maybe it was Hugo's son and something had happened to him. Sophie didn't feel she could cope with such sadness at the moment, and especially not with a drive to the hospital on the cards later that morning. She was nervous enough as it was, without allowing herself to get distracted.

However, while Hugo freshened up in the bathroom, Sophie found herself slipping into his bedroom for another quick peek at it.

She picked up the frame and turned it towards the window. Was that a family resemblance between the two men, or was she imagining it? Replacing it quickly, she darted into the hall and slipped her feet into a pair of pumps she'd left by the front door. Whoever the man in the picture was, he was wickedly handsome, and she wished she could meet him in real life, just to check that his good looks weren't a trick of the light or a bit of clever Photoshopping.

'Are you ready?' Hugo asked.

She nodded, although she didn't feel at all ready to tackle busy, unfamiliar roads.

Thankfully, the drive was better than she anticipated, although she didn't particularly like the motorway, and before she knew it she was parking the car and helping Hugo out of the passenger seat. He waved her away, but she hovered regardless, in case he needed her.

Once inside, she sat in the waiting area, wondering if she should offer to go in with him, but he didn't suggest it, so in the end she took a book out of her bag when he was called by a nurse and read until he was ready to leave.

As she sat there, her book open on her lap, she thought about what she loved most about Tenerife, besides the weather. And decided some of it was the large expat presence, which meant there were lots of home comforts if she wanted them, like familiar brands of food and toiletries, some British TV channels, and English newspapers and books. She'd bought the one she was reading from a shop in the town where she'd stayed when she was on holiday, and it made a nice change from trying to read on her phone.

Although she hadn't been on the island long – and she adored the flavours, colours and variety of the local food, the exuberance of the language and the culture – occasionally a wave of homesickness swept over her and she longed for the familiarity of the UK. Being able to read an English novel made her feel a little less cast adrift.

She'd had another one of those homesick moments earlier that day, which was why she'd planned on cooking a roast chicken dinner. Her delight when she'd discovered Bisto gravy granules on a shelf in one of the little shops in a side street in Playa de la Arena was beyond measure and had set the ball rolling for introducing Hugo to a traditional British roast chicken and roast potatoes with a selection of veg to go with it. Her mouth was already watering at the thought of dinner tonight.

She'd make another meal out of the leftovers tomorrow, and she planned on making stock with the carcass so they could have soup later in the week. With fresh crusty bread, it would be an ideal lunch for the pair of them.

She glanced up from her book once more, keeping an eye on the corridor Hugo had been ushered down earlier by one of the nurses, and saw him slowly walking along it. She was about to jump up and hurry to his side, in case he needed her support, when she realised he was speaking into a mobile phone, and she paused. For one thing, she hadn't realised he owned a mobile, having never seen him use it – then again, she'd never seen him use the house phone either – and she also didn't want to intrude on what was clearly a private conversation.

'*Sí*, Alejandro, *sí*,' she heard him say, followed by a stream of Spanish. He sounded happy and upbeat and she wondered who he was speaking to.

'Are you OK?' she asked him, after he'd finished his call.

'*Sí*, I am good. That was my nephew, Alejandro.' He was smiling. 'My sister's son, he is a good boy. He phones me more than she does.'

'That's nice.' Alejandro sounded thoughtful and considerate, and Sophie was glad Hugo had a relative who was taking an interest in the elderly man – although she did wonder why he hadn't visited him since she'd been living at the villa.

'Is everything all set for the operation?' she asked, bringing the subject back to the reason they were at the hospital.

He nodded. 'It will go ahead on Wednesday. If you can drive me here, then collect me in two days, I would be grateful. If anything changes, I will tell you.'

'Oh, no, you don't,' she said, as she helped lower him into the car. He tried to shake her off, but she could tell he was struggling so she ignored his silent protest and the cross look he gave her, and took his arm to steady him. 'If you think I'm leaving you in hospital for two whole days and not visiting, you've got another think coming. When are visiting times?'

'I will be fine,' he said. 'I do not need visitors.'

She glanced at him out of the corner of her eye. He'd become quite cranky all of a sudden, and she already knew he was very independent, but this was taking things too far. She decided to try a different tack.

'You mightn't feel the need for visitors, but what about me? It's not going to take me all day to do a bit of cleaning and walk Paco. I don't know anyone else on the island and I'm worried I'll be lonely.'

It was his turn to shoot her a look, and she could have sworn that the corner of his mouth turned up. 'If you insist, although I warn you, I will not be talking much.'

'What's new?' she retorted with a smile of her own to show she was teasing. 'You never do.'

72

It was true. Sophie suspected that even if he hadn't been in considerable discomfort, he'd never be the life and soul of a party. She had no idea how long he'd lived on his own in the villa, but he'd clearly become used to his own company, although he did talk to Paco on a regular basis. She'd found herself doing the same thing on occasion; Paco was a very easy dog to talk to.

She drove Hugo back to the villa and supervised his painful, slow progress into the living room, where she settled him in his favourite chair and opened the doors wide. Walking out onto the terrace she took a deep breath of sea air and turned her face to the sun, drinking in the warm rays.

'I'll just pop the chicken in the oven,' she said, 'then I'll take Paco for a walk.' After she got back, she'd have a go at tackling that spare room. It didn't look at though it had been cleaned in ages, and she was itching to get in there.

'You are a good person,' Hugo said. 'I am thankful you are here.'

Although their relationship was technically a business one, Sophie was thankful too. 'So am I. I've fallen in love with Tenerife.'

She turned to face him, leaning back against the balustrade, her arms stretched out either side, hearing the rhythmic boom of the waves at her back then the suck and drag of the pebbles, like the slow heartbeat of a giant beast.

'Have you seen much of the island?' he asked.

'A little. I've done some of the touristy things, like visited Teide and Masca Gorge.'

73

'There are many different sides to Tenerife,' Hugo said. 'The south with its noisy bars and nightclubs, and all-you-can-eat buffet restaurants, and shops selling plastic rubbish. Then there is the capital city of Santa Cruz in the north, with its culture and historic buildings. Do you know, it has one of the busiest harbours in Spain, and the most beautiful beach in Tenerife, which is made with sand from the Sahara? And everywhere there are mountains, some of them bare and others with kilometre after kilometre of trees.'

'Wow, it sounds wonderful.' She was also shocked to hear Hugo say so much in one go.

'It is wonderful.' He rested his head on the back of his armchair. 'Now, leave me, please. I am tired and I want to sleep for a while.'

He closed his eyes and Sophie noticed how wan he looked, and how much the lines on his face had deepened. The hospital appointment had really taken it out of him.

She prepared the chicken with Paco supervising her every move, his gaze never leaving the bird until she put it in the oven. Then she lifted his lead off the hook near the front door and called him to her. She decided to go north towards Playa de la Arena and pop into the little shop where she'd found the Bisto gravy to see if they had any packets of stuffing. She hadn't thought about it at the time, but a nice bit of Paxo's finest sage and onion would set the meal off a treat.

The sun was deliciously warm on her back and she remembered how much her mum had loved the summer. Although technically it was winter here, it was a far cry from the depressingly short days, the constant rain and the dipping temperatures she'd left behind. Her mother would have loved Tenerife, and for a moment her grief threatened to rise up and swamp her.

It often hit her when she least expected it, and she knew from experience that the only thing she could do was to let it wash over her. So she perched on one of the large rocks which lined the path and let the sorrow take her, knowing she'd feel better if she didn't fight it.

Paco, bless him, sensed there was something wrong and came and sat at her feet, his tail wagging gently as he stared up at her with a seemingly concerned expression. Absently she stroked his fluffy ears, taking some comfort from his presence.

She hated feeling so wretched and she knew her mother would have been appalled to see her like this, but a part of her never wanted to let go of the intense sorrow because that was all she had left of her.

Chapter 10

'Paco, sit,' Sophie commanded, snapping her fingers and pointing to the pavement outside Mrs Tiggywinkle's. Paco obediently sat, his tongue lolling. He knew what was expected of him, even if she wasn't totally sure he understood the English word 'sit'. He knew the drill and that he wasn't allowed inside.

She loved the name of the shop – it was so English, like a little piece of home. And that was exactly what it stocked, shelf upon shelf of familiar items that could be found in any British supermarket, from food to toiletries, and newspapers to books. She couldn't find all her favourite items (like Marmite-flavour crisps), but it was a start.

Expecting to see Mrs Tiggywinkle herself behind the counter, Sophie was surprised to see an unfamiliar man operating the till. He was about her own age, maybe a couple of years older, slim, fairly good-looking, with light brown hair which had been bleached to blond at the ends flopping over his forehead. British, she guessed, because... well, he just looked it.

'Er, excuse me, do you have any stuffing?' she asked when he glanced up.

He gave her a broad smile and she could have sworn there was an appreciative look in his eyes when he saw her.

'Just over there, next to the baked beans. I've no idea why my mother thinks that's a logical place for it, but she insists that's where it belongs, and who am I to argue?'

'You're Mrs Tiggywinkle's son?'

He laughed, his eyes twinkling. 'You do realise that's not her real name, right?'

She felt herself blushing. 'Of course I do, but I don't know what else to call her.' Actually, she hadn't been entirely sure that it wasn't her real name. She once knew someone called Henrietta Criebabie (pronounced 'cry baby'), so anything was possible.

'Tracey Brockman, and my dad's name is Ted. I'm Dominic, by the way. Are you here on holiday?'

'I'm Sophie.' She smiled back at him. 'I'm not on holiday, although I *was*. I live here now.'

'Cool.' He nodded at the packet of stuffing. 'Still missing the home comforts, though?'

'Yeah, there's only so much of this deliciously healthy Mediterranean food I can take before I crave a bit of stodge in the form of roast potatoes, Yorkshire pudding and gravy.'

'I know what you mean. I've been here since I was thirteen, but I still need egg, beans and chips now and again, with a dollop of brown sauce.'

Sophie looked horrified. 'Don't you mean tomato sauce?'

'Nope. Tomato sauce is so wrong. Except in a hot dog. And maybe a burger.'

She laughed as she paid for her purchase. 'You ought to have a sign around your neck, warning people of your weirdness.'

'Now you're just being rude,' he said, but he was laughing so she knew he was taking it in the spirit it was meant. He glanced at the door. 'Is Paco with you?'

Paco must have become fed up waiting for her, because he was standing half in and half out of the doorway and looking expectantly at her.

Sophie grinned at the sight. 'Yes. You know him?'

Dominic walked out from behind the counter and called the dog to him. Paco padded over, wagging his tail in that slow way of his. 'Good, I thought for a moment that Hugo's dog had taken it upon himself to go for a wander.'

'No, he's with me. I thought I'd combine walking him with a visit to your shop. A two birds and one stone kind of thing.'

'How is Hugo? I haven't seen him for a while.'

Sophie hesitated, not sure how much she should say about Hugo's health. He seemed a very private man and she didn't want to share anything she shouldn't. 'He's good,' she replied diplomatically.

Dominic was ruffling Paco's ears and the dog had a blissful look on his face. 'So, apart from the fantastic weather, the beautiful scenery and the wonderful atmosphere, what brings you to Tenerife?' he asked.

'Work, mostly.' She didn't feel it necessary to add the fact that the work in question came with live-in accommodation, which made it all possible, or that her employer was Hugo himself.

'Oh?' He was looking at her curiously, but she didn't explain. 'Are you living in Playa de la Arena?'

'Actually, I'm living at Hugo's place,' she said.

His eyes widened. 'You're at Villa Delfín?'

Was that what it was called? She'd had no idea. To her, it was simply 'the villa', and she'd never even thought to ask. There was no nameplate, no sign or plaque that she'd noticed.

'Yes, Villa Delfín.' She tried the name out on her tongue, liking the feel of it. 'I meant to ask Hugo what *delfín* means, but I keep forgetting,' she lied. Was it some kind of family name?

'It means dolphin. Years ago, they used to come in so close that you could see them from the shore, but there's a bit too much traffic out there now, so they tend to stay in deeper water.'

Dolphin? How lovely. There was a substantial tourist trade in whale and dolphin watching, and she often saw boats grouping around what she assumed to be a pod of the lovely creatures.

'I must get back,' she said, 'before my roast chicken becomes a charcoal chicken.'

'Nice to meet you,' Dominic said, straightening up as Paco backed out of the door. 'Maybe I'll see you again?' His expression was hopeful.

'Maybe,' she said as she left, smiling to herself.

He was nice; friendly and pleasant to talk to. And he was probably the only man who had looked at her twice in years.

Then she told herself to stop being so silly, because he was probably just as nice to everyone and she'd imagined the way he'd looked at her had meant anything. The last time she went out on a date was…? She honestly couldn't remember.

It would be lovely to have some romance in her life though, even if it did have to be relatively short-lived.

Chapter 11

The following day was yet another glorious one. The tide was in, which meant that the natural seawater pool on the edge of Alcalá would be full. She hadn't summoned the courage to take a dip yet, but she'd seen plenty of people swimming there, and Paco loved it. She'd asked Hugo what breed of dog he was, and Hugo thought he was a Newfoundland. The dog had a thick black coat, which Sophie enjoyed grooming, and Hugo had drawn her attention to the dog's webbed feet, a feature typical for the breed. He wasn't entirely certain Paco was a purebred, and neither was he sure of the dog's age, having obtained him from an animal shelter, but one thing was certain, the dog loved to swim, and no surf was too high or too rough for him.

Today she intended to let him swim in the *piscina natural*, and she took one of his balls along to throw for him. He loved nothing better than retrieving it from the water. Again and again and again. Never seeming to tire of it, Paco would happily retrieve all day, as long as there was water involved, and she guessed the constant immersion in the sea helped keep him cool.

She reminded herself to give him another grooming session after dinner to brush the salt from his fur. Then she quietly chuckled to herself; most people who were lucky enough to find themselves in her position might be planning on a more exciting evening, like opening a bottle of wine and watching the sun go down, or maybe checking out one of the nearby bars. Or even spending the evening somewhere far more lively, like a nightclub.

Not her – she was planning on grooming a dog.

It occurred to her as she spread a towel out on the rough rocks and sat down to dangle her feet in the salt-water pool that she was getting old before her time, that she should be living life to the full and wringing every second of fun out of it.

But all the fun had been sucked out of her from watching her mother's slow, inevitable decline. She felt that her youth had died along with her mum, and it was probably too late to do anything about it now. All of her friends – those same friends she used to giggle about boys with and share bottles of rosé with before going out clubbing – were now married, and many of them had children too.

A bolt of envy shot through her at the thought that life seemed to have passed her by, but she swiftly chased it away. She was hardly old at thirty-three. There was plenty of time for her to start living again. Her problem was that she didn't know how to any more. But for the moment, at least, she was happier than she'd been for a very long time, and she intended to make the most of her stay on Tenerife, to recharge her depleted batteries and work out what she wanted to do with the rest of her life.

She didn't have to make any decisions today, though. All she had to do right now was to keep throwing the ball, and she found she was taking a great deal of delight in making one shaggy dog very happy.

When they got back, Sophie wondered whether to visit Mrs Tiggywinkle's again. She didn't actually need anything, but Dominic kept popping into her mind. Apart from Hugo, he was the only person she'd really spoken to since she'd moved into the villa, except to ask the price of something. She wasn't feeling lonely; it was more a feeling of restlessness, a need to chat with someone closer to her own age (sorry, Hugo) or who could actually join in with a conversation (sorry, Paco). However, she'd been out once today walking the dog and she wasn't sure whether she could be bothered to go out again. She supposed she could always ask to borrow the car for an hour. Not that she had to ask, Hugo had assured her, but she didn't like to take it without him knowing.

'I met Mrs Tiggywinkle's son yesterday,' she said to Hugo, who was sitting on the terrace staring out to sea, deep in thought. He was having his operation tomorrow, and she guessed it must be playing on his mind.

'That is not her real name,' he said with a smile.

'I know. Dominic told me she's called Tracey Brockman.' She paused, then asked, 'What do you know about them?'

Hugo shrugged. 'They are English, they came here about twenty years ago and opened the shop. That is all I know.'

Since he'd told her he moved to Tenerife when he was thirteen, that would make Dominic about thirty-three, the same age as her. 'I haven't seen him there before,' she said.

'He has his own job.'

'What does he do?' Gosh, this was like pulling teeth.

Hugo turned to look at her. 'Why are you so interested?' There was a knowing expression on his face and a hint of a twinkle in his eyes.

'No reason,' she replied, and Hugo chuckled.

'He has a radio show in the mornings, an English show. You have listened to him sometimes.'

Her eyes nearly popped out of her head. 'I have?' She usually tuned into an English-language station in the mornings because she liked the music – a wide range from the seventies to the present day, and nearly all of it stuff she could sing along to. The presenter wasn't really the same Dominic as she'd met in Mrs Tiggywinkle's shop, was it? She hadn't for a moment thought his voice sounded familiar, though, so she vowed to listen to his show tomorrow morning when— Oh, actually, she wouldn't have time because she'd be taking Hugo to hospital in the morning for his operation, a thought that quickly sobered her. She hoped he'd be OK; in the short period of time she'd known him, she'd grown to care about the old man. Not that he was all that old, she conceded, being around her aunt's age.

'He surfs,' Hugo announced, breaking into her thoughts. 'Out there.' He pointed to the southern end of the small bay, where the waves crashed and surged against an outcrop of rocks. She'd noticed that the rollers tended to be larger there and start further out than in any other stretch along the coastal path. She'd seen surfers there often when the sea wasn't too rough, bobbing about in their sleek wetsuits like so many seals playing. While she admired their sense of adventure, she wasn't in the least bit tempted to take a dip herself in the chilly water.

She decided she'd look out for him the next time she walked to Alcalá, although in their black suits the surfers all looked very much alike.

But as she was making sure Hugo's bag was packed and that he had everything he needed for his short stay in hospital, she couldn't help wondering why she was bothering herself about Dominic. In a few short months she'd be back in England, and while Dominic might be good-looking and nice to talk to, she'd been on her own for so long that maybe she wouldn't recognise a spark if it burst into flame and set her hair on fire. She also didn't know for sure whether he fancied her, so it was a moot point anyway.

She came to the conclusion that she was being silly because her emotions were all over the place from the loss of her mother. A brief romance wasn't going to heal the big hole in her heart; she needed to give herself time to grieve properly and not try to fill the emptiness inside her by throwing herself at the first man who showed an interest (if indeed he actually had). She needed to concentrate on Hugo and her job, and to start planning for her future back in the UK. She was realistic enough to understand that it wasn't love that she needed right now – it was security. And at the moment she had neither, just a temporary job and a temporary home, and a temporary respite from her life in England.

With a despondent sigh, she added a bar of soap to Hugo's washbag, then zipped the whole thing up. The problem was, she much preferred this life to anything she could envisage when her time in Tenerife was up. By trying to run away from her problems she'd actually gone and created a few new ones. She'd fallen in love with the

island and the villa, and was becoming increasingly fond
of Hugo and Paco too, and she simply couldn't bear the
thought of having to leave any of them.

Chapter 12

Hugo had only been gone a few hours and already Sophie was missing him. Although he mightn't say a great deal, he was always there, another person in the house. Of course, Paco was also there too, but it wasn't the same.

Since she'd dropped Hugo off at the hospital (she'd waited with him until the very last minute), she'd cleaned the villa from top to bottom, weeded and watered the garden, washed the terrace down, taken Paco for a walk (no surfers today), and made herself some dinner which she'd eaten outside while watching the sun slip down over the misty island of La Gomera.

Actually, the sunset had been the most spectacular one she'd ever seen, and she wished she'd had someone to share it with. Hugo had probably seen hundreds, if not thousands, of such sights, but the display of scarlet, orange, peach and purple had taken her breath away.

It was only when she stood up to take her plate into the kitchen that she realised the sky to the west above Mount Teide looked rather weird. It was an odd ochre colour, and she wondered if there was a storm brewing.

Please not tonight, she prayed, not with her only having Paco for company. She had visions of the sea pounding the rocks and sending spray high into the air, and the wind whipping around the villa. She also had visions of the electricity going off, and the thought of being without light and all alone was rather worrying. She wouldn't mind if the villa was in a village, but it was on its own in the bay. There was the farmhouse near the headland, but even that was some distance away.

'Paco,' she called nervously, and the dog came padding over to her and leant against her legs. His weight made her stagger slightly, and she felt a little calmer at the feel of his solid body against her. Paco didn't seem worried and she trusted him to let her know if anything was amiss. She also trusted him to protect her, but considering he'd never shown the slightest hint of aggression, she had no idea why she thought that; it was just a feeling she had that he wouldn't let anything happen to her.

She wasn't going to take any chances, though, and if there really was a storm brewing, she wanted to be prepared, so with that in mind she made her way around the outside of the house, closing all the shutters and battening down the proverbial hatches. Once back indoors, she had to grope around for the light switch, as the interior of the villa was now in almost total darkness because she'd forgotten to turn any on before she'd gone outside.

'You can stop laughing,' she muttered to the dog. He was staring up at her, his tongue lolling to one side, and she could have sworn he was finding the whole thing amusing. 'You'll soon be coming to me for cuddles once the thunder starts,' she warned him. 'Let's see who'll be laughing then.'

To be honest, she suspected neither of them would be, so she checked the doors and windows again, this time from the inside, then dug around in one of the cupboards for a bag of tea lights. She'd found them while cleaning one day and had wondered at the time why Hugo needed such a large bag. She knew now, all right...

But to her surprise the lights didn't go out. The electricity was still on when she went to bed, although she did turn everything off at that point, including her bedside lamp, because no matter how scared of being alone she was, she couldn't sleep with the light on. Besides, she'd feel a bit of a baby if she didn't, and with Paco snuggled up beside her on the bed, she was sure she'd be safe enough.

As she drifted off to sleep, she sent a goodnight thought to her mum and another to Hugo. Although she wasn't a relative, the hospital had very kindly given her an update on his condition, and she'd been relieved to hear that the operation had gone well and that he was awake and had eaten some food. Or rather, that's what she thought the person on the other end of the phone had said, because their English was a little difficult to understand. At least she could go to sleep knowing that Hugo was OK, and she was looking forward to seeing him tomorrow.

That was her last thought before she drifted off, and she had no idea how long she'd been asleep when a noise woke her.

At first she lay there wondering if she'd actually heard the clang of the gates or if she'd dreamt it. But when the sound wasn't repeated, she turned over, deciding she must have imagined it, and stretched out a hand to stroke Paco. The dog wasn't there, so maybe she had heard something after all, and she tried to remember if she'd filled his water bowl before she went to bed. He had been known to give the metal dish a bang with his paw if it was empty, which would explain the clang—

Sophie froze; could she hear Paco growling?

Alert now, she sat up in bed, her eyes wide as she stared towards the bedroom door, trying to see if it was open. She'd definitely shut it before she'd climbed into bed, she recalled, but with the shutters closed, the inside of the villa was as dark as the underworld, and she couldn't tell if Paco had pawed it open.

The dog growled again, low and menacing.

'Paco,' she hissed, wanting the reassurance of having him by her side, 'Come here' – but he ignored her.

Should she lie there and hope that whoever it was would go away, or should she be brave and go and investigate? Oh, God, she didn't know what to do for the best.

A click of claws on tiles told her the dog was on the move and she strained to listen. Was that the sound of something in the lock? Someone was definitely outside the front door and it sounded as though they were trying to pick the lock.

Her heart hammering and her mouth dry, she reached out a trembling hand towards the lamp, hesitated, then withdrew it again. Switching the lamp on meant that she might be able to see whoever was breaking into the villa, but it also meant that the burglar would be able to see her. Maybe it was better to let Paco deal with the intruder? They wouldn't know what had hit them when a huge black dog launched himself at them from the darkness.

But what if they were armed? Paco might be injured, and she wouldn't be able to live with herself if anything were to happen to him because of her cowardice.

She reached out again, then stifled a yelp as a warm, wet tongue licked her cheek. 'Paco!' she hissed. How she wished she'd brought her phone into the bedroom, but she'd hardly used it since she'd moved into the villa and she wasn't sure where she'd put it. It was around here somewhere…

Oh, God, she could have sworn the front door had just opened – it tended to squeak a little – but the noise might have come from her own throat as she sat there clutching the sheet to her chin, terror surging through her.

She was going to die, she simply knew it. Or worse—

A bang, then a muttered curse – '*Mierda*'. She knew what that meant, having heard Hugo say it every time he dropped his walking stick. Shit, indeed, she thought hysterically; shit, shit, shit—

There was someone just outside her bedroom; she could hear the rustle of their clothes and the faint sound of breathing, and she held her own breath, but her heart was thudding so loudly in her ears she was convinced the intruder must be able to hear it too.

Where the hell was the dog and why wasn't he defending her? He could at least growl a warning. Perhaps he was just as scared, and the thought sent her pulse rocketing.

'Argh!'

Sophie wasn't sure who screamed the loudest as light flooded the room, her or the man standing in the doorway, one hand on the light switch, the other on his chest.

For a second neither of them moved and the only sound was Paco's soft panting and the thump of his tail on the floor as he wagged it.

'Get him, Paco,' she urged, coming to life before the intruder managed to gather himself and attack her.

Paco continued to sit there, tongue out, looking far happier than he should do under the circumstances. She was about to get murdered in her bed and all the dog could do was wag his tail and grin?

Sophie shrank back against the pillows as the man squared his shoulders and took a step towards her, firing a string of Spanish at her. Oh, God, he looked familiar too, and she desperately prayed that she hadn't seen his face on the news, being wanted for murder or something.

'Get away from me!' she shrieked. 'Stay back, I've got a gun.' To her immense surprise she found herself poking a finger under the sheet and pointing it in his direction. *What the hell was she doing?*

The man halted, a quizzical frown creasing his brow. 'A gun,' he repeated in English. He looked meaningfully at what was clearly a finger with a sheet draped over it.

Sophie looked down, then yanked her hand out from under the sheet and curled it into a fist. Her other hand still clutched the sheet to her chin. 'I won't go down without a fight,' she warned him. 'I'm stronger than I look.'

'I doubt that,' he said, taking another step into the room.

'I warn you, I'm going to scream so loud...'

'Go ahead,' he offered. 'Who do you think is going to hear you?'

She swallowed convulsively, all bravado abruptly draining away. 'Please don't hurt me,' she said in a small voice as the reality of her situation sank in. He was right – the villa was too far away for anyone to hear her, however much noise she made, and she was no match for a man of his size. She tried not to whimper as she begged, 'Take anything you want; my bag is by the sofa; the car keys are in the kitchen. Take it all, but please leave me alone.'

'I'm not going to hurt you, and neither am I going to take anything.'

'I don't understand,' she said. Please go away, just go away, she muttered silently to herself. 'What do you want?'

'A bed for the night, and to see my uncle. Why are you here, and more to the point, who the hell are you?'

'You can't sleep here,' she blurted, then she paused. 'Your uncle?'

'Yes, my uncle, Hugo Santana Negrin. He does still live here, doesn't he?' Suddenly this strange man looked far less sure of himself. In fact, he looked decidedly worried. And she now knew where she'd seen him before, and she wished the ground would swallow her up because she'd just made a total fool of herself. But then again, he had to take part of the blame for that: it simply wasn't right, breaking into people's houses in the middle of the night and scaring them half to death. And he had the better part of a week's worth of stubble on his face. He looked older too.

'Hugo?' he prompted as she sat there staring at him.

She swallowed, her mouth suddenly dry. 'Er, yes, I know Hugo. This is his house.'

'Okaay... does he still live here, or has he' – the man blinked slowly and took a deep breath, then let it out – 'rented it out to you?'

'He still lives here.'

'I see.' He nodded slowly. 'And you are...?'

'Sophie Lakeland.' She was still hanging onto the sheet for dear life, but at least now she wasn't fearful that she was about to be murdered in her bed. 'Are you Alejandro?'

'I am. But your name means nothing to me. Are you sleeping with my uncle?'

Sophie blinked, taken aback both by the idea and his bluntness. 'Does it look like it?' she demanded, indicating the empty space on the other side of the bed. The fact that Hugo's bed was also empty tonight was neither here nor there.

'No, but—'

'How dare you suggest that anything improper is going on!' Sophie had gone from petrified to incandescent with rage in the space of a heartbeat.

'It wasn't a suggestion; it was a question.'

'I don't care what it was! Just get out of my room. Go on, get out.'

'I'm going, I'm going.' He raised his hands, palms out. 'I'll go and speak to Hugo.' And with that he turned on his heel and strode out of her bedroom.

Sophie fell back against the pillows with a sigh of relief, but it was short-lived. No sooner had she made a move to get out of bed than he was back, clearly having discovered that Hugo wasn't in his bed.

'Where is he?' Alejandro demanded. 'What have you done with my uncle?'

'I resent your tone and the insinuation. What the hell makes you think I've done anything with him?' She was half in and half out of bed, and was very thankful that she'd worn her thick pyjamas tonight in anticipation of the encroaching storm.

'Because you're here and he's not?'

'The reason for that, if you'd care to ask and not jump to silly conclusions, is that he had his operation today and he's in hospital.'

'I'm sorry?'

'That's OK, I accept your apology.'

'I wasn't apologising.'

'Hmph! You should. It's not nice to accuse people when you don't know the facts.'

'What operation?'

'See, that's what I mean. Now, do you mind getting out of my room and shutting the door? I need to get dressed.'

'I haven't finished talking yet.'

'I have,' she replied firmly. 'Stick the kettle on. We'll have a nice cup of tea, and you can apologise properly.'

He gave her an incredulous look, but he did as he was told, and she heard him stomp off down the hall, Paco following him.

'Yeah, you were a great help,' she muttered at the dog's retreating back, then she dropped down onto the bed and blew out her cheeks. Crikey, that was an interesting few minutes, she thought. Thanks, Hugo. He might have warned her that his nephew was arriving.

He also might have warned her that the man who had scared her half to death was one of the most devastatingly handsome men she had ever set eyes on.

Chapter 13

'I'm sorry,' Alejandro said, as she warily sidled into the kitchen, wishing she'd taken the time to brush her hair, put on some make-up and a nice dress, shave her legs...

'You really didn't know Hugo was going in for an operation?' she asked.

'No. Is it serious?'

'Hip replacement.'

'Ah.' The kettle came to the boil and switched itself off. Alejandro stared at her as she popped a couple of teabags into some mugs. 'Tea? Really? That's so—'

'English?'

'Yeah.'

'I *am* English,' she pointed out frostily. He might be as heart-stoppingly handsome as his photo had suggested, but she didn't think he was all that bright. Or polite.

'So I gather. When did he have the operation?'

'Today.' She checked the time on the clock hanging on the kitchen wall. 'Yesterday,' she amended.

'How is he?'

'It went well, and he had eaten something when I phoned,' she told him.

'Good, good. Can I ask you a question? Why are you here?'

'Hugo needs someone to help around the house for a couple of months while he recuperates.'

'I see,' he said.

There was a pause.

Gosh, this was awkward, she thought, then something occurred to her. 'It's the middle of the night.'

'I know.'

'That's a strange time to be visiting.'

'I'm not visiting. Not exactly. I am here because of work.'

'Oh, I see.' Actually, she didn't. It was still the middle of the night. Couldn't he have arrived in the morning, like any normal person?

'It's the middle of the night because I flew in from Iceland via Madrid and spent a couple of hours with my parents before catching a flight to Tenerife. There was a delay at Madrid airport; otherwise I'd have been here much earlier. I was trying to be quiet,' he added. 'Why are all the shutters closed? I thought the place had been abandoned.'

'There's a storm coming.'

He frowned, a crease forming between his brows. He looked sexy in a glowering kind of way. 'I don't think so,' he said.

See, not too much going on in that pretty head of his... She thought she'd better explain. 'The sky was a strange yellowy orange, like when the sky back home is full of snow. So I closed the shutters and got the candles out, just in case.'

'It's the *calima*,' he said with a smile. 'A wind which blows across the island from the west, carrying dust from the Sahara Desert. What you could see in the sky wasn't clouds, but airborne particles. If the wind is strong enough it can blow Saharan dust right across the Atlantic to the Americas. It should clear in a couple of days, but if it gets really bad you might want to stay inside. Do you have asthma?'

'No.' She might have to revise her opinion of his intelligence, she decided, feeling a bit of an idiot. Perhaps he simply lacked basic social skills?

'Then you should be OK,' he told her.

'Oh, good. Tea?'

'I prefer coffee.'

'Right.' She removed a teabag from one of the mugs and set about making his drink, grateful for something else to focus on other than his handsome face and the way his T-shirt clung to his chest.

What the hell was the matter with her? Get a grip, she told herself. It wasn't as if she hadn't seen a good-looking guy before. Except this one had woken her in the middle of the night, had given her the fright of her life, and was now standing a few feet away from her, lounging against the kitchen worktop and looking like some sort of film star. Damn him.

She handed him his coffee and took a gulp of her tea, nearly burning her lips on the scalding liquid. 'Work, you said?'

'Yeah, there are, um, some things I need to check out.'

'I see.' She didn't. 'Where do you work?'

'The Pacific Rim, mostly.'

She was none the wiser. It must be a bar or a club of some kind; it sounded like the sort of place that could be found in Playa de las Americas, where things were altogether much more lively than here. But why had he flown in from Iceland? She guessed he must have been on holiday. Although it wasn't the sort of place she'd want to go for a week's R & R, it did appeal to some people. And maybe Alejandro wanted a change from the usually balmy Canaries, and be on the receiving end of some truly cold weather.

'You've come from Iceland? I bet it's cold.' Sophie bit her lip; she couldn't believe she was talking about something as inane as the weather.

'Just a bit, although it does get warm if you get too near a crater.' He smiled, a quirky upturn of his lips.

'Right.' She had no idea what he was talking about. Was he making some kind of a joke? 'What do you do, exactly?'

'Oh, I assumed you knew.' The smile disappeared and she could have sworn he looked embarrassed. 'I'm a research scientist, a volcanologist.'

Sophie closed her eyes slowly, before opening them again as his words sank in. He didn't work in Playa de las Americas, he probably hadn't been on holiday in Iceland, and the crater he was talking about was a volcanic one.

This man, who had sneaked into the house in the middle of the night and who she'd begun to think of as a bit dumb, was probably one of the most intelligent people she'd ever met.

Who was the dumb one in this kitchen now?

She tried a different line of conversation. 'Are you staying long?'

'That depends on whether there's a bed for me here. I usually sleep in the room you're in.'

The thought of him laying his head on the very same bed as she'd just risen from made her feel a little funny. Nice funny, as in a bit warm and fuzzy.

'Sorry… let me just… it won't take me a moment to…' Sophie put her mug down and glanced around frantically, wondering where to start. Should she just grab all the bedding off her bed (*Alejandro's* bed) and do a quick swap? But what about all her things? She didn't feel comfortable leaving her underwear in drawers he might use. Not that she thought he'd go rooting around in her knicker drawer… Oh, bugger.

'There's no need. I can sleep on the sofa,' he said.

'Oh, but—'

'No buts. I wouldn't dream of throwing you out of your bed.'

'But—'

He held up a hand. 'I'm serious. The sofa will be absolutely fine.'

'There's another bedroom,' she blurted.

'I know, but have you been in there? It's full of stuff from the floor to the ceiling.'

Sophie allowed herself a smug smile. 'Not anymore.'

Alejandro cocked his head to the side and gave her a thoughtful look. 'Is that your doing?'

She nodded. 'It won't take me a moment to pop some sheets on the bed.'

'That's OK, I can make up my own bed.' His gaze roamed around the spotless kitchen. 'I take it you're responsible for this too?'

'Yes.'

There was an awkward silence. At least, Sophie felt awkward; she wasn't sure how Alejandro felt. He did look perfectly at home, though, and she wondered how often he visited Hugo.

'Erm, Alejandro, when will you be going back to Iceland?' she asked.

'Call me Alex, everyone does. And that depends.'

'On what?'

'On… stuff. Things.' He looked at everything and anything but her, and she began to think that maybe he was running away from something, like a relationship. Or perhaps he was in trouble at work. He seemed rather reluctant to go into detail, and she narrowed her eyes at him, wondering what kind of trouble he might be in.

'Right. Good. It's late. Very late. I'm going back to bed. I think you'd better come too.' She didn't like the thought of him prowling around while she was asleep, even though he had more right to be here than she did.

Alex was smiling at her wryly, and she realised what she'd just said and how it had sounded. 'I mean, go to your own bed,' she amended, blushing furiously. 'On your own. In the other room.'

His smile turned into a low, sexy chuckle and her insides did a flip. She bit her lip. This was not the time nor the place to have these kinds of feelings, and Alex was definitely not the man to have them for. He was too handsome for his own good for a start, plus he was Hugo's nephew, plus the two of them were on their own in the middle of the night, and she was feeling lonely and vulnerable and in desperate need of comfort.

She suspected he'd give her more than comfort. And her stomach did that annoying flippy thing again at the thought.

Huffing out a sigh, Sophie strode into what she'd been calling the spare room, yanked open the top drawer of an old (but polished to within an inch of its life) chest, and dragged out a pair of clean sheets and a couple of pillowcases. As she proceeded to make the bed, she gave herself a good old telling off. She might be in the market for a little bit of romance (Dominic's face popped into her mind), but she wasn't prepared to get her heart broken on the way. And Alex was a definite heartbreaker, she could tell. Not that she'd had much experience of his type of man, but just by the way he made her feel, she knew she'd better keep her distance. She'd known him all of half an hour, and he was already making her feel distinctly un-Sophie-like.

Gradually she became aware of him leaning against the door frame, watching her.

'Leave that,' he said. 'I'll finish making the bed. You go get some sleep.'

'What about you?' she asked suspiciously.

'I'm going to sleep too. As you said, it's late.'

Reluctantly, she straightened up and moved away from the bed. 'Good night, then.'

'Good night. I'm sorry to have frightened you.'

'You didn't,' she retorted, although he most definitely had.

'Disturbed you, then,' he said.

He most definitely had done that too, and she lay awake for a long time after he'd stopped pottering quietly around in the spare room, and long after silence had descended on the villa, unable to rid herself of the feeling that her life was about to be turned upside down. Again.

Chapter 14

Sophie's first thought when she heard noises coming from the kitchen was that Hugo was up unaccustomedly early. Her second was to remember what had happened last night. Every single detail. For the first time since she'd moved into the villa, she wished she didn't have to share a bathroom. She'd dearly like to have a quick shower, wash her hair, put on some make-up, and dig out her nicest pair of jeans.

Then she realised that Alex had already seen her bare-faced, messy-haired and wearing her fluffy pyjamas, so did it matter if she wandered into the kitchen looking the same as she had done last night?

Yes, yes, it did.

But the fact that she was so bothered at the thought of him seeing her au naturel perversely persuaded her to do nothing more than grab her bathrobe off the hook on the back of the door and saunter into the kitchen as though the most attractive man she'd ever set eyes on wasn't already in there, peering at the contents of the fridge.

'Morning,' she muttered, envying him his fresh look. She felt as though she'd been run over by a steamroller. Twice.

'Good morning. Have you looked outside?'

She hadn't. The only thing she'd looked at was him. She noticed that he'd had a shower, and a shave too. His chin was bare and droplets of water clung to his wet hair. To distract herself, she hastily glanced out of the kitchen window, at the same time realising that something looked a little odd. Alex had opened all the shutters, but instead of the usual silver light preceding the sun rising over the mountains in the east, the sky was the same shade of pale orange-yellow that it had been last night.

'It will soon disappear,' Alex informed her. 'The wind will be coming from the north by the end of the day and will blow it away.'

'That's good.' Why were they talking about the weather again? In her limited experience the subject didn't hold the same fascination for people living in Tenerife as it did for those in the UK – possibly because there wasn't such variety on an almost hourly basis. Which made her wonder if Alex was feeling as awkward as she was. It couldn't have been easy for him, expecting to slip into the villa for a quiet sleep before having breakfast with Hugo the following morning, only to discover a strange woman in his bed and his uncle alarmingly absent.

'I'll phone the hospital later,' she said, 'and see what sort of a night Hugo had. Then I'll visit him this afternoon.'

'What time?'

'About three-ish.'

'I'll come with you. Do you mind if I take the car this morning? I need to go to INVOLCAN.' He saw her bemused expression. 'Volcanology Institute of the Canaries. It is the organisation for monitoring all seismic activity on the islands.'

She knew Mount Teide was a live volcano, but just how alive was it? And what was this talk of seismic activity? Was there anything she needed to be worried about? Was that why Alex was here?

'Everything is all right, isn't it?' she ventured to ask.

'Of course it is.'

Sophie squinted at him; he sounded far too bright and chirpy for a man who'd flown in from Iceland in the middle of the night to look at some 'things'. What sort of things, she wanted to know. Was there any danger?

He smiled at her. 'I promise to be back by three o'clock,' he said. 'Cross my heart and hope to die.' He crossed his heart, his expression earnest.

Oh yes, she thought, there definitely *was* danger. She was in serious danger of developing a serious crush on this man.

'Erm, what will you be doing for dinner tonight?' She wanted to know whether she should cook for him or not. She wished Hugo had given her some notice of Alex's arrival, and what, if anything, she was supposed to do with him. Was she expected to prepare meals for this man? It wouldn't be a problem because she had to eat something anyway, but it would be handy to know.

'Are you asking me to dinner?' he chuckled, a teasing expression on his face, and she narrowed her eyes at him.

'I cook for Hugo,' she explained haughtily. 'I just wondered if I was expected to cook for you too.' Then she realised how grumpy and surly she sounded, and added, 'I mean, it's not a problem; I'd just like to know because it would affect what I cook.' She'd been planning a simple salad because it would just be her, but now that it mightn't be, she'd make something more substantial.

'I'm easy,' he said.

I bet you are, she thought. Easy to fall for…

'Your English is very good,' she blurted. He even knew phrases like 'cross my heart'.

'English is the international language of science. Everyone speaks English, and I've lived abroad since my early twenties. The more you speak it, the better at it you get. You, I suspect, are pretty good at it.'

'So I should be, I'm—' She stopped. 'You're teasing me.'

'Yes, I am. I'm also late, so if you'll excuse me, I'll need the car keys.'

Sophie found them and handed them over. 'Dinner?' she reminded him.

'Dinner,' he agreed. 'But I don't expect you to cook. Let me take you out.'

Ooh, she hadn't been expecting that, and a shiver of excitement shot through her before she managed to rein it in.

'If it's not too much trouble,' she said doubtfully. Then, realising she was channelling her mum, she added 'I mean, that would be lovely.' Lordy, but she really was sounding more like a middle-aged woman every day. She finished off by saying, 'Fab,' in an attempt to sound more 'with-it', although with *what* she wasn't too sure.

Alex shot her an amused look as he headed for the door, and she knew she'd just made a total prat of herself.

'See you later,' she called after him, and he gave her a wave without looking back.

As soon as she heard the car pull off up the dirt track, Sophie slumped against the counter and groaned. He must think her terribly stuffy. To her own ears she now sounded like she had a plum in her mouth, and she guessed that if she said those words aloud it would have been with a cut-glass accent.

After breakfast and a good clean up all while listening to Dominic on the radio, she thought it wise to take Paco for a walk considering she mightn't get a chance to do so later on, and she also thought she might pop into Mrs Tiggywinkle's for some supplies for Hugo. She knew he was hoping he would be out of hospital in a day or so, but she wanted to make his stay there as comfortable as possible for him, so she'd pick up some grapes (naturally), a newspaper, and some of those weird chewy sweets he seemed to like which tasted of plastic and sugar and not much else.

'Paco, stay,' she commanded once they reached the shop, and Paco obediently sat. He really was a good dog, and she told him so before scratching him behind the ears and heading inside.

A familiar voice said, 'Hello, again,' and she saw that Dominic was manning the shop today.

She hadn't thought to see him there, assuming he'd be at the radio station, but thinking about it, it was going on for one o'clock and his show finished at ten a.m.

'Good show this morning,' she said, and was surprised when a bashful expression stole over his face.

'You caught it then?'

'Yes. Although I didn't realise it was you I was listening to on the radio when I spoke to you the other day.'

'Not many people do. I don't broadcast it. Broadcast it! Geddit?' He chuckled at his own joke.

Sophie rolled her eyes. 'I'm glad you don't make jokes like that on air. You play some good music, though.'

'Thanks. I tend to play the stuff I like, and it's great that my listeners seem to like the same music – otherwise I'd be out of a job. One of them, anyway. As you can see, I work here when I'm needed.' He waved an arm around the little shop. 'Do you surf?' he asked suddenly.

'Um, no. I can't say I do. It looks rather dangerous. I can see them on the little headland by the villa. Do you surf there?' Hugo had told her as much but she didn't want Dominic to know she'd been talking about him.

'Yes – well, bodyboard, actually. That headland is called Punta Blanca, and when the waves are right you can't beat it; short, foamy waves and powerful tubes.'

Now he was beginning to speak a different language. The waves bit she understood, but she had no idea what a tube was.

'I also surf at El Médano, but it ranks high with professional surfers so it can get a bit busy, and the wind's got to be offshore. It's a lovely shallow beach, though, with great swells, but it can be hard on the knees if you're not careful...' He trailed off. 'Your eyes have glazed over.'

'Oh, have they? I'm sorry, you sort of lost me at "powerful tubes". I don't know what they are.'

'Sometimes, under the right conditions, waves form a tube, or a cylinder, as they break, and you can—' He stopped. 'Tell you what, rather than me explaining it to you, why don't I show you? Come surfing with me.'

She shook her head. 'I already told you, I don't surf. I wouldn't know where to start and I'm not sure I want to find out.' She shuddered. 'That water looks pretty cold.'

'It is,' Dominic replied cheerfully. 'But with a wetsuit on, you don't really feel it. Besides, the adrenaline will keep you warm.'

'Really, that's very kind of you, but I don't think so.'

'Can you swim?'

'Yes…?'

'Then you'll be fine. I'm a good teacher and I promise I'll be gentle with you.' He had a twinkle in his eye and Sophie didn't think he was referring to just the surfing.

'Can I think about it?' She'd already thought, and the answer was a most definite no, but she wanted to let him down gently.

'Of course. But I have got another idea. If the conditions are right, I'll be bodyboarding near your villa tomorrow morning. How about if you come and watch, then we could go for a spot of lunch afterwards? My treat.'

Wow, two offers of meals out in less than a day. With two very different men.

'Good compromise,' she agreed.

'Let me have your number, and if it's too blowy we'll go straight to lunch.'

They swapped numbers, and Sophie made her way back to the villa, reeling slightly. Yesterday she'd been quite comfortable in this new world she'd made for herself, and today she had dinner and lunch out to look forward to. She was pretty sure the lunch with Dominic was a real date. The whole conversation with him had had a date-like feel to it – not that she could remember what being asked out felt like, because the last time had been several years ago; but if she had to bet on it, she'd bet her right arm that lunch with Dominic was a date.

She wasn't sure what tonight's dinner with Alex was. She was pretty sure it was just a meal, nothing more. But the way he'd looked at her…? Or had she imagined it? She'd been so bowled over by the unexpected attraction she felt for him that she might be projecting her wishful thinking onto what was, on his part, a perfectly reasonable suggestion that they have dinner in a restaurant to save her the hassle of cooking for him.

Strolling slowly back to the villa, with the scent of the sea filling the air and the noise of the waves pounding on the rocky shoreline, she imagined being out there in the water, at the mercy of the sea and those imposing surges, and the currents which undoubtedly ran beneath them, and she shuddered.

No thanks. Nope. No way was she doing more than dipping a toe into that water. Dominic might be a good teacher and she probably would be perfectly safe in his hands, but she seriously didn't fancy it.

She did fancy *him*, though. Not as much as she was attracted to Alex, but the two men were like chalk and cheese. Or rather, a domestic house cat compared to a leopard. The leopard was far more alluring, but at the same time far more dangerous.

But the leopard hadn't asked her on a date. The pussycat had. And out of the pair of them, if she wanted a gentle reintroduction into the world of dating and romance without running the risk of having her heart shattered, Dominic was the logical choice. He was also the only choice.

Anyway, all this soul-searching might be hypothetical – she might find that she and Dominic had little in common. He might find her reluctance to surf a total turn-off. They might have lunch, then never see one another again.

Just enjoy it for what it is, she told herself, and stop trying to read too much into it.

Feeling better, she called Paco away from whatever it was he'd been sniffing so avidly (probably something disgusting) and upped the pace. She needed some lunch before Alex arrived to pick her up to see Hugo. And a shower, and to put on some make-up. Just because she was visiting someone in hospital, it didn't mean she didn't need to make an effort with her appearance.

At least that's what she told herself....

Chapter 15

'Alejandro?' Hugo sounded surprised.

To Sophie's amazement, he was sitting in a large armchair next to his bed and not actually in the bed when she and Alex walked into the ward. He'd spotted them immediately and the expression on his face when he saw his nephew was almost comical.

'Alejandro?' he repeated, followed by a rapid stream of Spanish.

Alex answered in kind, then switched to English. 'I'm not sure,' he said. 'A couple of days, perhaps a week.' He turned to Sophie. 'Hugo asked me what I'm doing here and how long I'm staying. I don't think he's all that pleased to see me.'

'I am.' Hugo pulled a face. 'But I do not like for you to see me like this. I don't want to be a...' He looked at Alex. '*Una carga?*'

'A burden,' Alex translated. He put a hand on his uncle's shoulder. 'You can never be a burden. You should have told me you needed some help after your operation – I could have taken some time off work.'

Hugo chortled. 'You never take time off. You will say you will look after me, but instead you will be on the volcano.' He turned to Sophie. 'He lives for the volcanoes. Lava hunters, they are called.'

'That's not fair, Hugo,' Alex protested. 'I haven't seen any decent lava in ages.' His face clouded over. 'I hope I don't see lava anytime soon either.'

'Is that why you are——?'

'Yes,' Alex jumped in, cutting Hugo off. He shot Sophie a look, and she frowned at him.

What had Hugo been about to say? Whatever it was, Alex clearly didn't want to talk about it – not in front of her anyway.

'I didn't expect to see you out of bed,' Alex said, and Hugo shrugged.

'They do not let you stay in bed. They make you get dressed and get up.' He didn't look happy about it, and Sophie guessed he was probably in quite a lot of discomfort.

Still, the medical staff must know what they were doing, and if getting a patient mobile so soon after such an operation was the best thing to do, then Hugo would simply have to put up with it.

'I've brought you some grapes,' she said, holding up a bag, 'and a newspaper. Oh, and you forgot your sliders.' She took the shoes out of the bag and popped them on the floor underneath his bed. She'd searched his room in vain for a pair of slippers but guessed that slipper-wearing was probably more of a British thing. Over here people tended to wear flip-flops or sliders. Sophie owned a couple of pairs, but she'd also brought her slippers with her, along with her fluffy PJs. Just in case.

Hugo grunted his thanks, adding grumpily, 'There was no need to come. I am fine. You must have other things to do.'

Sophie smiled. 'This is what you employ me to do,' she reminded him gently. 'To look after you.'

'I do not need looking after.'

Alex caught her eye and they shared a look. Humour lurked on his face.

'Paco misses you,' Sophie said, changing the subject.

Hugo's grumpy expression softened. 'I miss him, also.'

'Have they said when you're likely to go home?'

'Two or three more days.' He shifted slightly in his chair and pain flashed briefly across his face.

Sophie reached out and placed her hand over his in sympathy, but he shook her off. She caught Alex's eye again and suppressed a smile. Her suspicions that Hugo was going to make a terrible patient were confirmed, and she guessed she'd have some fun and games trying to prevent him from doing too much. At least he'd had the foresight to employ someone to help, even if he'd done so grudgingly. He was realistic enough to know that he wouldn't be able to cope on his own directly after the operation, although Sophie suspected he'd taken her on more for Paco's sake than for his own.

The thought that Hugo mightn't need her now that his nephew was here flitted through her mind, but she pushed it to one side. Alex himself had said he was here because of work, and he wasn't sure how long he was staying, so she was probably worrying about nothing.

She'd accepted the fact that she'd have to return to the UK in a couple of months. She *had*. Honestly. But the thought of leaving any sooner than that filled her with dread.

No, she was fretting for no reason. Alex would be gone in a few days, maybe a week, and the three of them

– Hugo, Paco and herself – would slot straight back into their old routine.

Suddenly feeling awkward, Sophie got to her feet. 'I expect you've got some catching up to do,' she said to the pair of them. 'I'll go for a wander and find somewhere to get a coffee.'

Hugo waved her away and Alex merely nodded, and as she slipped out of the ward, she heard them talking to each other in quick-fire Spanish.

By the time she returned (having found a vending machine and a hard plastic seat on which to perch while she drank her coffee and tried to read a couple of pages of the book she carried with her everywhere), Alex looked ready to leave, and Hugo looked ready to go back to bed.

From the sallowness of his skin and the deep lines around his eyes and mouth, Sophie could tell he was in some pain. She attracted the attention of a nurse and then they said their goodbyes, Sophie promising to return tomorrow afternoon.

'It'll be a bit later than today because I'm going out to lunch,' she said. 'Is there anything I can bring you?'

'No. Who are you lunching with?'

'Dominic Brockman. He offered to give me some surfing lessons, but I'm not too keen on the idea. I'm going to watch him in the morning, though, as he's going to surf off the end of the bay.'

'Be careful and don't get too close to the waves,' Hugo warned.

'I won't.' She hesitated, wanting to give him a peck on the cheek but guessing he wouldn't appreciate it.

'Who's Dominic Brockman?' Alex asked as they made their way back to the car.

'He's on Radio TEX in the mornings. His parents own Mrs Tiggywinkle's shop in Playa de la Arena.'

'Have you known him long?'

'Not really. A few days.'

'And he's offered to teach you to surf?'

'Yes.'

'Hmm.'

'What's wrong with that?'

'Nothing.' He unlocked the car and they got in.

'Yes, there is. You've got a face like a bulldog chewing a wasp.'

'A what?'

'You look grumpier than Hugo,' she explained. His English was exceptionally good, but unsurprisingly it didn't seem to stretch to some of the more obscure English sayings.

'It's just…' He paused for a moment, concentrating on pulling out of the car park and onto a busy road. 'I thought you were here to look after my uncle, not to spend your time dating.'

Sophie inhaled sharply. The cheek of him! She was rather hurt too, to think that was the impression he had of her. 'I *am* here to look after Hugo,' she replied stiffly. 'Please be assured that I don't intend to allow anything to affect that.'

'Tell me, do you have a contract? What qualifications do you have that make you suitable to care for him?'

'No, and none. Look, if you're not happy with me, then speak to Hugo.'

She didn't appreciate having her integrity or work ethic called into question, especially when this man knew nothing about her. Hell, he'd not even been aware that

Hugo was having his hip replaced, so what right did he have to question his uncle's arrangements for his care? Or her ability to do precisely that? And the sort of care she'd provided for her mother was miles apart from the basic household tasks Hugo wanted her to perform. For Alex to suggest she needed a bloody degree for that was insulting.

'For your information, I nursed my mother for years until she died, and I didn't need any sodding qualifications for that!' Tears were close to the surface, threatening to spill over onto her cheeks, and she gulped them back. There was no way she was going to let this obnoxious man see her cry. She refused to give him the satisfaction.

'I'm sorry about your mother,' he replied stiffly. 'When did she pass away?'

'At the beginning of October.'

'Not long.'

'No.'

'I'm sorry for your loss.'

No he wasn't. He couldn't care less. He clearly didn't like her, didn't want her living in Hugo's house, and wasn't happy about leaving his uncle in her care.

'If you give me a couple of days to sort out a flight, I'll be out of your hair.' Dear Lord, she needed to sort out more than a flight – she had nowhere to live, no job…

She glanced at Alex out of the corner of her eye, hoping she was wrong about him wanting her gone, but his expression gave nothing away.

'I can't leave any sooner,' she said. She really couldn't – she didn't want to turn up in the UK with nowhere to stay, although at this precise moment she didn't have the foggiest idea what she could do about that.

'Why do you want to leave?'

She frowned. 'You said…?'

'I didn't say you should leave. Hugo needs you. But more importantly, he likes you.'

'He said that?' Her anger began to drain away, along with her distress.

'Yes. Please don't take offence; I'm simply looking out for him. I don't want him to be exploited.'

'*What?*' The plug was back in her tub of anger and the bowl was rapidly filling up again. 'You think I'm exploiting Hugo? *How?*' she demanded furiously.

'The villa is worth a lot of money. He is a single man living on his own…' Alex shrugged a shoulder.

'*How dare you?* How bloody dare you!' Sophie was almost incandescent with rage. She couldn't believe what she was hearing. Hugo was old enough to be her father. The fact that she and Hugo had separate bedrooms should tell Alex that nothing was going on between them. And he'd already asked her that question last night when he'd barged into her room. Clearly he hadn't believed her. Hang on a minute…

'You can't have it both ways,' she cried. 'One minute you're accusing me of playing around with Dominic off the radio, and the next you're saying I've set my sights on your uncle and accusing me of being some kind of gold-digger. Which is it? Eh?'

Alex inhaled deeply and let out a long, slow breath. 'Look at it from my point of view,' he said levelly. 'I arrive in the middle of the night to find a strange woman in my uncle's house and my uncle in hospital having an operation which I know nothing about. He's not told the family about either his need for a hip replacement or about you.

You hear of old people being preyed on and I don't want it happening to Hugo.'

'If you're that concerned about him, how come you didn't know he needed an operation? Hips don't suddenly go overnight, you know. He's had this problem for a while.'

'Touché.' His lips twisted into a rueful smile. 'You are right, of course. I should have known. My family should have known. All I can say in our defence is that I have been working abroad a lot and my parents – my mother is his sister – live in Madrid. We don't come home as often as we'd like, or as frequently as we should. I also think Hugo deliberately didn't share details of his health with us. My apologies.'

'Not accepted.' Sophie crossed her arms. 'Don't try to ease your guilt by having a go at me. You can't blame Hugo for sorting out his care himself. He obviously didn't feel he could ask you to help. So either you leave me alone to get on with what Hugo is employing me to do, or you tell me to go and you can look after him yourself.'

There was silence for the rest of the drive. She had no idea what Alex was thinking, but her mind was whirling with the problem of how soon she could get a flight – she had no intention of staying where she wasn't wanted – and what the hell she was going to do once that flight landed. It would have to be a guest house in the short term, she imagined. There really wasn't any other option.

Alex unlocked the barrier and drove down the track towards the villa, with Sophie sitting rigidly beside him, wanting nothing more than to flee into the relative privacy of her bedroom and sob. She was just about holding herself together and thinking she'd done well not to fall apart when Alex, damn him, spoke.

'Are we still going out to dinner?'

Chapter 16

Sophie leapt from the car, slammed the door as hard as she could, and whirled to face Alex. 'No! Of course we aren't going out for dinner. What's wrong with you? Some of us have got packing to do and a flight to book. And no, I don't want a lift to the airport. I can find my own way there, thank you very much.'

'I wasn't offering to give you a lift.'

'Why doesn't that surprise me?' She threw her hands up in frustration.

'Because,' he said, a smile playing about his lips, 'you're not leaving.'

'Watch me.' She was aware she was behaving like a toddler having a tantrum, but dear God, this man seemed adept at bringing out the worst in her.

'Please,' he said.

'Please what?'

'Don't go.' That smile was still there. More of a smirk, she thought, and she wanted to wipe it off his lips and carry out her threat.

But he'd given her a way out, and did she really want to cut off her nose to spite her face? As she'd told herself earlier, he'd be gone soon, out of her hair, and there'd be just her and Hugo once again. That's if she could tolerate this obnoxious man for a few more days.

'Please,' he repeated, sounding a little less certain of himself this time. 'I know I haven't been fair with you, but try to see it from my side. I honestly didn't know what to think or what to believe, and the fact that Hugo didn't tell any of us about the problem with his hip makes me feel awful. Did he think we wouldn't care?' Guilt and worry were written all over his face.

'OK,' she said, thinking he might have a point, although he had reacted unfairly, and she decided to give him the benefit of the doubt. 'I'll stay; but no more allegations.'

'Agreed.'

'And you don't interfere in the house.'

He gave her a level stare and she thought he was going to object, but all he said was, 'Fine, no interfering.'

'And you can take Paco for a walk while I get ready.'

'Get ready for what?'

'Dinner.'

His lips twitched again, but he didn't say anything. He simply nodded and strolled past her to unlock the front door.

She waited for him to go inside, and heard him talking to Paco before she slunk into the hall and shot to her bedroom, where she leant against the closed door breathing deeply. Despite his obvious suspicion of her, she couldn't help being attracted to him. He was far too handsome for his own good, too sure of himself, too confident, and he was a threat to her carefully constructed and very new equilibrium. She neither needed nor wanted to feel so disconcerted by him.

Hoping the way was clear, she opened her bedroom door and crept slowly out.

Alex was in the hallway, putting a lead on Paco.

'He doesn't need that,' she said. 'He won't go far. You can take him to the natural pool over there.' She waved vaguely in its general direction. 'He likes the water.'

'I know where it is.'

'Oh. Of course you do.' She felt a bit silly. He probably knew the area much better than she did, and she wondered if he'd lived around here once. It was strange to think she was sharing a house with him and yet she knew so little about him, apart from his name and what he did for a living; although the details of his job were equally as unknown. She didn't know how old he was either, although she could take an educated guess at mid-thirties.

'Um, can I ask a personal question?' she said.

He straightened up. 'You can ask. I might not give you an answer.'

'How old are you?'

'How old do you think I am?'

'That's not fair.'

'Isn't it?'

'Er... thirty-five?'

'Thirty-seven. How old are you?'

'Thirty-three.'

'It's good that we've got that out of the way,' he said, and she could tell he was laughing at her, even if those perfect lips of his hadn't moved. 'Is my age important?'

Sophie shrugged. 'Not really. I was just curious.'

'We can get to know one another a little more over dinner,' he said. 'Shall we leave at around eight, to eat for nine?'

Nine was late. She was already starting to get hungry. She recognised that she was programmed to eat earlier than was usual for the locals, but Hugo had happily fitted in with dinner at six thirty, and she suspected that he was so grateful to have a wholesome meal put in front of him that he wouldn't have cared what time it was served at.

'Eight is fine,' she said. The upside was that it would give her more time to find something suitable to wear, because she was as sure as God made little green apples that a pair of shorts and a strappy T-shirt simply wouldn't do.

After Alex left, Sophie had a quick shower and dried her hair, then spent the next half an hour searching through her wardrobe.

There wasn't a great deal to choose from. The summer clothes she had brought with her were years old. Thankfully she'd never tended to buy high fashion clothes, and shorts, T-shirts and bikinis didn't tend to date much, but nevertheless she felt dowdy in the six-year-old dress she'd picked out.

It was pretty enough with its turquoise and pink colours, and she supposed it was quite flattering, but it was old and she'd worn it loads of times previously (although not for a couple of years) and she didn't feel special in it. Though why she felt the need to feel special when she was only popping out for a bite to eat with her employer's nephew was beyond her. It was hardly a date. Tonight's dinner was born of a need to eat and Alex's kindness in not having her cook for him.

Or maybe it wasn't kindness. Kindness wasn't a word she associated with Alejandro. So if it wasn't that, then it must be that he didn't trust her skills in the kitchen. Or that he felt uncomfortable having a strange woman prepare his dinner in his own house. Not that it was *his* house, but she knew what she meant. Dinner for two in the little dining area, or out on the terrace with the sun setting over La Gomera might be a little too intimate for his liking. Whereas dinner in a busy restaurant was far less romantic.

Romantic? Ha! Why was she thinking about Alex and romance in the same sentence? She most definitely wasn't having any kind of romantic thoughts about him whatsoever. And she was pretty certain he wasn't having any about her. They rubbed each other up the wrong way for a start, and he definitely got on her nerves. Not only that, but he was rather rude and a bit too brooding for her liking. A bit too Mr Darcy-ish.

His melted chocolate eyes and faint hint of stubble, not to mention the accent, were quite gorgeous, though. Now and again he reminded her of a younger (although not by much) Álex González, but with shorter hair than his Riptide character in that *X-Men* film.

Handsome and arrogant with a hint of dark menace (was she reading too much into him?) was a worrying and dangerous combination, and she made a vow to keep her distance. Alejandro seemed like the sort of man to gobble a woman up (ignore the shiver, she told herself at the unsettling thought) and spit her out when he was done, with no regard to her heart. And Sophie had enough problems already, without adding yet more heartache into the mix.

Now Dominic, on the other hand, was more boy-next-door surfer dude, and an altogether different proposition. She didn't feel at all threatened by him, nor unsettled or discomforted when she thought about him, and she found she was very much looking forward to having lunch with him tomorrow.

Not as much as you're looking forward to dinner this evening, a treacherous little voice in her head whispered.

'Oh, shut up,' she muttered, giving herself one last look in the mirror.

It was dinner. Nothing more, nothing less.

So why did she have butterflies in her tummy and a sense of anticipation in her heart?

Chapter 17

Sophie had expected to be taken to one of the many restaurants in Playa de la Arena or Alcalá. What she hadn't been expecting was a biker café in Santiago del Teide, a town perched high in the mountains above Los Gigantes and those famous cliffs.

The fact that the place (she was fairly sure the name 'restaurant' wasn't warranted, and neither could it be called a bar) was heaving was some consolation. That it was chock full of people (mostly guys) in leather, with helmets dangling from the crooks of their elbows, wasn't. The gleaming chrome and black bikes sitting neatly in rows on the road outside hadn't inspired her with confidence either. In fact, they reminded her of a row of horses outside a saloon in the American West, and she was almost expecting a shoot-out between the sheriffs and the bad guys at any moment.

Feeling extremely out of place and rather threatened, Sophie stuck close behind Alex's broad back as he strode into the depths of the café, figuring he could take the brunt of it, if anything should kick off.

The smell of cooking was making her mouth water, though, and she stole glances at people's plates as she trotted behind him. The food did look delicious, she conceded, and her stomach gurgled loudly enough for her to hear it over the laughter and the talking. Music was playing in the background, but not so loud that it was obtrusive. It was seventies stuff, leaning towards heavy metal, and she recognised the sound of Deep Purple's *Smoke on the Water*. If she wasn't feeling like a fish out of water, she might have been tempted to tap her toes.

A rotund man in a navy apron looked up from behind the counter and broke into a broad smile when he saw Alex. He put his (too-large) knife down next to the onion he had been chopping and walked out to greet him, his arms open wide.

The only word Sophie could make out was 'Alejandro' before her non-date for the evening was enveloped in a meaty hug and an incomprehensible stream of Spanish.

The two men drew apart after much backslapping, and the man in the apron held Alex at arm's length and looked him up and down. Another hug followed, along with more slapping and patting before he finally let go and Alex was able to take a step back. Unfortunately, this meant that Sophie was in the man's direct line of sight, and she smiled uncertainly as his gaze came to rest on her.

More Spanish followed, and she guessed he was asking Alex who she was.

Finally Alex introduced her. 'Sophie, this is my good friend Bartolo. He owns this place, and he serves the finest *conejo en salmorejo* in the whole of the Canaries.'

'Ah, my friend, you are too kind. It is nice to meet you,' Bartolo said to her. He wiped his hand on his apron and held it out to her. When she took it, he leant forward and planted a kiss on the back of her hand.

'Nice to meet you too,' she replied politely.

'Take a seat,' he said to them. 'I've reserved a table for you over there. Carlos! Bring wine. Lots of wine!' He clapped his hands.

A waiter came over to them. 'The good wine or the not too good?' he asked, and Bartolo clicked his tongue.

'Carlos, he is joking. I only serve good wine.'

'I'll have water,' Alex said. 'I'm driving.'

'Pah. It won't taste the same,' he warned. 'Food without wine is like church without prayer.'

Alex shook his head, grinning. 'I'll take my chances.' He caught hold of her arm just above the elbow, to guide her to their table, and her eyes shot to him in shock as his touch raced along her nerve endings, startling her. The warmth of his fingers on her skin sent her heart racing and she inhaled sharply before letting the breath out slowly.

It was unexpected, that's all, she told herself when he released her in order to pull out her chair, and she collapsed into it, grateful to sit down before her legs betrayed her.

What on earth was wrong with her?

Then she remembered that it was hours since she'd eaten, and she put her sudden weakness down to that.

Alex took his own seat, then looked at her, concern in his eyes. 'Are you OK? I know this place mightn't be to everyone's taste, but believe me, the food is amazing.'

'I'm fine,' she said. 'What are we having?'

'Rabbit in *salmorejo* sauce. The meat is marinated overnight in red wine and herbs and once it is cooked, it's so tender...' He put his thumb and two fingers together and brought them to his lips, making a kissing motion.

Mesmerised, Sophie watched his lips pucker, and for a fleeting moment she imagined them on hers, the taste of them, the feel of them—

'It can be a little bit spicy, but it is good with *papas arrugadas*.' He mistook her bewilderment for incomprehension about the dish he'd mentioned, and he went on to explain. '*Papas arrugadas* are potatoes boiled in very salty water, drained, then tossed in sea salt. Probably the most famous Canarian dish.'

'It sounds lovely,' she said weakly, her attention still on those lips of his.

'Don't let all these bikers put you off,' he added, once again misreading her – thankfully, because she'd be mortified if he knew what she was thinking. 'They come here for the food too. And because Bartolo makes them welcome. His own bike is out the back under a tarpaulin. I keep urging him to sell it to me, but he's a stubborn man.'

'Do you ride a motorbike?' She was grasping at straws here; anything to take her mind off the thoughts he'd inadvertently put in her head. It really had been a long time indeed since she'd been kissed.

'I have done in the past, but with the increase in traffic on the roads since I was a teenager, it can be a bit scary.'

'Were you brought up on Tenerife?'

'Yes, partly. My parents ran a hotel in Costa Adeje until I was sixteen, and then we moved to Madrid. They're still there, managing a boutique hotel in the city centre. But I'd always come back to the island whenever I got the chance.'

'To see Hugo?'

Alex looked a little sheepish. 'That too. But I'm ashamed to admit that it was Teide that drew me back. Ever since I was old enough to understand what they were, I was hooked by volcanoes. The thought that we live on the slopes of one of the most destructive – and creative, but that's another story – forces of nature both terrified and fascinated me.'

'But we're not on the slopes of the mountain down at the villa,' Sophie pointed out, thinking that he was speaking hypothetically. Up here in Santiago del Teide, they were admittedly a bit closer to the enormous volcano, but they still weren't *that* close. She remembered passing through this picturesque little town on the way back from Masca Gorge when she'd gone on the coach tour, and she'd seen Teide in the distance, peeking through a circlet of clouds. It had looked so very far away.

'Don't you believe it,' Alex was saying. 'The villa is about fifty-two kilometres from the cone. That's about thirty miles. In volcanic terms, it is nothing.'

'Thirty miles seems a nice, safe distance.'

For a second Alex paused, then he said, 'It is.' But Sophie had the feeling he had been about to say something else.

'You say you're here for work? Is that to do with Teide?' she asked.

'Yes...'

'Can you tell me about it?'

'Not really.'

Why was he being so reticent? Then a horrid thought occurred to her. 'Is Teide about to erupt?' A mild panic invaded her mind at the very idea of such a thing.

'Not at the moment.'

'*Not at the moment?*' Sophie squealed, then lowered her voice. 'So it *is* going to erupt? Just not right now. Do you know when?'

'Teide and all the other volcanoes on the island—'

'There are *others*? Where?' she interrupted, taking a quick glance out of the window, almost expecting to see another volcano growing in front of her eyes. Teide was hard to miss as it rose up in the centre of the island like a giant, rocky, upside-down ice cream cone, and although she hadn't seen a great deal of Tenerife, she would have thought that another mountain the size of Teide would be hard to miss.

'Everywhere,' he said. 'Teide is the largest and the most recognisable, but there are over three hundred that form the island.'

Sophie was about to ask for more details when their food arrived and her attention was diverted by the dishes placed in front of them. She wasn't sure about eating rabbit, but it was a common sight in the supermarkets, she'd noticed, sitting alongside breasts of chicken and huge slabs of beef. It wasn't something she'd tasted before, but she was willing to give it a go, and the stew looked and smelt amazing. Her tummy gurgled once more, and her mouth watered.

To her surprise, the meat tasted a little like chicken, and although the sauce was quite spicy, she found it extremely tasty. Before she knew it, she'd cleared her plate and was using a hunk of the bread which had accompanied the meal to mop up any stray sauce. The spicy red salsa – *mojo*, she was told – accompanying the potatoes also had a bit of a kick and she took a large mouthful of wine to ease the pleasant tingling in her mouth.

'That was delicious,' she said, finally pushing her plate away and sitting back. She was so full she didn't think she could move.

'Have you got room for some *queso asado*?' Alex asked her, dabbing his mouth with a napkin.

She didn't, but she was willing to give it a try. 'What is it?' She knew *queso* was cheese, but *asado* was an unknown word.

'It's smoked goats' cheese, usually fried or baked in the oven, and today it's served with palm honey.'

'Cheese and honey? Hmm, I'm not sure.'

'Try it, it's wonderful.'

So she did, and it was, and when she had eaten every last morsel, she was fairly certain she wouldn't need to eat again for a week. She drank the rest of the wine in her glass too, then stared at Alex with heavy-lidded eyes. Replete didn't begin to describe the way she was feeling. Surprisingly, she was also feeling calm and relaxed, and she wondered why on earth she had felt so intimidated by a few people in leather. From what she could see, they were simply normal folk out for a bite to eat and a nice evening. Just like she was.

Her gaze was drawn to Alex again, and she caught him studying her.

A warmth spread through her, starting in her chest and culminating in her cheeks, and she knew she was blushing. Cross with herself, she looked away. 'Fancy a coffee?'

'Why not? Bartolo,' he called, 'two espressos please.'

Good, she needed a strong shot of caffeine to counteract the effects of the wine, as she was feeling rather giddy and not quite herself. She couldn't remember the last time she'd drunk this much, and she made a promise to herself not to drink so much in future if it had this effect on her. After two glasses she was feeling rather tipsy. And hot. It was really rather warm in here. No wonder her cheeks were aflame.

And the more she thought about how warm she was, the hotter her face became, until she was fairly sure she must resemble a tomato. Oh, *that was it* – she understood now. It was the food. The rabbit dish had been rather spicy... That explained it.

Feeling a bit of an idiot and anxious to draw Alex's attention away from her glowing face, she asked him about some of the places he'd been to in the course of his work.

'You must have visited some wonderful countries,' she mused enviously.

'Yes, and no,' came the cryptic reply. 'Hawaii, Japan, Guatemala all sound lovely – and don't get me wrong, they are – but they are dangerous places too. The parts I see, anyway. Fresh lava fields where the heat is so intense it can strip the skin off your bones. Craters where you need breathing apparatus to survive, or you wouldn't last five minutes. The threat of seismic activity, boulders the size of houses spewing from an erupting volcano...' The excitement and passion on his face were unmistakable.

'You love it,' she observed.

He sighed. 'You're right, I do. But there are also the endless hours trekking to remote places to set up equipment, and the even more endless hours analysing what those pieces of equipment tell you. Most of my work tends to be done sitting in front of a computer.'

'I wish I had something I was as passionate about,' she said wistfully.

'Washing Hugo's socks doesn't inspire you?' he joked, and she wrinkled her nose at him.

'It most certainly does not, although I do love living at the villa, and your uncle is an easy man to share a house with. He might not be as easy when he comes out of hospital, though.'

'He most definitely won't be,' Alex agreed, calling for the bill. 'He'll be a pain in the behind. I'm glad it's you who is looking after him, and not me.'

'Are you?'

He gave her a rueful grin. 'I am, truly. Despite the impression I gave.'

'You're not sending me back to the UK?'

'No. It'll be nice to have someone to wash my socks too.' He winked, and she threw her napkin at him.

'If you think I'm going to be running around after you, you've got another think coming,' she warned.

'Aww…' The proprietor arrived at their table with a small platter holding their bill. 'Thank you, Bartolo, it was delicious, as always.'

'You must come again before you leave.'

'I will.' Alex glanced at Sophie. '*We* will.'

She reached for her bag and drew out her purse, but Alex was way ahead of her, his credit card already in Bartolo's hands. 'Let me pay my half, at least,' she said.

'No chance. Dinner was my idea. Besides, I am old-fashioned. If I take a lady out for a meal, then I want to pay.'

'I'll get it the next time,' she said, then heat flooded her cheeks once more when she realised what she'd said. 'I mean, if there is a next time. Which there might not be, so don't feel obliged,' she garbled.

'I'm sure there will be,' he said, pushing his chair away from the table and getting to his feet.

Sophie jumped up, nearly knocking her own chair over in her haste, and she bit her lip in consternation. She really needed to stop acting like such an idiot. Anyone would think she was nervous. Ha!

The journey back down to the coast was made in comparative silence, Alex concentrating on the steep, twisting, unlit road, Sophie trying not to concentrate on Alex and failing miserably. She was acutely conscious of his every move, and with each breath she took she could smell his aftershave and an underlying scent that seemed to be his and his alone.

Pheromones. That was it. Some people were more attractive to others because of the chemicals they gave off. She'd seen it on a documentary once. And alcohol didn't help either, although she was starting to feel a little less squiffy.

By the time they pulled up outside the villa, she was feeling more herself. The trauma of last night, the argument with Alex today, a meal eaten far too late and with too much wine… There was a rational explanation for everything, and she'd discovered hers.

'I think I'll take Paco for a quick stroll,' she said, even though it was extremely late (for her anyway, because she was normally in bed by ten thirty), but the poor dog had been on his own all evening and he probably needed to water a rock or two.

Alex unlocked the front door and held it open for her before following her inside. 'You can't go on your own,' he said. 'It's too dark. I'll come with you.'

She honestly didn't think she wanted him to. It would have been nice to clear her head a little before she retired for the night, and having him by her side wasn't going to help her get herself straight.

'Better still,' he added, 'you stay here, and I'll take him out.'

'Paco is my responsibility,' she protested. 'I should be the one to walk him.'

'Fine, then I am coming with you,' he repeated.

Grumpily she swapped her sandals for a pair of trainers and slung a cardi around her shoulders, in case the breeze coming off the sea was a bit fresh.

Alex and a sedately excited Paco were waiting for her outside.

'Which way?' he asked.

Sophie shrugged. 'That way?' She pointed south towards Alcalá.

He began walking, the dog bounding ahead on large fluffy black paws and barely visible despite the full moon. Black dog, black volcanic rocks, dark ocean with the glitter of reflected light on the waves. Stars littered the sky and the lights of Alcalá twinkled in the distance. The night was bordering on magical, she thought, turning her face to the sky as she walked and marvelling at those distant diamond chips, losing herself to the vastness of space.

'Oomph!'

She'd only gone and bumped straight into Alex, who steadied her, his hands catching the tops of her arms in a firm grip.

For a second she was facing his chest, her nose inches from the open V of his shirt, and the smell of him invaded her senses, making her head spin.

She let out her breath in a soft sigh. It was a long time since she'd been held by anyone, especially anyone male, and an urge to melt into his arms swept through her. When she took an involuntary step forward, his hands slipped from her arms and worked their way around her back, encircling her, and she relaxed into his embrace. It felt right, him holding her. It felt natural. It also felt incredibly reckless, but she couldn't seem to help herself. Her reaction to him was instinctive and visceral, and totally out of her control.

She tilted her head back and their eyes met. The depth in his made her senses reel; she could lose herself in them, drown in the desire she read in them, and she wanted nothing more than for him to kiss her. His mouth hovered above hers and his soft, warm breath fanned her cheek as he stared down at her. Her lips parted of their own accord and her eyes began to close…

Paco bumped her leg.

Sophie drew in a sharp breath and the mood was broken.

Abruptly Alex dropped his hands to his side and she stepped smartly away from him, her legs trembling and her heart thudding so hard he must surely hear it above the rhythmic pounding of the waves.

He cleared his throat, and she gave a little cough.

'Thanks,' she said. Her voice was higher pitched than usual and sounded a bit breathy.

'You're welcome.'

She risked a quick glance as they carried on walking, but it was too dark to see his expression clearly, although the glitter of his eyes told her he'd returned her glance.

Sophie wasn't quite sure what had just happened. Had he been about to kiss her? Or, considerably more mortifying, had she assumed he'd been about to kiss her when he hadn't intended doing anything of the sort?

She bit her lip, her attention on Paco, who was busily sniffing every rock and then cocking his leg against the ones that were acceptable to his discerning canine nose. Neither she nor Alex spoke until they reached the headland, and the only thing Alex said then was, 'Shall we head back?'

She nodded, not trusting herself to speak in case anything she uttered came out as a squeak, and they turned around and made their way wordlessly back to the villa. The waves crashing against the shore and the distant rumble of traffic from the coastal road barely broke the awkward silence, and she was extremely glad when she was able to dart into the house and into her room, with a muttered 'good night' as she did so.

With the door firmly shut, she leant against it, her heart beating so loudly it drowned out any other noise for some time, and she waited for her heart rate to slow before she moved away from the door. And all the while she was listening intently for any sounds from the rest of the villa.

But for a big man Alex was remarkably quiet, and all she could hear was the click of Paco's claws on the tiled floor and the ever-present pulse of the sea.

Eventually she undressed and climbed into bed, imagining Alex doing the same thing on the other side of the wall, and wondering how on earth she was going to survive the next week or so until he flew back to Iceland. Because even after only one day, she was finding it almost impossible to keep her cool around him. Unbeknown to him, he'd woken something in her that she hadn't even realised was dormant.

And now that her libido was well and truly awake, she had no idea what she was supposed to do with it.

Chapter 18

How the pair of them managed to avoid each other the following morning was a work of choreographic art. Sophie was awake early, having spent the night tossing and turning as a result of having several disturbing dreams, and she was up and out of the door with a bemused Paco before she'd rubbed the sleep from her eyes.

This time, instead of turning back at the headland as they had done last night, she'd carried on into Alcalá until she found a café and sat outside with a much needed coffee and a bowl of water the owner had thoughtfully provided for the dog.

She'd hoped that by the time she got back Alex would have left for the day, but as she approached the villa she noticed the car was still there, and when she stepped into the hall she heard the shower running. Pausing for a second, she thought of him in there, standing under the falling water, without any clothes on, and her treacherous imagination began to—

Stop it! This was ridiculous, she told herself.

She knew exactly what this was. She'd heard of people who'd had near-death experiences wanting to validate their lives, and she suspected that this was her mind telling her that she wasn't the one who had died, and that her life was still to be lived.

Okaaay, that made a weird kind of sense, but did this new-found enthusiasm for life and love have to focus on the one man she really shouldn't be getting involved with?

The shower stopped and Sophie held her breath, imagining him stepping out of it, towelling himself down and—

With an annoyed snort she dashed into her room and softly closed the door, but it seemed an interminable time before she heard him leave and was able to venture out again.

Most of the rest of the morning consisted of her trying to keep busy in order not to think about dark chocolate eyes and a hint of stubble. She was acutely aware that in a couple of hours she'd be meeting another man for lunch, and in order to refocus her mind she switched on the radio to the TEX station and listened to Dominic's cheerful voice, catching the last half-hour or so of the show.

Before long she found she was singing along to the music and enjoying his upbeat banter with those listeners who had phoned in with requests. By the time the show ended, she was feeling more like herself and realised she was looking forward to watching him surf. He was a nice guy, she thought, and good-looking to boot. In fact, the two men were like day and night, and it seemed fitting that she'd spent last night with Alex (not all of it, obviously) and today would be spent with Dominic. Chalk and cheese. Night and day. Yin and yang.

She knew which was the safer bet, which one she'd be less likely to lose her heart to; and, if she did, which one of them would take the most care of it.

Alex's world was so far from her own, his experiences so far removed from hers that he might as well live on another planet.

Never mind the fact that Dominic had lived on Tenerife for a big part of his life, she had the impression that he was British through and through, that he'd understand her and the subtle nuances that only someone brought up in the same culture could truly appreciate. And she wasn't just thinking of language, either.

Oh, who was she kidding? She was reading far too much into everything. Alex hadn't been going to kiss her, and Dominic was just being friendly. And that's the way she wanted it to be, and the way it had to be. In around two months' time she'd return to the UK and begin the next phase of her life. Tenerife was a pleasant interlude, nothing more, and any hint of romance could only be temporary. Just go with the flow and enjoy it for what it was, she told herself, as she got ready to watch a man in a wetsuit splash around in the surf like a seal.

As she approached the headland, she saw that the waves were quite strong, but not too high. Even in the short amount of time she'd been living at the villa, she found she was able to anticipate when the surfers would be in the water, and when the sea was too rough and dangerous for them to venture into it. In her limited experience today looked to be perfect, and there were already several dark heads bobbing about, and a few more people on the rocks, holding their boards.

She'd done a spot of research (purely not to look like a total idiot when Dominic talked about his hobby) and she realised that what the people here were doing was bodyboarding, not surfing, as no one stood up on their boards. Instead they lay across them and rode the wave in. Actually, it looked fun, but the temperature of the water and the fact that those exciting waves broke onto rocks put her off. Now, if there was a wide expanse of gently shelving golden sand and the sea was as warm as bathwater, she might seriously consider it. As it was, she was content to watch.

It wasn't easy to tell who was who in those black suits that most of the bodyboarders wore, but there appeared to be an array of different colours when it came to the boards themselves, and when one of the surfers gave her a wave, she guessed it was probably Dominic. Waving back, she noted his bright green board, and from then on she found it easy to track his progress.

It was incredibly pleasant sitting on the rocks, watching other people play in the waves. The sun was almost directly overhead, and it would have been too hot to stay out if it wasn't for the breeze and the occasional fine misting of spray from the larger waves. There was something terribly relaxing about listening to the sounds of the sea, and she wasn't surprised when she felt her eyes starting to close. If she'd been sitting on something more comfortable, like a padded sun lounger and not a lump of rock, she might easily have fallen asleep. Last night hadn't been the best night's rest she'd ever had, and she could seriously do with a nap, but suddenly a shower of cold droplets cascaded over her and she was jerked out of her semi-doze by a laughing and totally unapologetic Dominic, who was standing above her, dripping all over her.

'Wake up, sleepyhead. Was I really that boring? I think I'd better work on my technique,' he joked, and shook water over her again.

Sophie leapt to her feet with a squeal. 'That's *cold*,' she cried, giggling, brushing the drops of seawater off her warm arms. 'And I *was* watching you, honest.'

'What do you think?'

'Oh… you were brilliant—'

'Not me! Although I was pretty fantastic,' he added, then laughed as a passing wetsuited man snorted with laughter.

'In your dreams, Dom. You looked like a stranded whale,' the man called out.

'Meet Shaun. He's supposed to be my friend, but clearly he's just a guy who hangs around with the best in the hope that my fantastic boarding will rub off on him.'

Shaun flung a towel at him, and Dominic caught it and threw it back. The two men were grinning, and Sophie envied them their easy banter. It was a long time since she'd—

Oh, for goodness' sake! Everything was 'a long time since'. She should stop feeling sorry for herself (because, let's be honest, she wouldn't have had it any other way and caring for her mum hadn't been a chore but an act of love) and embrace this new life. Stop thinking about what had been and concentrate on the now. It's what her mum would have wanted, and she could almost hear her scolding her for being so morbid.

'I meant you,' Dominic was saying, 'before we were so rudely interrupted.'

'Me what?'

'Bodyboarding, silly. How about you giving it a go?'

Sophie looked over her shoulder, just in time to see a black figure go one way and his board go the other as a wave took him out. 'No chance,' she said. 'And that's the reason.'

Dominic laughed. 'Immie's wiped out again,' he shouted over to Shaun, and Shaun gave him a thumbs up.

'Immie is Shaun's girlfriend. She loves the sport, but spends more time in the water than on her board.'

'Which is exactly what I would be doing and why I don't want to try.'

'Not here, obviously. I'd take you to a nice beach with gentle waves and a cocktail at the end to celebrate.'

'Nope.' She shook her head. 'I can do the cocktail bit, though, that sounds more like my type of thing.'

'I'll persuade you,' Dominic said. 'I'm a very persuasive guy. Now, how about lunch?'

'Lovely, I'm starving.' It must be all the sea air, because she couldn't believe she was hungry so soon again after the meal last night.

Swiftly she shoved the thought of last night to the back of her mind before she began to think about something other than the food, and she turned to watch the remaining figures in the water while Dominic went to change behind one of the rocks, using only his towel for modesty. To her consternation, she wasn't the slightest bit tempted to peek, but she had a feeling that if it had been Alex under that towel, she would have had trouble keeping her gaze away from him.

Dominic came back with his board tucked under one arm and holding a bag in his other hand. 'My car is parked just over there.' He pointed to the farmhouse, which was the closest house to the villa. 'The owner, Luis, lets us leave our cars on his road. We used to park on the road to Villa Delfin but we kept blocking it and Hugo got cross. Besides' Luis' place is nearer and we're a lazy bunch. We'll happily spend all day in the water, just don't ask us to walk any further than from a table to the bar.'

Sophie gazed around with interest as they strolled past the whitewashed farmhouse and its assorted buildings and along a track which passed between banana fields on either side. These, she noticed, were in considerably better shape than the semi-abandoned fields which lay behind Hugo's villa.

'Does Luis also own the fields between Hugo's villa and the coastal road?' she asked, taking note of the healthy-looking plants with bunches of unripe fruit hanging on them that she could see through the neatly mended netting.

Dominic gave her a quick look and shook his head. 'Don't you know? Those belong to Hugo.'

'Do they? He never said.' She'd had her suspicions, though.

'He's been having more and more trouble with his hips,' Dominic said, 'and for the last year or so he's not been able to do a great deal on the plantation. It's a shame to see them in such a state, but it won't be for much longer, hopefully.'

'Oh, I don't know about that. It'll be a good three months before he's back to full mobility, and even then I don't think he'll be able to do a lot of the sort of physical work getting those fields back in order would entail.'

Dominic frowned at her. 'I'm talking about the offer to buy his property.'

'What offer?'

His eyes widened and he suddenly looked uncomfortable. 'Oh, I… er, I'm not sure I should say.'

'You've already said.' She came to an abrupt halt and pulled at his arm, forcing him to stop and turn to face her.

'That's because I assumed you knew about it. If Hugo hasn't told you, then I don't think it's my place to.'

'You can't leave it there. If he's selling up, then surely I have a right to know because it affects me too.'

Dominic took a breath and stared into the distance at the sea still visible between the fields. 'OK, I suppose it's common knowledge around here anyway, so it's not a big secret. Hugo owns the land from the start of the coastal path at Playa de la Arena to the edge of Luis's fields, and from the road up there' – he indicated the coast road at the top of the fields with a jerk of his head – 'to the path down there.'

He started walking again, Sophie following, and as they rounded a slight bend a couple of cars came into view, parked where the track widened. He pointed a key at them and one of them beeped into life.

'A Russian conglomerate wants to buy it and plonk a ruddy great hotel complex on it,' he continued, opening the hatchback and throwing his bag in. The board was gently placed inside with a great deal more care.

'Go on,' Sophie said, once they were settled and Dominic had done a five-point turn in the narrow lane.

'I don't think many people are happy about it because there are already enough hotels and apartments in the area. There isn't a need for more. And this section of the coast between La Arena and Alcalá is unspoilt and wild. It would be ruined if a massive hotel was to be built here. But what with Hugo's health and the fact that he's not getting any younger, I wouldn't be surprised if he sells up.'

'It kind of makes sense from a financial point of view,' she said. 'If he's not able to keep the banana plantation going any longer, and he can't afford to pay people to help...' She thought back to her 'interview' and how Hugo had been at pains to clarify that most of her own wages would be in the form of bed and board. 'At least if he sells the fields he'll have enough money to live on for a good long while.' She hoped so, having no idea how much a banana field cost. 'He might even be able to do a bit of updating to the villa.' An image of the run-down kitchen sprang into her mind. It was OK and she could manage perfectly well in it, but it could do with a bit of TLC.

'Oh, the villa would have to be included in the sale, which is why we think Hugo has been hanging on for so long,' Dominic informed her. 'He doesn't want the villa torn down to be replaced with a beach bar. Not that there's much of a beach to speak of, what with it being so pebbly and rocky, but I've heard rumours that the new owners would build some kind of a pool and sunbathing area. I'm not sure of the details, but it all sounds very luxurious and extremely expensive. Right, we're here. I hope you like fish.'

Sophie nodded automatically, her mind whirling. Hugo was considering selling the villa? How could he? It was gorgeous; a little dated, admittedly, but that only added to its charm. And the location was to die for. The thought of a hotel with all the associated staff and guests marring such a beautiful place filled her with dismay.

She wondered if Alex knew about this. In fact, maybe that was the reason he was here, to help his uncle negotiate the sale. Alex had said it was for work, but if that was the case, why had he been so secretive about it last night? Why didn't Hugo want her to know about it? Was he worried she'd leave? Or was it hush-hush because the Russian conglomerate (what was one of those anyway?) wanted it to be? No, that couldn't be it, because Dominic knew about it, and if he knew, then his parents probably did and so must a load of other people. Besides, he'd just said that it was common knowledge…

Her head was spinning as she tried to work out what was going on and she became progressively more confused.

It wasn't until she was sitting at a table overlooking the sea and the smell of food wafted under her nose that she began to get a grip, telling herself that the sale of the villa was none of her business, and she was on the island for such a short time that she would most likely have left long before anything was finalised. But the thought of the villa not being there was rather upsetting. She loved the place, and she'd been anticipating being back in the UK and dreaming about it when she needed a respite from whatever her life would be like once she'd returned to reality. Because this wasn't reality. This whole Tenerife experience was a delaying tactic, and an opportunity for her heart to heal a little and for her to grow stronger. And she'd been banking on holding onto the villa in her mind to serve as a light when things grew dark.

She was handed a menu and she made a valiant attempt to concentrate when she opened it. There they were, at a lovely restaurant overlooking the sea, and there she was being miserable and distracted. The situation wasn't Dominic's fault and it wasn't fair for her to behave in this manner.

'What do you recommend?' she asked him, putting a bright smile on her face, even as she winced internally when she caught sight of the prices.

'*Sancocho canario* is particularly good here. It's fish served with sweet potato, *gofio* and *papas arrugadas*, a recipe which gives you sweetness, spiciness and saltiness all together on the same plate.'

'I know what *papas arrugadas* are, but what's *gofio*?' she asked.

'It's a kind of toasted flour which is used in various dishes in the Canaries, but here it's mixed with honey and almonds, and a little olive oil, then rolled into a sausage and sliced. It doesn't sound great, and if I'm honest it doesn't look too appetising either, but it's a nice mixture of savoury and sweet, and goes really well with the fish.'

'Go on, then, you've sold it to me.'

'*Sancocho canario para dos, por favour,*' Dominic said, handing the menus back to the waiter and then ordering some wine. 'White,' he informed her. 'It's chilled and delicious with the fish.'

That was twice in less than twenty-four hours she'd let a man choose her meal, and she wondered if all the men on the island were as knowledgeable about food as Alex and Dominic were. She was aware that for most islanders lunch and dinner were long-drawn-out affairs. They took the time to savour their food and lunch could last a couple of hours, with wine often being served. She recalled eating a hurried sandwich at her desk during those long-ago lunch breaks, and even afterwards, when she'd given up work to look after her mum, she tended to eat quickly in case she was needed.

This was incredibly civilised, and she thought she could get rather used to it. Actually, come to think of it, she already had. There was nowhere more beautiful than sitting on the villa's terrace with the sun setting behind La Gomera and the smell and sound of the sea all around. Now all she needed to do was cook a two-course meal, add some wine, and top it all off with a cup of strong coffee. There was no need for expensive restaurants when she could create the same thing at home, with a bit of practice on the cooking front. So far she'd stuck to dishes she knew, but maybe she could experiment? And she was fairly sure that Hugo would appreciate some traditional Canarian cooking to balance out all those English meals she'd served him lately.

It would be rather romantic — if it wasn't for the fact that she'd be sharing the meal with Hugo.

And Alex… but she didn't want to think about him right now.

The food was delicious, and Dominic was good company. They swapped life stories (as much as she was prepared to share with him, because he really didn't need to know how traumatic the last few months had been) and he was shocked to be told that she'd moved to Tenerife on what was little more than a quick meeting and a promise of a job and somewhere to live.

'I admire you,' he said, placing his knife and fork down on the plate. 'It takes courage to do what you did.'

'I don't know about that. I don't think courage came into it. It was more of an opportunity to extend my stay here so that I didn't have to go back home and start over again.'

'It's still a ballsy thing to do,' Dominic insisted. 'I don't know if I'd have had the guts to do what you did.'

'Don't forget, it's only temporary. I can go back home anytime I want to. Oh...' She put a hand to her mouth and stared at him in surprise.

'What's wrong?'

Sophie blinked, her eyes wide. 'I've just realised that when I said "home", the image that came to mind wasn't my mum's house, or my old flat. It wasn't even England. It was Tenerife.'

'It does tend to have that effect on you. I remember when we first came over here for a holiday and my mum said she wanted to live here. She dragged me and my dad back the following year and they both said it felt like they'd come home, so it wasn't that much of a shock when they started talking about moving here.'

'Do you wish they'd stayed in England?'

'Hell, no. If you want cold water, you should try swimming off the coast at Scarborough. It's bloody freezing. And it rains all the time. There are only about six days of the year when you can sit outside and eat, and even then you need to keep an umbrella handy, just in case.'

'I think you might be exaggerating a bit.'

'A bit,' he conceded with a grin. 'Seriously, life on Tenerife is so good, and it's not solely down to the weather, although that does play a big part. It's the whole pace of life thing. There's simply no rushing around as a rule. Take this afternoon – how often do you get to have a two-hour lunch break in the UK?'

'You're lucky your job allows you to do that,' she pointed out, somewhat more tartly than she'd intended.

'I am,' he admitted. 'But I'm right too. There's not the same degree of busyness and rush here as there is in Britain. Yet we still manage to get things done. Eventually.'

'I'm going to miss Tenerife,' she said after a long pause. 'It's silly that I'm already thinking about leaving when I've only been here a few weeks and there's ages to go yet, but…'

'Don't go. Stay.'

'What?'

'Live here permanently.'

'I can't do that!'

'Why not? Loads of people do.' His grin widened. 'We're not all tourists, you know.'

'Now you're being silly.'

'I'm being serious. You've said yourself that you've got nothing to go back for.'

'But that doesn't mean I can just up sticks and move over here.'

Dominic reached out a hand and placed it on top of her own. He stared at her, his usually sunny and smiling expression sobering. 'I think you'll find that's exactly what you have done.'

And when she thought about it, she realised he might be right.

Chapter 19

Sophie didn't have time to think about Dominic's suggestion. As soon as he dropped her off with a double kiss, one on each cheek, and a promise to get together again soon, without the bodyboarding element but with a trip to the beach for a toe-dip in the Atlantic as a prelude to submerging more of her in the sea, she was confronted by Alex. Why the sight of him was such a surprise to her was anyone's guess, considering he was staying at the villa and it was getting near the time to leave to visit Hugo.

'Good lunch was it?' were the first words out of his mouth when she bumped into him in the hall.

'Yes, lovely, thanks.'

'Did you go somewhere nice?'

'A little place down by the sea at Alcalá. They do fantastic fish.'

Alex frowned. 'I know it. Are you ready?'

'Just let me fetch a few things for Hugo,' she said, and trotted into the living room to pick up the bag she'd set aside for him earlier.

'Can we go now?' Alex asked crossly when she reappeared a few seconds later, and she wondered what had rattled his cage. He was behaving as though she'd kept him waiting for ages when, in fact, it had been mere seconds. And she also felt a subtle criticism emanating from him, as though she was being remiss in her duties to Hugo by going out to lunch.

What on earth was he being so grumpy about, she wondered, as she got into the car and they began the journey to the hospital, when a thought occurred to her. She debated whether to mention the possible impending sale of the villa and the surrounding land, but decided against it. After all, it was none of her business, and if Hugo and his nephew didn't want to talk to her about it, then she had no right to ask.

Sophie tried not to stare at Alex out of the corner of her eye as he drove down the motorway, but she couldn't help sneaking little glances at him.

He was so different to Dominic, who had driven with some panache, one elbow draped out of the open window, the other merely resting on the steering wheel as he had darted in and out of the traffic. She'd had the feeling that he drove like that all the time and he wasn't putting on a show for her. Whereas Alex handled the car with the minimum of effort and showmanship, just an understated competence and the occasional flickering glance in the rear-view mirror.

He slid the car expertly into a parking space, and Sophie slithered out of the passenger seat on unsteady legs. His nearness disconcerted her and made her heart beat a little faster, despite her wish that he'd disappear back to where he came from. She really could do without such a distraction in her life, no matter how handsome the distraction was.

Hugo, she discovered on reaching his bedside, was just as grumpy as his nephew, but at least he had good reason to be. No one liked being in hospital and Hugo must still be in some discomfort despite the pain medication. He grumbled that he was being forced to do physio, the food was awful, he'd had no sleep last night because of a man snoring in the opposite bed, the nurses were horrid to him… Plus a list of other complaints that Alex didn't bother to translate. Hugo's English was pretty good, but he seemed to enjoy grousing in his own language, complete with arm gestures and lots of eye-rolling.

She hoped his mood would improve once she got him home; otherwise the next few weeks weren't exactly going to be a barrel of laughs. Maybe having Alex there to share some of the load for a few days wouldn't be such a bad thing, she conceded.

Once again she left uncle and nephew to it, and went off to find a coffee and a quiet corner in which to read.

Unfortunately, though, she simply wasn't able to concentrate on the novel and her eyes kept sliding across the words without taking them in. When she realised she'd read the same sentence at least three times, she admitted defeat and put her book away. Clearly her brain had more important matters for her to think about than the romantic comedy she had been vainly trying to lose herself in.

Dominic was playing on her mind. Or, more specifically, his suggestion that she didn't have to return to the UK.

Was she brave enough?

Maybe. She'd been brave enough to ring a bell and look where that had led.

She leant her head back against the wall and closed her eyes. Think logically, she urged herself. What are the pros of staying here? For a start, she loved the island, the way of life, the weather, the language (even though she could only recognise one word in a hundred, and even then she couldn't be totally sure she'd got it right), the food, the culture. She loved that there were enough expats out here so that she didn't feel totally isolated and that she could pop into Mrs Tiggywinkle's if she wanted a blast of Britishness. She loved the mix of tourists and locals, and the many different languages she could hear, from Russian to Japanese, Swedish to French. It made for an eclectic melting pot. She loved the contrast of the many different blues of the ocean with the varying shades of rock, from coal black to russet, and jagged shards through to smooth, striated marble. She also loved the plants that grew wild, their roots burrowing into every nook and cranny, determined to find a foothold. Down here, in the south of the island, and also around the villa on the coast, they were mostly succulents and cacti, but up in the mountains, where rain fell more frequently, she'd noticed other types of plants, some of them sporting delicate flowers in soft pastel shades.

OK, now for the cons. No job. Nowhere to live. Can't speak the language, which made getting a job that much more difficult. And without a job, there would be no apartment. Then there were things like healthcare – what if she became ill? How did that work? Did she need a visa or a permit to work here? Was there a time limit on how long she could stay?

She also suspected she might miss England – the greenness, the soft mists, the snow (not that they usually had much), British TV, hearing a familiar language and accent.

But what she'd really miss about home – and this was the biggie – was her family. Aunty Anne and Denise were the only family she had left. Could she stay here and not watch those gorgeous twins grow up? Could she be happy with a yearly visit back home; twice yearly, if she saved hard?

On the other hand, Anne would be understandably wrapped up in helping her daughter care for the twins and would probably have little time to spare, so Sophie mightn't see a great deal of her, especially once she'd started a new job and her days were taken up with work.

It wasn't a decision to be taken lightly, or to be made on a whim. She'd have to have a serious think about it. Make sure it was the right decision for her, and that she wasn't simply running away and delaying the inevitable.

'Oh, Mum, what should I do?' she murmured, and she smiled sadly at the thought of what her mother would say. She'd tell her to follow her heart. But that was the problem – she didn't know what her heart wanted or where it was leading her.

When she opened her eyes, it was to find Alex standing a few feet away, studying her. She gave a bit of a start and wondered how long he'd been lurking there, spying on her. His expression was inscrutable, but he nodded to her once, then turned on his heel, and she guessed she was meant to follow him.

'I'll drop you off at the villa,' he said when she caught up with him as he marched down the hospital corridor. 'Hugo will be discharged tomorrow afternoon. Someone will visit the villa in the morning to ensure it is suitable and make any necessary adjustments.'

'Like what?'

'A chair in the shower, blocks under Hugo's armchair to raise it up so he doesn't flex the new joint too much, bars in the shower to help him sit and stand, the addition of an elevated toilet seat. Please make sure you are in. If they can't gain access to the property, he won't be allowed home.'

'I'll be in,' she said tightly. There was no need to make it sound as though she spent all her time out gallivanting and couldn't care less about Hugo's care. If Alex hadn't been there this evening, she would have been told all this herself by the doctor. As it was, she thought she was being tactful by giving the two men some time alone. Clearly it had been viewed in a different light by Alejandro.

For the second time that day, she was dropped off at the villa, but the contrast between the two events couldn't have been any starker. This time there was no double-cheeked kiss, no hug, just a gruff 'goodbye', and a brief meeting of eyes in the rear-view mirror as he drove back up the track. He was probably checking that she wasn't haring it along the path to meet Dominic, whereas she was feeling an odd mixture of relief and abandonment at his departure.

A part of her wanted him to stay because she didn't fancy being on her own this evening – her thoughts were too chaotic and swirling – and the other part was thankful there wouldn't be any tension and no snide comments. The easy(ish) companionship they'd shared over dinner last night had dissipated, to be replaced by awkwardness and a sense he was watching her, waiting for her to trip up.

Well, she'd show him. She hadn't spent years caring for her mum to not know what she was doing now. She'd show him just how professional she could be, despite not having any formal qualifications. BTECs and NVQs were all well and good, but they weren't a substitute for experience, and she had that by the bucketload. She also had compassion and empathy, and she really did care for Hugo. She'd get him on his feet and mobile again in no time, just you wait and see, she thought at Alex, as the car pulled out onto the main road.

Then, once Hugo was more capable of taking care of himself, she'd have a good long think about whether she could stay on this beautiful island, or even if she actually wanted to.

One thing was certain, though. The next few days, until Alejandro left, were going to be interesting.

Chapter 20

'Are you OK?' Sophie asked Hugo, possibly for the fourth or fifth time that evening. He'd only been home from hospital for a couple of hours and she couldn't help fussing around him. It was nice to have someone to look after, and even nicer to know that he'd eventually recover. She was looking forward to playing a part in that and anticipating a job well done.

True to their word, a couple of people from the hospital had visited earlier and had made the necessary adjustments to the villa, but Hugo still needed some help in getting about until he was a little steadier on his feet.

'I can do it myself,' he protested when she leapt to her feet in order to help him get to his, and he tried to shake her off as she put a supporting and steadying hand on his elbow.

'You might well be able to,' she said, 'but this is one of the reasons I'm here, remember? Not just to wash your clothes and walk Paco. I'm here to help you recover and make sure you don't do too much, and that's what I'm jolly well going to do.'

Ignoring his scowl, she brought his walking frame closer and held onto him while he caught his balance, then hovered behind him as he shuffled out of the living room, anxious in case he slipped on the marble-tiled floor.

It was only when he was safely tucked up in bed, with a glass of water on the bedside table next to him and his glasses on his nose as he prepared to read for a few minutes, that she allowed herself to relax.

After promising that she'd check on him in the night whether he liked it or not, and reminding him he was to shout for her if he needed anything at all, she headed for the fridge and the white wine chilling in it. She'd have one glass while sitting on the terrace watching the stars, and then go to bed herself.

The moon was still full, although beginning to wane, and the light it cast on the sea made the wavelets glitter and shimmer. The evening was an especially calm one with hardly a hint of breeze, and the surface of the ocean was smooth. The smell of briny water was strong and she took a deep breath, allowing the tang, along with the first sip of fruity wine, to ease the tension in her shoulders. The usual crash and pound of the waves had been replaced by a gentler rhythm as the sea splashed on the nearby pebbles and sucked them back down the shore, and tonight she found it even more soothing. For once her soul was at peace and her heart was filled with quiet serenity. She wasn't happy exactly – she still felt the loss of her mum too keenly for that – but she was contented with her lot for the moment. The future was some weeks away yet, and she vowed to try to enjoy every minute she was here.

The changeable nature of the view that she loved constantly amazed her, and she didn't think she'd ever tire of looking at it, whatever the weather was doing. Although, to be fair, it tended not to vary that much. Certainly not to the same degree that it did in England. Some days were cloudier than others here, and some days were windier than others. She hadn't seen any rain yet, although Hugo had informed her that the higher in the mountains you went, the more likelihood there was of a shower or two, and the north of the island had more precipitation than the south.

Then there was the difference in light between the early morning and midday, and between mid-afternoon and sunset. Not to mention how dark and mysterious the sea looked at night, and how even a sliver of moonlight could transform the whole scene.

She had no idea how long she'd been sitting there letting the calm tranquillity of the seascape wash over her, but when she heard the rumble of a car trundling down the track towards the villa her mood soured.

She debated whether to disappear off to bed, but she hadn't finished her wine yet and she'd be damned if she was going to let Alex drive her from the terrace. She had as much right to be here as he did. More, maybe. She mightn't be family, but at least she actually lived here, which was more than could be said for His Gruffness. She wasn't sure who was the more irritable – him or Hugo – but Hugo did have a valid reason. She wondered what Alex's excuse was.

Listening to him quietly opening and closing the front door, then the sound of the fridge being delved into and the soft gurgle of wine into a glass (she'd recognise that noise anywhere), she prayed he'd remain in the living room.

Her luck was out, she saw, as he sauntered slowly onto the terrace, his attention on the same view she'd been looking at a few moments before. Now, though, her focus was on the man himself, and she obtained some satisfaction when he jumped as he saw her.

'I didn't realise you were out here,' he said.

'It's only nine thirty. Too early to sleep,' she replied, even though she'd been contemplating doing exactly that only a short while ago. Now, though, any tiredness had fled, to be replaced by wary watchfulness.

'I mean, I didn't think you were in.'

Sophie's mouth dropped open. 'Where did you think I'd be?'

'I don't know.' He sank into a chair and waved his glass in the air. 'Out somewhere.'

'With Hugo only just discharged from hospital? What do you take me for?'

He shrugged and she itched to throw the contents of her own glass over his annoying head.

'You've got an awfully low opinion of me,' she whispered furiously, trying to keep her voice low so as not to disturb Hugo. 'I don't know why, as I've done nothing to deserve it.'

He shrugged again and arched an eyebrow, which she took for disagreement.

'Go on, then. Tell me why,' she demanded.

Alex sipped at his wine and shuffled around in his seat to look her in the eye. 'I think you're more interested in a good time than my uncle.'

'Oh? And how do you work that out?'

'You were out most of the day yesterday with—'

'Hold it there, fella. Yes, I went out, but before I left I cleaned the kitchen and the bathroom; I walked Paco, weeded the vegetable patch then watered it, swept the terrace and hung a load of washing out to dry. What else would you have me do when the person I'm employed to look after is being looked after perfectly well by people far more qualified than I am?'

'You said it.'

'That's it, is it? My lack of qualifications? Would you prefer to do it yourself?' Sophie leapt to her feet, hands on her hips, and glared at him.

'No, I would not. It's just—'

'Well, I'm not leaving, not unless Hugo tells me to. He's the one paying my wages, not you—'

'How much *is* he paying you?' Alex interrupted.

'None of your business.'

'Hugo is my uncle. It *is* my business.'

'No, it isn't. But if you really want to know, ask him.'

'I will.'

'Good.'

'Fine.'

Sophie glowered at Alex and Alex glowered back. They seemed to have reached an impasse, and with nothing left that she wanted to say to him, she took herself off to bed, muttering darkly under her breath as she did so. God, the man was insufferable. She'd never met anyone so annoying in her whole life; not even when her desk had been next to a bloke who'd constantly sniffed between noisily sucking on sherbet lemons and tapping his pen against his teeth. Oh, and when he didn't have a lemon sweet in his mouth, he'd whistled. Tunelessly.

Alex, she decided, was more annoying. A lot more. With bells on.

The fact that he still thought she was some kind of gold-digger infuriated her.

Abruptly the penny dropped. *The offer!* Of course. That must be what was getting up Alex's nose. He must think that she was here because of the potential gold mine Hugo was sitting on. But she hadn't known about Hugo owning the banana fields until yesterday, and she certainly hadn't been aware of anyone, Russian or otherwise, desperate to get their hands on the tract of land and the villa. She thought she should set Alex straight and, thoroughly pissed off now, she yanked open her bedroom door and marched through the villa and out onto the terrace, her bare feet slapping on the cool tiles.

Sophie could just make out Alex's surprised expression as she came to a halt in front of him, folded her arms across her chest and launched into the attack.

'For your information, I didn't know about the offer on the villa until yesterday, when Dominic told me. And even if I had, I resent you thinking that I'm the type of person who'd try to take advantage of anyone, because I wouldn't. And just because Hugo has had a hip replacement doesn't mean he's old and decrepit, or that he's lost his marbles. And you seem to forget that he's old enough to be my father, and it's simply wrong on so many levels that you think—' She halted, unable to put her disgust into words. She honestly had trouble imagining what was going through Alex's head when it came to her relationship with Hugo. Ew.

Alex was studying her the way a nasty small boy might study a fly that he was about to pull the wings off. Not that she had met any small boys who she thought capable of doing such a thing, but she could guess what their expression would be.

'I demand an apology,' she said.

'For what?'

'For what I just said.' For a highly intelligent guy, he could be seriously stupid, she'd noticed.

'You didn't make any sense.'

'Oh! Argh!!'

'You're still not making any sense,' he informed her.

'*The offer!*' she cried, rather too loudly, and hastily lowered her voice. 'The offer,' she repeated. 'You think I'm after Hugo because of the money he might get.'

'What offer?'

'The one a Russian conglomerate made.'

'To you?'

'Why would they make an offer to me?'

'I have no idea. As I said, you're not making any sense.'

'To Hugo.' She took a deep breath, hanging onto her temper by a thread.

'Someone has made some kind of an offer to Hugo?'

'Grrr.' Alex was speaking to her as though she was a young child. 'Yes! *The offer.*'

'No, I have no idea what you mean. You are speaking to me as though I am supposed to understand you. Now, I know English isn't my first language, but I am fluent and—'

'Stop. Just stop. I'll spell it out for you, shall I, so there's no language barrier? God, you're the most annoying man on the planet.'

'Is that what you want to spell out, that I'm annoying?'

'No!' She ground her teeth so hard she thought she might have cracked a molar. 'I know what you think of me, that I'm planning to take advantage of Hugo when he sells Villa Delfin and the rest of his property to the Russian conglomerate, but you are so far from the truth you might as well be on the moon.' Sophie flung her arm out and pointed at the sliver of moon which was still visible behind a cloud. 'For one thing, I didn't know anything about it until yesterday, and for another, I simply wouldn't. I don't know what you take me for – or rather, I do, and it's not nice – but I'm not like that. Even if I had known, which I didn't, I wouldn't, and...'

She stopped, realising she was repeating herself and going around in circles. It was up to Alex now. Either he'd believe her, or he wouldn't. She suspected the latter, but at least she'd done her best.

He was still staring at her, but this time a deep frown creased his brow and his mouth was drawn into a thin line. 'What offer?' Alex asked slowly.

Sophie rolled her eyes, took a deep breath and prepared to launch into yet another explanation when it hit her – *he didn't know.*

Oh, shit.

The air whooshed out of her lungs, and she bit her lip and grimaced. 'You didn't know?'

'Clearly not.'

'I see.'

'You had better explain.'

Yes, she better had, hadn't she?

So she told him what Dominic had told her, finishing with, 'Hugo's not paying me much. Not actual cash. He's paying me in bed and board, with a little extra thrown in. Oh, and the day I moved in Hugo said something a bit odd. Well, what he said wasn't all that odd, but it was the way he said it, and I remember thinking at the time that he sounded sad, regretful almost.'

'What did he say?'

Sophie paused for a second to make sure she got the wording correct. 'He said, "I don't want to have to live anywhere else".'

'Why did you think it was odd?'

'As I said, he sounded sad, as though he was going to have to move and he wasn't looking forward to it.'

'Maybe he was worried that he wouldn't be able to cope after his hip replacement?'

'Maybe, but have you seen the state of those fields? He hasn't been coping for a while.'

'I'm sure he'll be fine when he's fully recovered,' Alex said. 'But thank you for telling me about the "offer".' He exaggerated the word, setting her teeth on edge again. 'And for putting me right about your motives for being here,' he added.

'You still don't believe me, do you?'

'Actually, I do.' He drained the last of his wine and placed the empty glass on the table, then got to his feet.

Sophie huffed, unsure if he meant it, then rested her head back against her seat wearily. All this distrust was tiring and she seriously couldn't be bothered to argue with him anymore. She watched him walk away, relief flooding her, then he hesitated. What now, she wondered.

'It's not only Hugo I find myself being protective over,' he said, and when his eyes met hers, she shivered at what she saw in them.

And she simply knew she was in for another restless night.

Chapter 21

In deference to Sophie's (very) limited Spanish, Hugo and Alex spoke mostly English when she was around, for which she was extremely grateful. So her ears pricked up when, on the tenth day after Hugo's surgery, he asked Alex when he was returning to Iceland.

'In a couple of days,' Alex said, picking up a bread roll and breaking it open.

Hugo nodded. 'All is well?'

'Yes.'

'Good. I am pleased.'

The three of them were having dinner on the terrace, and Sophie paused in the act of spooning some chorizo and soft-boiled egg salad onto her plate, her eyes shooting from one to the other as she tried to make sense of the hidden meaning behind the words. Something was, or had been, going on, she was sure of it, and it was to do with Alex's job and the reason why he was on Tenerife. It was better focusing on that than on Alex's imminent departure, because she really wasn't sure how she felt about that.

Ever since that night out on the terrace the two of them had exercised excessive politeness around one another. If Hugo had noticed the slightly strained atmosphere, he didn't say anything. And, as far as Sophie knew, Alex hadn't mentioned to his uncle that he was aware of the Russian conglomerate's offer.

She put the spoon down, pretending to study the salad as she contemplated the prospect of the villa without Alex in it. It would be strange. She'd become used to his presence and found herself listening out for him, his voice, his soft footsteps. She even liked the way he smelt, and that she could tell if he'd been in a room recently by the scent of his aftershave in the air. The place would seem emptier without him.

'You two should go out this afternoon,' Hugo said, breaking into her thoughts.

'Pardon?' Did he mean her and Alex? Surely not.

'Take her up that volcano you love so much. Now that it is safe.'

'Wasn't it safe before?' she asked.

'Yes, it was. But there were some anomalies,' Alex said, frowning at his uncle.

'She is not a tourist,' Hugo said around a mouthful of green leaves.

'Yes, but—'

'It is not secret,' Hugo said.

'No, but—'

'Take her out. Show her the real Tenerife.'

'The volcano?' Sophie asked. 'I've seen it.'

'Did you go to the top?' Alex wanted to know.

'Yes. The view was fantastic.'

'The real top? The edge of the crater?'

'Er… no. Not that far. I went up in the cable car.'

Alex put his cutlery down and reached for the glass of water at his elbow. 'What about you, Tío? It's less than two weeks since your operation.'

'I have physio this afternoon, then I shall have a siesta.'

'I don't like leaving you on your own—' Sophie began, but Hugo interrupted her.

'Nonsense! I will be fine for a few hours. I have my phone, and I will not be on my own for long.'

She nibbled her lip; an afternoon out sounded wonderful. Apart from taking Paco for his twice daily constitutionals and the occasional trip to the supermarket to pick up groceries and other supplies, she'd hardly left the villa recently. Not that she felt the need to, but the change would do her good. Besides, it might be the last time she'd really see Alex. If he was leaving the day after next, then apart from at dinner tomorrow evening, she might not see him at all. And despite the harsh words between them, she discovered that she wanted to spend an hour or so with him – she wanted to be with him more than she'd previously admitted to herself.

She glanced up and found him staring at her, his liquid chocolate eyes unreadable, but there was a softness to his lips, and he nodded.

'If Sophie wants to come, then I shall take her. No one who visits Tenerife should leave without looking into her heart.'

A tremor ran through her at the thought of being alone with him and she offered him a tentative smile.

'And I'll even give you a couple of hours off tomorrow and take Hugo to the hospital to have his stitches out,' Alex suggested. 'I might also take him out to lunch. How does paella at Ramon's sound, Tío?'

'Good, but Sophie should come too,' Hugo said. He wiped his mouth with a napkin and reached for his stick.

He'd come such a long way in a short space of time, she mused, gazing at him fondly. From the walker, to crutches, to using a stick. He'd been doing his exercises religiously (she'd made sure of that) and had taken several gentle strolls along the coastal path, turning back when he got tired. He'd not gone far, but it was a start.

'No, you two spend some time together. Hugo and I can go another day,' she said. After all, she had no idea how long it would be before Alex returned and it would be nice for uncle and nephew to spend what little time remained together.

'Go.' Hugo levered himself to his feet and waved a hand in her direction. 'Enjoy.'

'If you're sure...'

'He's sure,' Alex said. 'I'll wash the dishes, you go and get ready. You'll need walking boots if you have them, old trousers or jeans, and a fleece. It can be cool at the top.'

She smiled, remembering the temperature difference between sea level and twelve thousand feet, and hurried to do as he suggested.

After she'd fussed over Hugo (much to his annoyance), Alex finally dragged her out of the villa, one hand on her elbow, and steered her towards the car.

Once she was in the passenger seat, instead of starting the engine, Alex swivelled to look at her.

'I was wrong,' he said. 'Forgive me?'

Astounded, all Sophie could do was nod. Who'd have thought he'd apologise to her? And it was very welcome too.

'I didn't really think you were after Hugo's money, but I couldn't see any other reason for a young, beautiful woman like you to shut herself away in a villa in the middle of nowhere with an invalid,' he said. 'But you're not really in the middle of nowhere, and Hugo isn't really an invalid.'

'No to both of those things,' she replied, but what she was really focusing on was the fact that he'd said she was beautiful. He was being very kind, and she didn't think he meant it, but it was nice of him regardless and her heart gave a little jump.

'You are, you know,' he continued. 'Beautiful.'

'Aw, you're making me blush.'

He chuckled. 'Sorry. Shall we go?'

'Yes, please. Do you want to tell me what the anomalies were? You and Hugo were very hush-hush.'

Alex started the car and they trundled up the track towards the road. 'Over the past few weeks, there has been increased seismic activity, greater carbon dioxide emissions and more frequent fumaroles – gas and smoke which seeps out of vents in the crust – on the southwestern flank of the volcano, and in the Las Cañadas caldera itself. Now, this isn't unusual, and it does happen periodically, but it nevertheless has to be taken seriously.'

'Were we, *are* we, in any danger?'

'No, I don't believe so.'

'What's the Las Cañad… caldera…?' She glanced out of the window but Teide was obscured by the walls surrounding a field and the mountain slopes it covered.

'OK, well, a hundred and seventy thousand years ago there was an even larger structure than El Teide standing where Teide is now. When it collapsed, a caldera – a large crater – was formed. El Teide and its sister peak, called Pico Viejo, rose out of this crater to form two cones. You know Teide has a relatively pointed peak, well, Pico Viejo's summit is an explosion crater over seven hundred metres wide. As we go further into the caldera, you'll see its steep sides forming a rough circle. We will go up in the cable car, and from there we go on foot to the rim of Teide.'

'Gosh. I didn't know you could do that.'

'The top is accessible if you have a permit, but you're only allowed on the mountain for a short period of time.'

'Because of the fumaroles?'

'Because it is a national park and the authorities wish to prevent too much erosion by footfall.'

'Ah.'

'I have a special permit, however, and we can remain at the summit for as long as you wish.'

'Lovely.' She couldn't wait. Her mother would be thrilled when she told her she'd— Oh. Furiously Sophie blinked back unexpected tears. Grief wasn't a predictable linear thing; it rose up to swamp her at the most inappropriate and unanticipated moments, and every now and again she actually forgot her mum was gone, and the loss of her was felt as keenly as though it had just happened.

Trust Alex to notice. 'Are you OK? We don't have to go to the top if it worries you, though I assure you it's perfectly safe.'

'I'm fine. Honest.'

'No, you are not. Tell me; maybe I can help.'

Sophie took a steadying breath, willing her eyes to stop filling with tears. 'I was just thinking about my mum, that's all,' she said. 'It's nothing.'

'It's not nothing, please don't be ashamed of your tears. You loved her very much, I can tell.'

'Yes, I did. Sometimes I forget she's gone and when I remember it hurts all over again.'

'I haven't lost anyone close to me, thankfully, and I can't imagine what you are going through, but from what other people have told me the pain does get easier to bear. Although I don't believe it ever goes away entirely. And maybe that's not such a bad thing. Emotion is what defines us, what makes us who we are, and keeps our memories alive.'

'Wow. Insightful.'

'Is it? I know words can't help, but that's all I can offer you.'

You could offer me a hug, she thought, then immediately shook the idea off. How ridiculous she was being, but she couldn't help reacting to his nearness, to the compassion she saw in his eyes as he looked at her, the scent of him, male and citrusy, the fine black hairs on his powerful forearms.

Hormones. Pheromones. That's all, she rationalised. It was the woman in her reacting to the man in him. Nothing more. Pure animal attraction, and as far as specimens of the opposite sex went, he was a gorgeous example. Apart from that, they had nothing in common. His way of life and experiences were so far removed from hers that they might as well be on different planets. They had no points of similarity; and, to be honest, his personality often left a lot to be desired. He was hardly Mr Tactful. And he could be quite rude and abrasive.

He could be empathic too, though, and he wasn't afraid to apologise when he was in the wrong. That had to count for something, didn't it?

Oh, give it a rest, she said to herself. No matter how attracted she was to him, or how much he was starting to grow on her, he'd be out of her life in a couple of days. She'd probably never see him again as long as she lived.

There – how was that for a dampener? Not only was she feeling incredibly sad because of her mother, she was now also imagining never setting eyes on Alex again. Well, she certainly knew how to kill a mood...

Alex, aware of her melancholy (she hoped he put it down to lingering sorrow at the loss of her mum) kept up a running commentary regarding the formation of the islands, Tenerife in particular. He pointed out various items of interest as they travelled deeper into the national park.

'Here you can see Los Roques de Garcia,' Alex informed her as they drove past, and Sophie saw several strange rock formations towering in the distance, stacks of layered rock which had been eroded at their bases, pointing like fingers towards the heavens. 'They have names like "Finger of God" and "the Cathedral",' he said.

She studied the weird, twisted pinnacles of rock in awe, craning her neck for a final view of them as the car swept past. 'It's very beautiful and extremely fascinating,' she said, recognising why Alex was so enamoured with his job. He was also a good guide, not blinding her with science but informing her in layman's terms and making it interesting as he did so. Even though she'd been on this road before when she was on the coach tour, she was seeing it with fresh eyes as she learnt more than she ever thought was possible about the geology and history of the area. She was right, her mother would have loved it. As she gazed at the magnificent rock formations around her and at the raw, rugged splendour of the landscape, she vowed to enjoy every second of it, in her mother's memory.

You only live once, and she'd be damned if she was going to let grief hold her back. Her mum would want her to live her life to the full and she was going to make sure she did exactly that. And if this stunning scenery taught her anything, it was that the world keeps turning and she had to make sure she claimed her tiny place in it.

Chapter 22

The guard on the gate waved them through and Sophie took a last lingering look at the safety of the cable car station before turning her attention to the path ahead. Instead of following the other tourists who had a permit to hike from the station to the summit, Alex led her around the side of the mountain and the others were soon lost from view.

'This is what is known as Route 11 and it leads to La Fortaleza viewpoint, but more importantly, we can reach the crater rim without having all those people around us,' Alex explained.

'Is it allowed?' There was a track of sorts, but it wasn't particularly well defined, and it was much rockier than she'd anticipated.

'It is for me.' He turned around to smile at her.

She smiled back before the astounding views claimed her attention. She simply had to stop to take them in, because walking and gazing around was an accident waiting to happen on the uneven surface. Although the path was better in some places than others, she didn't want to risk a sprained ankle or worse. Then an image popped into her head of having to be carried back down in Alex's arms and her insides did a little roll.

As they carried on around the topmost cone – which was far higher than she'd imagined – the whole of the north of the island hove into view, spread out before her, and she recalled flying just above the tip of the volcano when her plane had navigated the island in preparation for landing.

In the distance she was certain she could see another island, but the haze and clouds made it difficult to tell. When she mentioned it to Alex, he said, 'You can see Gran Canaria from here, and on a particularly clear day you might even be able to make out the coast of Africa. Remember the *calima*?'

She nodded.

'I've been up here when the prevailing winds have changed from northerly to easterly, and seeing a bank of orange cloud bearing down on the island is a sight to behold. As you know, thankfully it doesn't happen often, but when it does, it takes your breath away.'

The whole island was taking Sophie's breath away, especially this part. The contrast between the wide roads, the palm trees, the white villas and hotels near the sea and this primeval landscape was awe-inspiring. Up here, she felt the raw power of nature; she was simply a little speck on the side of the third highest volcano in the world. The thought was humbling, but she'd never felt more alive than she did right now.

Her eyes wide with wonder, she drank in the majesty and the splendour and was so glad Hugo had insisted Alex brought her here. When she'd visited Teide last time, as part of the coach tour, she had been astounded by it – but that visit now seemed a little too safe, too secure. The cable car station allowed people to enjoy the volcano without having to risk broken ankles, and that was great for those who would otherwise be unable to get to the top. But walking on the rocks directly, feeling their rough surface under her feet, and more importantly, being on her own with no one else in sight, made Sophie feel like an intrepid explorer.

But she wasn't on her own, was she? Alex was by her side…

'Are you ready to go up there?' Alex asked, intruding into her thoughts.

She followed his finger as he pointed towards the conical peak towering above them. 'Up there?' she squeaked.

'That is the top. I'm not going to lie, it's a bit of a trek and the gradient is hard, but you've come this far…'

She took a deep breath of the thin, cool air. 'I suppose I must. How long will it take?'

'About forty-five minutes.'

Sophie craned her neck and gazed at the tip of the mountain. It looked really high and very steep, and from what she could see there didn't appear to be much of a path. It was more of a narrow trail of trodden down loose volcanic rock.

'We'll end up at roughly the same point on the crater rim as all the other people,' he told her, 'but without having them on the same trail, so it's a bit more private.'

'Right then, let's get started,' she said, placing one foot on the loose pumice and feeling the ground give a little. This would be like walking on sand, she guessed – difficult, hard-going and extremely tiring. She'd certainly sleep well tonight!

The pair of them trudged up the slope in relative silence, with only their laboured breathing to be heard over the sound of their boots crunching on the rocks.

Nothing grew on this uppermost peak, she noticed, not even a tiny blade of grass or a cactus.

Gasping, she clambered up the last stretch on all fours, levering herself up to the crater edge, and peered over it.

Her eyes widened. She was expecting something more...

'Don't tell me, you thought you'd see a lava lake?' Alex said.

Hearing the amusement in his voice, she replied, 'No. Not really.' Then, after a pause as she took in the bowl of what looked like white dust beneath her, she admitted, 'Kind of.'

He scooted down beside her, his thigh touching hers. 'Teide is an active volcano. It might not be erupting now, but it has done so in the recent past and will do so again. What you see here is a layer of dust covering a plug of rock. The dust is from the fumaroles. Notice it is yellow in places? That's caused by sulphur dioxide. It's best to be upwind of it. For one thing, it smells like rotten eggs, and for another it's not advisable to breathe too much of it.'

Sophie noticed that the wind was at her back, blowing away from her and across the volcano's summit, and she inhaled deeply. She couldn't seem to get enough air into her lungs, and while she understood it was due to the altitude, she also had a feeling that Alex himself was partly to blame for her breathlessness. She was acutely conscious of his leg next to hers and she could feel the heat of his skin through his hiking trousers and her jeans. In fact, if she didn't move away from him right this second, she thought she might spontaneously combust. Hot now (because of the exertion of the climb, she told herself), she unzipped her jacket and fanned the collar.

To her annoyance, Alex appeared to be neither out of breath nor warm. In fact, he looked as cool as the sea in the distance, and she tore her gaze away from him and shuffled slightly so they were no longer touching.

Either Alex didn't notice, or he didn't care, because he continued to stare intently at his surroundings, and she guessed his mind must be on his job and the volcano they were perched so precariously on.

'I wish I didn't have to go back to Iceland,' he said, after a long pause, and for a moment she was surprised until she realised that he must mean he wasn't ready to leave Teide yet. To her dismay, she also wished he wasn't going. But for her peace of mind and to protect her fragile heart, she knew it was for the best. She could so easily see herself falling for this complex, charismatic man, and that was something she most definitely didn't want to do.

The hike back down to the cable car station was easier, and with every step she took Sophie felt revitalised as more oxygen entered her lungs, so that by the time they got out of the swinging glass and metal box, and she stood on terra firma again, she was positively bouncing.

'That was brilliant,' she cried. 'One of the best experiences of my life.'

'Really?' A smile lit Alex's face, and she blinked at the delight and passion she saw there.

'You really do love your job, don't you,' she said, as they headed back to the car.

'I do. It's fascinating and I could spend all day up here. Unfortunately, for every hour I spend in the field, I have to stare at a computer screen for twenty. Still, I couldn't imagine doing anything else.'

'I know you said you'd been looking after your mother for a long time, but what did you do before that?'

She grimaced. 'Worked in an office doing routine admin. Not very exciting.'

'Um, no, maybe not... What about interests?'

'I like to read. A lot. Walking, watching films and documentaries. That's not very exciting either, is it?'

'Do you enjoy these things?'

'Yes.'

'Then it doesn't matter if other people think they're not exciting. It's what you enjoy doing that's important.'

'I do envy you, though,' she said. 'You have a calling, a vocation. To you, what you do isn't just a job.'

'No, it's not,' he agreed. 'But it's not all spewing lava and pyroclastic flows, either.'

'Pyro-*what*?'

He laughed as he opened the car door for her, and she got in. 'A pyroclastic flow is a mass of volcanic matter and deadly gases which is ejected from a volcano. It can reach speeds of more than five hundred kilometres an hour. If you're in the path of one, you're toast. Literally.'

She expected him to laugh, but his expression was sombre.

'It's a terrible thing to witness,' he said, 'but compelling too. I'm just glad they don't happen too often.' He started the car and brightened. 'How about a snack in a little place I know, followed by impenetrable darkness?'

'Er... the snack sounds good. I'm not so sure about the darkness bit.'

'You'll love it, I promise.'

Bemused, Sophie sat back and let the scenery unfold as Alex negotiated the route through the caldera. She remembered travelling this way on the coach, and she looked forward to driving along wooded roads with gaps between the trees where pretty villages could be seen. It was undeniably a beautiful and impressive part of the world, and as they descended she wound her window down to let the warmth of a Tenerife afternoon flood the car.

After coffee and a delicious pastry – and Sophie making a quick call to Hugo to check he was OK, only to be given short shrift for waking him from his nap – they resumed their journey.

'It's not far,' Alex told her, 'but it does involve some more walking.'

'You do know it's still light and will be for another couple of hours?' she pointed out.

'Not underground, it's not.'

'What? Are you serious?'

'We are going to the Cueva del Viento – Cave of the Wind – and it's one of the longest volcanic tubes in the world. Well worth a visit.'

Really? While she admired his enthusiasm for all things volcanic, she hadn't been expecting to visit a dank cave. Thank God this wasn't a date, because she'd be most disappointed. Sightseeing was one thing but rooting around in the depths of the earth was something else entirely. What was wrong with exploring one of those gorgeous villages she'd seen along the way? Her version of an afternoon out was considerably removed from Alex's. She'd quite happily wander down a cobbled street or two, and maybe browse in a shop, even though she wouldn't have any intention of buying anything. She might even visit one of the lovely little churches she'd read about.

But a cave? No thanks.

'It's really interesting,' Alex tried to assure her, and she gave him a sideways look in return. He gave her one back. 'If you don't come out of there with a smile on your face, I'll clean the villa from top to bottom,' he promised.

'It doesn't need cleaning.'

'OK then, I'll weed the garden and water the plants.'

She considered his proposition, then held out a hand. 'Deal.'

He took it and shook it quickly before returning his hand to the steering wheel, but the fleeting touch sent shivers of excitement through her and she had to suppress a gasp. Oh, Lord...

All she needed to do was to maintain her equilibrium for the rest of the afternoon. Despite the fact that she was enjoying herself immensely, she needed to focus on not enjoying herself too much. It would be over soon, both the afternoon and Alex's visit. She only had to keep her composure for a short while and not do anything daft, then he would be out of her life and she could move forward with her heart and her dignity intact.

'You do realise that I'm not going to smile, don't you?' she warned him. 'No matter what.'

'We'll see,' was all he said, and she steeled herself to keep her expression blank. There was no way he was getting a smile out of her afterwards, not with weeding and watering at stake.

'Here we are,' he said, after driving up one of the steepest streets she'd ever seen and pulling into a car park.

'Let's get you kitted out with a helmet, then we're good to go.'

'Do they let people wander in or is there a tour guide?' she asked.

'Entry is by organised tour only, usually. But not today. Today you are with me, and I'll be your guide.'

He was greeted warmly at the visitor centre and, once he'd explained what he wanted, was given a set of keys and two helmets. The keys, she discovered, were for a Jeep — which Alex drove along a winding dirt track through a lovely forested area — and for the gated entrance to a steep flight of steps.

Sophie would have been quite content to stop there and explore a bit, but Alex was determined to get her underground.

He made sure her helmet was secure (she tried not to look into his eyes as he fiddled about with her chin strap), then he unlocked the gate and ushered her down the steps.

'Is it safe?' she asked, touching the yellow plastic helmet nervously and thinking she must look a sight with it on.

'Perfectly. The roof is low in places, which is why we need to wear a helmet. There are several tours a day, and the authorities wouldn't allow that if there was any danger. Now, let me tell you about this astounding place.' He switched on a torch and she saw a tunnel before her, stretching into impenetrable darkness beyond the meagre spill of light.

'This tunnel is eighteen kilometres long, making it one of the longest lava tubes in the world. It's actually a labyrinth of passages formed over three levels...'

She let his voice fade out as she concentrated on where she placed her feet and tried not to let the darkness beyond the torchlight frighten her. It was extremely disconcerting to think that if those batteries failed, they'd be in utter darkness, and anything could be lurking in these tunnels. Anything!

To her surprise, though, once she had a grip on her totally rational fear, she found the experience utterly absorbing. Once again, Alex proved to be a great guide, explaining things to her and making everything sound incredibly interesting.

There was one moment, however…

'I'm going to turn the torch off in a second,' he said. 'You might have experienced what you think is total darkness in the past, but it's nothing like you're about to experience now. Don't be frightened, I'll hold your hand so you know I'm still here, but I want you to try to be as quiet as possible and let your ears and your nose take over. Ready?'

Sophie gulped. No, she wasn't ready for this, but she nodded anyway, even though she knew that if she told him she didn't want him to turn the torch off, he would leave it on. She didn't want him to think she was a wimp and afraid of the dark, even though she most definitely was. Normally darkness didn't bother her, but the thought of being trapped down here with absolutely—

'Eek!' The light had gone out and they were immediately plunged into the most complete blackness Sophie could ever imagine.

'Are you OK?' he asked, and she felt his hand slip into hers and close around it, holding her in a firm grip.

'Yes,' she whispered, although she wasn't; not really. This must be what it was like to be blind, she realised, lifting her free hand up to her face and seeing nothing.

Eyes open as wide as they could possibly go, she strained to see something, anything, but the darkness was absolute.

Heart hammering, she tried to be quiet as Alex had suggested, but all she could hear was her own heartbeat thundering in her ears.

She could smell him, though, she realised. His usual citrus aftershave. Soap too, and the washing powder she bought. She could smell another scent below them, and that was the scent of Alex himself. He smelt of the outdoors, of wide open spaces, of the sea. It was his own unique smell and it sent a wave of longing through her.

She could feel him too. His hand held hers, warm and strong, and she absent-mindedly rubbed her thumb across the back of his, his skin feeling smooth to the touch. She wanted to let go and run her fingers up his arms, to caress the fine hairs that she knew were there.

Then she noticed she could feel the heat emanating from him. Even if he hadn't been holding her hand, she would have known he was there. Finally, the sound of him breathing softly could be heard and the tiny rustles of his clothing. For a moment, she was sure she could hear his heart beating.

'I'm going to switch the torch back on now, so you may want to close your eyes for a second, so you aren't blinded,' he said quietly in her ear, and the sound of his voice made the skin on the back of her neck tingle. She knew his lips must be inches away from her ear, as his breath fanned her cheek, and she itched to turn her head and discover what they tasted like.

Obediently she closed her eyes, just as he switched the torch on, and light flooded her eyelids in bursts of orange, red and yellow.

Cautiously she opened them again to discover she was right – his lips *were* awfully close to her own. And she did exactly what her head was screaming at her not to do. She pushed her helmet back slightly, tilted her chin, closed her eyes again and waited for his kiss.

It seemed a long time coming.

His sharp intake of breath and the way he tightened his grip on her hand told her that he wasn't going to pull away. His warm breath was soft on her cheek and the scent of him filled her completely until her senses swam and she felt giddy.

All this, and he hadn't even kissed her yet.

At first, she wasn't sure whether she was imagining it, because his lips were so light on hers, a feather-light touch, barely there. Her pulse soared and she parted her lips, tremors coursing through her.

He needed no further encouragement and his mouth claimed hers, the kiss deepening as he let go of her hand and his arms came around her, pulling her into him, his helmet bumping against her forehead before he pushed it back.

She went willingly, eagerly, tasting him, moulding herself against him, her heart swooping and her head spinning until she was utterly lost in him.

It could have been one minute, it could have been an hour, before they broke apart. She'd lost all track of time. God, she'd lost all track of herself.

Had she really kissed him so passionately, so ardently, the same way he'd kissed her?

Cocooned in the darkness, with the torch only a tiny circle of light, the real world seemed very far away indeed. Light years away.

Slowly she opened her eyes, her lips still tingling from their kiss, the scent of him still on her skin, his arms still encircling her, to find him gazing at her with an expression in his eyes she couldn't read. She saw desire and hunger there, but she saw something else too. Was it sadness?

Yes, that was probably it. He was already regretting kissing her and... But if that was true, why were those delectable eyes coming closer, and why could she feel his mouth on hers once more?

Lost again, she surrendered to the undeniable feelings consuming her, and it was only later, when they emerged blinking into the early evening light, that she realised she'd be doing her own weeding and watering.

And she found she didn't mind, not one little bit.

Chapter 23

Despite the smile, despite her somersaulting heart and the butterflies dancing in her stomach, and despite knowing that if she had to live those moments over, she'd do exactly the same again, Sophie couldn't help wondering if Alex had kissed her on purpose in order to win the bet. Not that it was a bet exactly, because she hadn't wagered anything, and she hadn't lost anything either, but she still wondered if he might have cheated.

If he had, it was quite a gamble on his part, she acknowledged, because she could have just as easily rebuffed him and given him a piece of her mind.

But she hadn't. She'd practically thrown herself at him, and she wasn't entirely sure who had made the first move anyway. She had a feeling it might have been her, with her closed eyes and her face lifted towards his in a blatant invitation to be kissed.

And he'd certainly done that. Several times. And with a great deal of skill too. And ardour. Don't forget the ardour. He'd wanted to kiss her as much as she'd wanted to kiss him. Six of one and half a dozen of the other, as her mum used to say.

The atmosphere on the drive home was subdued, each of them lost in their thoughts. Sophie's were mostly of the self-doubt and beating herself up variety. As usual, she had no idea what Alex was thinking, as he didn't say very much and his expression was guarded. She hoped he wasn't regretting what had happened and she prayed that his last couple of days at the villa wouldn't be awkward.

She desperately wanted to discuss it, yet she couldn't work up enough courage to broach the subject. Then her thoughts led her to the conclusion that it didn't matter anyway because his life was in Iceland and hers was... well... nowhere. On Tenerife for the time being, but after Hugo no longer needed her then it was probably going to be back in the UK, unless she made the decision to stay. Even that was easier said than done; she still didn't know how she felt about leaving her family, and she had yet to find a job and somewhere to live, which would be hard enough in England where she could speak the language. Over here, it was an impossibility.

To her relief, Hugo was up and about when they got back, oblivious to any awkwardness between her and his nephew, and she spent the time preparing the evening meal telling him what she'd seen and learnt, hopefully in a neutral tone of voice and without excessive references to Alex.

Alex, for his part, had a quick shower, then retired to his room. In between chatting to Hugo, she caught the sound of his voice and guessed he must be on the phone. She wondered who he was talking to. It could be anyone, but...

It was only then, hearing his occasional murmur, that she considered the possibility that there might be someone anxiously awaiting his return to Iceland. Someone special. Someone who he was on the phone to right this very minute, keeping his voice low and intimate.

Suddenly she felt sick. Had he been playing with her? Was she just a passing amusement to him?

It would be so easy to do — she would be long gone by the time he returned, and who would know? Even if Alex's girlfriend were to meet Hugo and Sophie's name was mentioned, it would be purely in the context of employee, the woman who had been paid to look after him.

The sound of the front door shutting as Alex left the villa made her jump, and she glanced up from chopping an onion to find Hugo studying her.

'It's the onion,' she said unnecessarily as she used the back of her hand to dash away the tears which had gathered in the corner of her eye and were threatening to spill over. Hugo uttered a noncommittal grunt, which she chose to take for agreement. Because what else could those tears be but a reaction to her butchering of the poor onion on the chopping board?

'I am happy you enjoyed your afternoon,' he said after a while. 'It is many years since I walked on El Teide.'

'Now that you've had your hip done…' she began, but Hugo shook his head.

'My days of climbing up that mountain are over. I am too old, too tired.' He brightened. 'I bet Alejandro told you the science and did not tell you the story of the true heart of the volcano. Do you want to hear it?'

'Yes, please.' Anything to take her mind off Alex, the phone call and whether he'd return to join them for dinner.

'A people called the Guanches lived on these islands before my ancestors came here,' Hugo began. 'They said the volcano held up the sky. They also said El Teide was the way to the world below… I am not sure how you say it…?'

'Hell?' Sophie offered, fascinated.

He shook his head. 'That's not it.'

'The underworld?'

'*Sí*, the underworld. That is the word. OK, long ago Guayota, the devil, locked Magec, the god of light and the sun, inside Teide, and this made the world turn to night. There was no sun, no light, and the Guanches were afraid there would never be another day. They prayed to the god of gods, Achamán, to bring the light back, and so Achamán, he fought Guayota. Achamán threw the devil into the volcano and put a… what do you call that?' He pointed to a bottle of wine on the counter.

'Wine?'

'No, the top. It stops the wine from coming out.'

'A cork?'

'Yes, a cork. He let Magec out and put a cork – not a real one, but one made of rock – in the top of the crater to keep Guayota in. The light came back to the land, and from then on, the Guanches lit big fires outside when the volcano erupted, to scare Guayota and keep him in the underworld. It makes sense, no? The world was dark because of an eruption and the old people thought it was because of the devil. I love this story. It is better than the science. Science is so cold; there is no heart to it.'

Oh, I don't know about that, Sophie thought, recalling Alex's passion for his subject and his passion when he kissed her.

'Alejandro, he does have a heart, but he keeps it deep inside here.' He thumped his chest. 'Like Guayota, hidden from the world. I had thought…'

Despite her better judgement, she felt compelled to ask. 'What?'

'That you might set his heart free. I have seen the way he looks at you.'

'You have?' She gulped and her knees felt a bit wobbly.

'*Sí*, I have.'

'I can't say I've noticed,' she replied. 'You're probably imagining it.'

'Perhaps yes, perhaps no.' He sighed. 'Ignore me. I am an old man. I make mistakes.'

'You're not that old,' she pointed out and he smiled sadly at her. 'Thank you for the story, it's definitely more romantic than magma chambers.' Then, feeling the need for some fresh air to clear her head, she announced that she was going to water the vegetable patch and, leaving Hugo to keep an eye on dinner, she headed outside.

She loved the terrace with its wonderful views, but this little area of garden was her peaceful place. Under her care the vegetable patch was thriving. It took a lot of work, admittedly, because not many of the things that she grew liked being so near to the sea, and she had to water both the plants themselves and the soil in order to dilute the salt from the spray caused by the waves. It was a daily task and one she found quite therapeutic.

Not this evening, though, as her thoughts churned in her head. Hugo must be mistaken. Alex did not look at her in that way. He hardly looked at her at all.

What about those kisses? a treacherous voice asked, and she shook her head to get rid of it. They were a mistake, an accident. *All of them?* A one-off, she said to herself. Never to be repeated. People kissed all the time without it having to mean anything.

It meant something to you, her heart insisted, and her brain crossly told it to shut up.

Eventually, after she'd watered everything in sight, twice, she turned off the tap, picked a sprig of parsley and went back inside.

Then she spent the rest of the evening and long into the night waiting for Alex to come home and feeling incredibly annoyed for letting herself get into this position. The sooner he left the villa, the better, as far as she was concerned, and she could try to forget those kisses had ever happened.

Chapter 24

'I'm popping to Mrs Tiggywinkle's while you're at the hospital,' Sophie called to the villa in general. 'Do you want anything?'

'You English, you do a lot of "popping",' Hugo teased, coming into the hall, and she noticed that he wasn't using his walking stick.

'You'd better take your stick with you to the hospital,' she advised, avoiding Alex's eye as he joined them, hovering behind his uncle. 'They might tell you that you have to keep using it for a while.' She moved towards him and kissed his whiskery cheek. 'Good luck, not that you'll need it. You're doing brilliantly.'

Hugo pulled a face, but she could tell he was pleased.

'Right, I'm off. I'm taking Paco, in case you get back before me and wonder where he is.'

'It doesn't take that long to walk to Playa de la Arena,' she heard Alex mutter, but chose to ignore it.

If she wanted to stop off somewhere for a pastry and a coffee, then she bloody well would, and she didn't have to answer to Alex either. Although she actually didn't intend to be too long, because she didn't want to leave Hugo on his own for any length of time in case Alex had plans for after the hospital appointment.

It was another glorious day (when wasn't it?) and she basked in the feel of the warm sun on her back and the salty tang in the air as she strolled along the path. The sea was on her left, the neglected fields on her right, and she couldn't help staring at them as she walked past. It was a pity something couldn't be done about them – and she didn't mean building a whopping great hotel on them. If those walls were taken down, and the dying plants removed, then the land could perhaps be allowed to return to nature. Or, and here was an idea, the whole area could be landscaped like the stretch of coast where Alcalá began. The authorities had made a start with the paved coastal path, but they could take it one step further and do something with the land; if they were willing to buy it, which they probably weren't. And if they had the funds, which they probably didn't.

Thinking of funds led her to think about Hugo's predicament. She knew he couldn't be receiving any income from the banana fields, and she wondered if he was living off his savings. Or maybe a pension – he was old enough to have one.

Once again she was filled with dread and incredible sadness at the thought of the villa being torn down and replaced by a fancy bar to service the new beach that no doubt would be constructed once that Russian conglomerate got their greedy hands on the property.

She imagined a bear of a man, smoking a cigar and speaking with a heavy Russian accent, as the face of this nameless organisation, and she shuddered.

'Why so glum?' Dominic asked as she stepped into Mrs Tiggywinkle's.

Although she'd visited the shop several times since she'd had lunch with him, she hadn't seen him in there. 'Oh, this and that,' she said. 'Long time, no see.'

She was struck once more by just how good-looking he was, with his open expression, clear blue eyes and longish hair, which was bleached by the sun and falling over his forehead. He was dressed in a T-shirt with a wave emblazoned on the front, a pair of navy shorts and sliders on his feet, looking every inch the surfer dude.

'Yes, it's been a while, hasn't it?' he agreed.

'I've listened to your show a few times.'

His face lit up. 'You have?'

'Yep, so I feel as if you've been in my kitchen on a regular basis.'

'I wish I had been,' he said, giving her a meaningful look.

'Are you flirting with me, Dominic Tiggywinkle?' she demanded, and he threw his head back and laughed.

'Yes, and I'm not ashamed of it either,' he replied. 'I was going to give you a call, but I remembered you said you'd be busy looking after Hugo. How is he?'

'Doing really well, thanks. He's walking without a stick now, although I do think it might be a bit too soon.'

'That's great news. Does it mean you'll have some free time for that surfing lesson?'

'Not just yet, but I could manage a coffee.'

'When?'

'I'm free now, but I can see you're working.'

'Actually, Mum and Dad have just arrived back from the wholesalers, so if you give me ten minutes to hand over the reins, I'll be with you.'

'Great. I've got a spot of shopping to do while I wait.' She wandered up and down the little aisles, picking up a few items and popping them into her basket. Robinson's marmalade, yum; she'd have that on toast in the morning. And she added Heinz baked beans to the basket too. Hugo didn't see the attraction, but she loved them with a jacket potato and some cheese. Then there was real honest-to-goodness British chocolate, which she simply couldn't live without. Spanish chocolate was lacking somehow, and didn't taste half as good. She put a couple of bars in the basket and went to the counter to pay.

'Hello, love, how's Hugo?' Mrs Tiggywinkle asked. She'd been asking about him regularly since the operation, and Sophie told her what she'd told Dominic.

'He'll soon be back to full fitness, then,' Mrs Tiggy-winkle observed, and Sophie's heart sank. Yes, he would, wouldn't he? She really must get a move on and do something about her future.

'Ready?' Dominic appeared at her elbow and took her shopping bag from her, leaning over to put it behind the counter. 'You can pick it up on the way back.'

They wandered out of the shop, Paco padding behind them, and headed for a row of bars and cafés.

'You didn't answer my question,' Dominic said. 'I asked why you looked so glum.'

She hesitated, wondering where to start, but knowing it shouldn't be with Alex. In fact, she shouldn't mention Alex at all. 'Oh, you know, just worrying about the future and stuff.'

Dominic frowned. 'What do you mean? Shall we sit here?' He indicated a collection of tables and chairs arranged outside a café, and she took a seat.

They ordered a couple of drinks and a slice of cake each, then Sophie tried to explain what was on her mind, without mentioning what was really on her mind right at this very moment – Alex.

'So you see,' she concluded after explaining her job and home situation to Dominic, 'I've got some big, life-changing decisions to make, and I really don't know what to do.'

'You've got to go with your heart,' he said. 'Life's too short to do anything else.'

'That's easy for you to say; you've got a job and some-where to live. I'm assuming you have your own place, and even if you didn't you could live with your parents.'

'Yes to the somewhere to live bit, but the job isn't as secure as you think. I'm on a contract, and there's no guarantee it'll be renewed when it's up, because it depends on a number of factors, like listener figures and advertising revenue. It's the advertising that pays for the station to broadcast – more or less – and the advertising is only as good as the number of people who tune in. It can be quite a fickle business.'

'You're still better off than I am,' she grumbled.

'I know. I have what I think is the perfect lifestyle. I've got a job I love, which gives me loads of time to do what I love – surfing, natch – a great apartment with sea views, a— Wait a sec. I've got an idea. How about if you move in with me?'

'What?' Sophie had just taken a sip of hot coffee and nearly choked on it. She stared at him, her mouth open. 'You want me to move in with you?'

'Think about it. We get on well, and it would solve your accommodation problem.'

It would certainly do that all right, but she'd only known him for a couple of weeks and they'd only been on one date. It was all happening a bit too fast for her liking.

'Er... um...'

'You don't have to decide now. Think about it and let me know, yeah? You said you've got a couple of months left at Hugo's place.'

Sophie was astounded. Never in a million years had she expected Dominic to ask her to move in with him, and especially on such a short acquaintance. He knew nothing about her, for goodness' sake, nor she him.

But, she mused as she walked back home, it had given her something to think about, and as long as she made it clear there was to be no funny business and that she was there as a lodger only, then it could be the answer to her prayers in the short term. She was under no illusion that it would be a permanent thing. It was just until she sorted herself out.

What did she have to lose? She could renew the lease on the storage unit back in the UK, and if things didn't pan out, then she could always return to England. She'd not be any worse off. And it might be exactly what she needed to enable her to remain in Tenerife. Besides, she didn't have to decide just yet. She wanted to get to know Dominic a bit better first, and she decided that as soon as she felt she could leave Hugo for a decent stretch of time, she'd take Dominic up on his offer of bodyboarding lessons.

Feeling suddenly more optimistic and positive about the future, she almost skipped back to the villa.

But before she got there, the image of a certain dark-haired, dark-eyed volcanologist popped into her mind, and all she could think about was that she wished it was Alex who had asked her to move in with him.

She might even have said yes...

Chapter 25

The villa was empty and the car wasn't in its usual spot, so after she'd put her purchases away, feeling unduly restless, she decided to take advantage of Hugo's absence to give his bedroom a thorough clean. It could certainly benefit from it, and doing something useful might help burn off some of the energy surging through her. She had an urge to clean Alex's room too, but she fought it off. He'd be gone soon enough, and once he was, she could clean and scrub to her heart's content. Anyway, doing so now would be an invasion of his privacy.

Hugo, though, was an altogether different matter, because she went into his bedroom on a regular basis to do things like change the sheets on his bed, gather his dirty laundry, or throw open the window and let that wonderful sea air blow through.

Today she intended to do those things and more. She hadn't given the room a good cleaning since he'd come out of hospital, and it could do with a proper scrub down.

Rolling her proverbial sleeves up, she grabbed a dustpan and brush, ran some hot soapy water into a bucket, retrieved a duster and a tin of furniture polish from the cupboard under the sink, and prepared to do battle.

Half an hour later, she had stripped the sheets off the bed, cleaned the window, and taken the rug onto the terrace and beaten it to within an inch of its life until her arm ached and she was breathless. She'd also turned the mattress over and was now vigorously sweeping the floor and thanking God that whoever had built the villa had used marble tiles on the floors and not carpet, because Paco's fine fluffy fur got everywhere. It didn't seem to matter how frequently or how thoroughly she groomed him, she still found it all over the place. Vacuuming every day would be an absolute pain, but giving the floor a quick sweep had soon become part of her daily routine and it only took a few minutes. Unless she was giving it a deep clean, like today, when she was actually moving furniture and dusting skirting boards, when it took quite a bit longer.

Putting the brush down and being careful not to tread in the small pile of debris she'd already amassed, she eyed Hugo's humungous chest of drawers with trepidation. She knew that the wardrobe – dark wood and immensely solid – was beyond her ability to shift, although she did her best to squeeze the brush underneath it, and awkwardly flicked the duster behind it, to get at as much dust as possible. But the chest of drawers, for all its impressive dimensions, could surely be moved. If she pulled one side of it out from the wall, then the other, alternately, she could manoeuvre it until she could reach behind the darned thing with her brush.

Determined not to be defeated by a piece of furniture, she set to work, dragging and pulling with all her might. Crikey, Hugo must be storing bricks in it, she mused as she heaved and panted, even though she'd put enough of his clothes away in the drawers to know exactly what was in them.

Finally she had the thing where she wanted it, and she took a moment to wipe the sweat from her brow and drink a glass of cold water. Who needed to go to a gym when this lot wanted cleaning? Between the garden, walking Paco and lugging great lumps of furniture about, she was probably fitter now than she'd been in a long time. And healthier too. Being outdoors a lot helped, as did the mainly Mediterranean-type diet she was eating, despite Tenerife being nowhere near the Med and her occasional forays into British comfort food.

She grabbed the brush again and walked around the back of the chest. Gosh, it was a bit of a mess. There was a thick layer of dust on the skirting board and all kinds of nasty stuff on the floor behind: dust bunnies, what looked like a fossilised piece of bread (God knows how that had got there), a couple of folded pieces of paper stuck together with sticky tape, a button, a small screwdriver and a smattering of dog biscuits. Lovely.

She picked up the paper and the screwdriver and placed them on top of the chest of drawers, then swept the rest of the rubbish into a pile and brushed it into the waiting dustpan. Finished, she began pushing the hunk of stubborn wood back into position, shoving and shunting until she was happy that it was in the exact same place as before.

Then she turned her attention to the pieces of paper, wanting to give them a quick once-over to make sure they were nothing important before she tossed them in the bin. Gingerly, she prised them open, and when she saw that the topmost piece of paper was a bank statement, she realised it was too important to throw away.

She was about to fold the sheets of paper back up, when the summary figures at the top of the page caught her attention, and once she'd seen them, it was impossible to unsee them.

Hugo was overdrawn. Badly.

Her heart sinking to her pumps, she looked at the date. Two months ago.

Feeling a heel but unable to stop herself, she checked the other papers. One was a letter from the same bank as the statements. The other was from a company called The Zykov Corporation, and it had an elaborate logo of an intertwined T, Z and C emblazoned across it. What drew her eye, though, was the mention of a large sum of money in euros. Both letters were in Spanish. All three documents had been hidden, she realised, as she abruptly understood what the sticky tape had been for.

And she would never have discovered them if she hadn't decided to clean Hugo's bedroom from top to bottom, and even then she might not have noticed them if the sticky tape had done its job. Hugo hadn't anticipated either of those things, and she was tempted to put the documents back where she'd found them. After all, Hugo's financial affairs were none of her business.

But she didn't.

Instead, she fetched her phone from her room and used an online dictionary to translate Spanish to English.

Then wished she hadn't.

Hugo was drowning financially. The bank said so. His bank statements corroborated it. The letter from The Zykov Corporation contained the offer from the organisation that wanted Hugo's land. She might be naive and more used to UK property prices, but the figure TZC mentioned in the letter seemed ridiculously low. And, if the translation was correct, they'd upped it from a considerably lower one. It still wasn't enough, she thought, but it should be sufficient for Hugo to buy a small apartment and not have to worry about money for a long time. If ever. Together with his pension, he would have plenty to live on, as long as he wasn't rash.

Sophie had no idea what his total outgoings were, but from what she could tell, he still had to pay a considerable amount in tax for the banana fields, even though he was in no position to farm them and hadn't done for quite some time.

Paco gave a low woof and Sophie jumped.

She paused, listening intently, and after a moment the sound of an engine reached her.

Alex and Hugo were back.

Rushing now, not wanting to be caught, she folded the papers and stuffed them down behind the chest of drawers. With any luck, Hugo would never know she'd been snooping. Hastily, she gathered up her cleaning things and darted out of the room.

She was busy putting Hugo's washing into the machine when uncle and nephew sauntered back into the house. Hugo was walking-stick-free and grinning widely.

'Did it go OK?' she asked, hoping they would mistake the heat in her cheeks from having been bent over. She straightened up. Should she say anything to Alex? Did she have any right to?

'I had the stitches removed and they are pleased with the wound.'

'He has to go back in another two weeks, and they've given him additional exercises to do at home,' Alex said.

'I will soon be as fit as a guitar!' Hugo announced, and Sophie laughed.

'Yes, you will,' she agreed. He was making excellent progress, performing his exercises diligently, and being careful to move only in the way he had been shown so as not to overextend his hip.

She wondered if his desperation to get fit again had more to do with the hope that he could farm his fields once more. Because if he couldn't...

Making a decision, she waited for Hugo to go into the living room, then brushed past Alex and whispered in his ear, 'I need to talk to you in private, and you're probably not going to like it.'

With that she grabbed an armful of clean bed linen out of the cupboard, so she had a legitimate reason to be in Hugo's room, and when she was satisfied that the two men were out of her line of sight, she reached down the back of the chest of drawers and wriggled her hand into the gap. Wincing with the effort of stretching as far as she could, her fingers finally touched the folded pages. Carefully, praying that she wouldn't drop them, she pulled them out.

She might be doing wrong, but her conscience would not allow her to let it lie. She knew she wasn't in a position to help Hugo, but Alex might be, and she'd never forgive herself if she didn't at least try. Even if it cost her her home and her job.

Chapter 26

Sophie waited until Hugo retired for the night before she said anything more to Alex. Alex kept sending her meaningful looks, but every time she met his curious gaze, she shook her head, a tiny movement so as not to alert Hugo.

'What is it?' Alex asked, as soon as Hugo had closed his bedroom door. 'Please don't tell me you are returning to the UK and leaving Hugo to cope alone?'

'No! What makes you think that? It's—'

Alex jumped in before she was able to explain. 'Because you warned me that I'm not going to like what you're about to tell me, and I am aware of your predicament.'

Sidetracked, Sophie gawped at him. After the intimate moment they had shared in the lava tube, she assumed that he'd realised she was a better person than he'd previously thought. But clearly he was still of the same opinion. Which made those exquisite and wonderful kisses all the harder to reconcile with the way he thought of her. Obviously her instinct had been right last night, and he had merely seen an opportunity for a snog and had taken it. More fool her for encouraging him.

'I might not have a "predicament" anymore,' she informed him smugly, although she'd not yet made her mind up regarding Dominic and his generous offer. It was nice to have options, though, and nicer still to be able to tell Alex about it. He'd probably think even less of her now, but she honestly didn't care. 'Dominic has asked me to move in with him.'

As soon as she said it, she realised it sounded as though she was going to be living with him as boyfriend and girlfriend; but if she backtracked now, she'd probably dig herself a deeper hole than the one she'd already dug. So she let the words hang there, without further embellishment or explanation. Alex wouldn't care anyway. He was leaving tomorrow, and he had someone waiting for him in Iceland. It made no difference to him what she did.

She did address what she thought was worrying him, though. 'Of course, I'll stay until Hugo no longer needs me,' she said.

'I see.'

Alex's expression was blank, though she was certain there was a hint of disappointment in the depths of those chocolate-brown eyes.

'But that's not what I wanted to talk to you about,' she added.

He cocked his head to the side slightly. 'I'm all ears.'

She ignored his sarcastic tone. Hugo's plight was more important than picking a fight with the most obnoxious man she'd ever met.

'Wait a sec.' Biting her lip, she fetched the documents from where she'd secreted them in her own room, and then wordlessly held them out.

He gave her a long look before he took them from her, and she held her breath while she waited for his reaction as he studied them.

When it came, it wasn't what she expected.

'Where did you get these?' he demanded, his lips a thin line, his jaw clenched.

'They were in Hugo's room, behind—'

'I don't believe this,' Alex interrupted her, his voice hard.

'Neither did I, at first. Of course, I couldn't read the letters straight away, but I translated them on my phone and—'

'I can't believe that you thought it was OK to snoop in my uncle's personal things,' he snapped. 'You are taking advantage of your position.' He waved the papers at her. 'These are private.'

'I know, but—'

Alex slapped them down on the table, making her jump, and glared furiously at her. 'There is nothing you can say that will excuse what you did.'

'What?' She didn't believe what she was hearing. There she was trying to help, and all this man could do was accuse her of the most horrible things. She had not been snooping. *She hadn't.* But she could see that it wouldn't do any good to try and explain, and she wasn't sure she actually wanted to now. *How could he think that of her?*

Tears pricked the back of her eyes and she blinked hard. There was no way she was going to let him see how upset she was, nor how much his words hurt. If he wanted to believe she'd been rooting through Hugo's private things, then let him.

'Fine,' she said. 'Believe what you like, I don't care. I was only trying to help.' She marched off to her room, shut the door firmly (she really wanted to slam it, but she didn't want to disturb Hugo) and flung herself on the bed, letting the hot tears fall.

She had no idea how long she lay there sobbing quietly, but when there was a soft knock on her door, she was more or less done. Her weeping had finally trailed off to hiccups and lots of nose blowing, and she felt drained and exhausted.

'What?' she hissed, knowing it was most likely Alex on the other side of the door. Hugo would have made too much noise getting out of bed (not his fault; he still struggled with that particular movement) and she would have heard him.

'Can I come in?' Alex's voice was soft through the door.

She clambered off the bed, catching sight of her reflection in the mirror. Her face was red and blotchy, her eyes red and puffy, and her nose was red and sore. She looked awful, a total mess. She had an urge to dab on some make-up and run a brush through her hair, but she shoved it away. Why should she care what she looked like? And the more hideous she looked, the more Alex might realise how much he'd upset her.

'What do you want?' She opened the door a crack and peered out. 'If you want me to leave, I'll…'

'What is it with all this talk of leaving?' he asked abruptly. 'You keep mentioning it. Have I said I want you to leave?'

'Isn't that what you want to talk to me about?'

'No.'

'Oh. What then?'

'May I come in? Or you can come out? How about a glass of wine on the terrace? We can speak there without waking Hugo.'

'Why?'

'Why what?'

'Why do you want to talk to me?'

'I thought it would be obvious.'

'Not to me it isn't.'

'About the letters you found.'

'Oh, I see… you're saying I *found* them now, are you? You've changed your tune.'

'I might have been a bit hasty,' he admitted. 'Have you been crying?'

'Duh.'

His gaze was soft as it lingered on her face. 'I'm sorry. I didn't give you a chance to explain.'

'No, you didn't.'

'Would you like to explain now?'

Would she? Yes, she thought she would. It would serve Alex right if he felt guilty when she told him how she'd come to find the statements and letters. And she was looking forward to receiving a grovelling apology from him.

'White wine?' she asked, suddenly thirsty.

'You can have whatever colour wine you like.'

'Give me a minute.' She shut the door on him and spent the minute, plus a few extra, making herself a little more presentable.

When she joined him on the terrace, Alex had poured her a glass of chilled white wine and was sitting on one of the decrepit loungers, his eyes closed.

She picked up the glass, took a large mouthful, and sat down.

'You weren't snooping, were you?' he said, his eyes still firmly shut. He probably didn't want to have to look at her poor ravaged face and see the damage he'd done, she thought.

'No. I'd decided to give Hugo's room a thorough clean. I found those letters when I swept behind his chest of drawers.'

He opened his eyes and gave a small laugh. 'Do you mean to say you managed to move that monstrosity all by yourself? It weighs a tonne. It's old too. I remember it from when I was a child.'

'It took some shifting,' she admitted, 'and there was enough dust and other stuff behind it to fill a skip. I think the letters were originally taped to the back, but they'd fallen off. I only looked at them to make sure I wasn't about to throw out anything important.'

'I thought there would be a reasonable explanation,' he said.

'Hmm.'

'I'm sorry I jumped to the wrong conclusion. I didn't mean to, but when you said you were going to live with Dominic Brockman, I kind of flipped.'

She frowned. 'Why would that bother you?'

'You kissed me.'

She wrinkled her nose. 'You kissed me too.'

'Was it so bad?'

Sophie hesitated. 'It was lovely. But your life is in Iceland, and mine might be here or in the UK.'

'You haven't decided?'

'No.'

'Are you and Dominic…?' He let the sentence hang in the air.

'No.'

'Oh, I thought…'

'He's a friend.'

'But you still might move in with him?'

'I might not have any choice if I want to remain in Tenerife.'

Alex's expression was thoughtful, his attention on the dark water beyond the balustrade. Sophie tore herself away from staring at him. She'd been drinking him in, trying to memorise every line of his features, every curve, every lock of hair. He was already emblazoned on her heart, but she wanted to make sure his image was seared on her mind, in case she never saw him again.

'Poor Hugo,' he said, bringing her focus back to what really mattered.

'Any ideas?'

'One or two. But I need to speak to him, and I hope he'll be honest with me. He's a proud man, independent. No one in the family knew he needed a new hip. No one realised he was having problems with the plantation. It's not a huge farm, as farms go, but it has been enough for him to live on. I spoke to my parents when I first arrived and saw the state of things here, and they had no idea either. The problem is, I don't think he'll be able to cope even when he is back to full fitness. This much land is too much for one man.'

'But what's the alternative? Surely you don't mean for him to sell up?'

'Preferably not. I'll have to see what I can do.'

'But this is his home! He loves the villa. What if—'

'Sophie?' His voice was low and soft, and the way he said her name made her pulse race and her insides melt.

'Yes?'

'Do you trust me?'

Actually, she did. She didn't trust him with her *heart*, but she did trust him to do his best for Hugo. It was clear that he loved his uncle. It was also clear that he was leaving tomorrow, and his destination was God knows how many thousands of miles away (just over four thousand, actually – she'd looked it up). She hoped he'd be able to work something out, despite that.

She put her empty glass down, not remembering having drunk the contents, and got to her feet. It was time she went to bed. She'd done all she could and at least she and Alex would be parting on good terms.

'What time is your flight?' she asked.

'Seven thirty-five in the morning.'

'Do you need a lift to the airport?' She felt she should offer, although she wasn't certain she could face it.

'I'm fine. One of the guys from INVOLCAN is picking me up.'

'OK. Well, I guess I should say good night.'

He rose from the chair in one fluid movement and took a step towards her. 'You'll look after him, won't you?'

'You know I will.'

He nodded. Then took another step until he was so close that she thought she could hear his heart beating.

When he opened his arms, she didn't hesitate, her body moulding to his as his lips found hers, and when he kissed her, she lost herself for long, long moments.

Releasing him and walking away was one of the hardest things she had ever done.

She didn't look back.

Chapter 27

It was dark and quiet, except for the eternal sound of the waves and the soft movement of the breeze through the leaves of the palm trees in the garden. The sun wouldn't be up for a few more hours yet and Sophie was sitting on the same lounger that she'd sat on earlier, a lukewarm mug of coffee in her hand and a blanket around her shoulders. Paco had draped himself next to her, his rear end on her feet, his nose on her shoulder, and she was grateful for his warmth. It wasn't cold as such, but she'd been out there for ages and the nights in Tenerife at this time of year could be a little chilly.

She wished the dog could warm her insides too, because her heart felt as cold as one of Iceland's glaciers. So what if she'd spent half the night looking at images of the country, and imagining Alex striding over a lava field, or walking down a street in Reykjavik? This vigil was her way of saying goodbye to him, because she had no intention of saying it to his face. She wouldn't be here, for a start.

Stiffly, with some protesting from the dog, she got to her feet.

She was fully dressed and all she needed to do was slip a jacket on and stuff her feet into her pumps. Paco could come with her. Despite his grumbling at being disturbed, she knew he'd be up for a walk.

Leaving a brief note saying she was out for an early morning walk with Paco, which was aimed at both Alex and Hugo, she called softly to the dog and the pair of them slipped silently out of the door.

She thought she heard a noise coming from the depths of the house, but she ignored it. There was no point in drawing anything out, prolonging the pain. The time she'd spent in Alex's arms last night had been a perfect way to say goodbye. There was no need for any words this morning. Besides, she had a feeling she might cry, and she didn't want Alex to see she was upset.

The sea didn't care what she felt, and she was drawn to its indifference. It carried on breaking over the rocks, oblivious to her sadness, as tears gathered in her eyes and slowly spilled over to trickle down her already damp cheeks.

'I wish you were here, Mum,' she whispered into the darkness. She missed her mother terribly, and she suspected she would miss her for the rest of her life. But in the early hours of this particular morning, her grief was especially raw and close to the surface.

She made for the headland where she'd watched Dominic bodyboarding and chose a rock to perch on, drawing her knees to her chest and wrapping her arms around her legs, resting her chin on them. Paco plonked down beside her with a soft whine and cuddled in close. She turned her head to look at him for a moment, her sad gaze meeting his gentle eyes, then she turned back to stare out to sea.

The occasional rumble of distant engines reached her from the road, only just discernible above the waves, and when she eventually heard one of them idling, then the slam of a car door, she swallowed. This was it, Alex was leaving, out of her life for good.

She remained where she was as she imagined his journey to the airport and his wait in departures. Did he think of her while he drank his coffee as he was waiting to board? Or was his mind on Iceland and what (*who*) waited for him there?

Seven thirty. He'd be taking off in a minute. The flat silver light of dawn had spread across the sky, driving the night away, and one by one the stars had disappeared.

Seven thirty-five. The sky was cloudless, promising another lovely day.

Seven forty. There was a flashing light high above, moving from south to north, and the faint noise of a jet engine. She watched it, her eyes following its progress. It wasn't the first aircraft she'd watched leave Tenerife this morning and she had no idea whether Alex was on this one or not, but she continued to watch until it had climbed too high and travelled too far to see any more.

And still she sat there.

Hugo would be fine for a while. He was able to get himself out of bed and his breakfast would consist of fruit, ham, cheese and olives, which didn't need much in the way of preparation, so she could stay out here for a while. Anyway, he might not even be awake yet.

Eventually, reluctantly, she levered herself stiffly to her feet, dusted off the backside of her jeans and headed for home, her heart heavy, her soul aching.

But for all her sorrow and the pain that was yet to come, she had no regrets. She'd hold the memory of Alejandro and their embraces close, and some day, when she felt able to, she'd bring it out and look at it, and imagine what might have been.

Chapter 28

'You need to get a life,' Hugo told her.

Sophie stopped hoeing and wiped the beads of sweat from her upper lip, before turning around. 'Get a life? Where did that expression come from?'

'One of your English radio programmes. I mean it. You are young, pretty. You should not be stuck here with an old man.'

'I'm not "stuck". I chose to be here, remember? It's a job. I'm not just doing this,' she gestured towards the soil she was grubbing about in, 'out of the goodness of my heart.' Actually, that wasn't true, but she could see that Hugo was feeling guilty and she didn't want to add to that.

'It has been five days,' he said.

'What has?'

Hugo gave her a knowing smile. 'Since Alejandro left.'

'Has it?' She tried to sound nonchalant but was fairly sure she was fooling no one.

He made a derisive sound and Sophie returned to her gardening, pretending to ignore him and his insinuations.

'What about Dominic Brockman?' he asked. 'You like him, yes?'

She shrugged. 'I suppose.' Was now the best time to tell Hugo that Dominic had offered her a place to stay once

225

her time at the villa was over? She still hadn't come to any decision – her mind had been too full of trying not to think about dark, liquid eyes and full, warm lips. She was nearly halfway through the three months which had been agreed on. She had to start planning soon. Procrastination wasn't going to help.

'I've… er… Dominic has…' She trailed off and cleared her throat nervously.

Hugo continued to watch her, his expression inscrutable. He reminded her of Alex.

'Dominic has suggested I move in with him,' she finally said in a rush. 'When you don't need me any longer. Just as friends,' she added. 'There's nothing going on.'

'And are you going to do this?'

'I don't know.'

'Do you miss England?'

'Hardly! It's cold. It's probably raining too.' She didn't miss England, what she missed was her mum. And Alex.

Hugo must have sensed her mood, because he said, 'When I am better, I shall prepare a special meal for us.'

'You?'

'Yes, me. Did you think I lived on bread and water before you came here?' He chuckled heartily. 'I can cook.'

'Great! What are we having?'

'It will be traditional Canarian food,' he promised.

She suppressed a smile. Clearly her cooking was too traditionally British for him, and he was craving some decent local food. She wasn't sure what he had in mind, but if he were to supervise, she was sure she could make a decent job of whatever dish he fancied.

'If you tell me what we're having, I'll cook it,' she offered. 'That's what I'm here for.'

'You are not a slave. I shall cook.' He thumped his chest, his expression stubborn.

'OK, but at least let me help.'

'We shall see,' he said, and she had to smile – her mum used to say the same thing when she meant 'no' but wanted to avoid being pestered.

God, but she loved this old man!

Suddenly, the sadness threatened to overwhelm her. Not only had she lost her mother and Alex (not that he was ever hers to lose), but she'd be losing Hugo too, in a few short weeks. Every day saw an improvement in his health. He'd soon be able to drive again, and he was already able to manage short walks on the flat. It was debatable whether he'd be able to farm those fields again, though. They would take more work than Hugo was capable of doing on his own, and even if he did return them to their former glory, it would be far too late to bail him out of his current financial mess.

Wondering if Alex had managed to do anything about his uncle's predicament brought Sophie back to thinking about him again. She pushed the image of his face (the one just before his lips joined with hers was her favourite) out of her mind with an impatient sigh.

She wished she was in a position to do something – anything – to help Hugo, but she was powerless. If she returned to England, she'd worry herself silly about him, she knew she would…

Abruptly she straightened up and took a deep breath. Aunty Anne didn't need her – Hugo did.

Her decision was made.

Hugo had unconsciously made it for her.

She had to remain on Tenerife to keep an eye on him. And the only way she could do that at the moment was to take Dominic up on his offer.

Biting her lip, hoping the man in question wasn't regretting suggesting she go and live with him, she reached for her phone.

Chapter 29

Sophie dipped a toe in the chilly waters of the Atlantic Ocean and squealed, the temperature difference bringing her out in goosebumps.

'Don't be a baby,' Dominic called as he raced past her, his board under his arm. She appeared to be the only person on this beach who wasn't wearing a wetsuit and didn't have a bodyboard.

She didn't care. It was bad enough paddling (her feet were already numb) and she had no intention of plunging into the surf with only a bikini between her and hypothermia. It didn't help that she'd been sunbathing while Dominic donned his suit, fiddled about with the leash (apparently you had to attach the board to your wrist or ankle, or risk losing it) and put his fins on (she'd been told they were called fins, not flippers). Because she'd been lounging around on the sand, soaking up the rays, her skin was pleasantly hot. In contrast the water was freezing.

Content to watch, she returned to her towel and flopped down onto it, although she did feel a bit of an outsider. This lot clearly knew each other well, and from what she could see, the group was fairly fluid. If you were there, great; if not, no worries. The women were all slim and fit, with wind-tousled hair and a spray of tattoos across their bodies. Come to think of it, the men were quite similar in that regard too. It was like being on an episode of *Baywatch* (her mum had liked to watch reruns of the programme, saying it brought back memories). Maybe she ought to get a tattoo if she wanted to fit in?

Everyone was very open and friendly, though, welcoming her without a second thought when Dominic introduced her, and later she was able to join in a bit more when someone fired up a barbecue. She might not be able to surf the waves, but she could cook a mean sausage, and she set to slicing rolls in half and tossing the onions until they were deliciously charred.

Sitting back with a hot dog in one hand and a can of fizzy apple juice in the other, she finally felt herself relax. She could get used to this beach lifestyle, she thought, and suspected it might become part of her weekly routine if she lived with Dominic.

When he dropped down beside her, smiling and daubed with sand and salt, she couldn't help smiling back. He was as easy to be with as he was on the eye. There was none of the Darcy-esque smouldering she associated with Alex, just—

Stop damned well thinking about Alex, she told herself crossly. She had to move on; although she realised it wouldn't be with Dominic. Or any other man, for that matter. Not for some considerable time, at least. She had to give herself some breathing space, some time to recover from the last few months and sort herself out, before she jumped into a relationship.

'You know what you said about me coming to live with you?' she said to Dominic, who was tucking into his hot dog with enthusiasm. 'Did you mean it?'

'Of course I did. I wouldn't have offered if I hadn't. Herrick is staying with me at the moment too, until he gets a place of his own.'

'You take in waifs and strays on a regular basis, do you?' She wasn't sure she felt better or worse about the idea after hearing that.

'Yeah. No sweat. If someone needs a place to crash, they can stay at mine.'

'Is Herrick here now?'

Dominic shook his head, unable to speak for a moment because of the huge mouthful he'd just bitten off. When he'd finally chewed and swallowed it, he took a slug of beer from the bottle he was holding before he answered. 'He's doing the lunchtime shift at the restaurant where he works. Are you still interested?'

'I am, but not for about a month.'

'That's OK, as long as I know, I'll make sure one of the rooms is free.'

'Where do you live, exactly?'

'I've got an apartment in Playa San Juan.'

'That's just down the coast, past Alcalá, isn't it?'

'Yep. You can actually walk to it from Villa Delfín, if you wanted to come and have a look, although it's a bit of a trek. Or I could show you on the way back.'

'Yes, please.' She'd like to see where she'd be living, and it was good to know that she'd be able to pop in and visit Hugo.

After everything had been packed away and goodbyes had been airily exchanged, Sophie and Dominic made their way back to his car and started the drive to the villa, stopping off along the way to see the apartment.

The building was located down a side street not far from the marina, with a decent-sized balcony and a view of the sea if you craned your neck. There were two double bedrooms and one single, a large living/dining room, a separate kitchen and two bathrooms. It was spacious and light, and she could easily imagine herself living there. What she couldn't as easily imagine was living there with Dominic. He was so exuberant and larger than life, despite his laid-back attitude, and his presence completely filled the apartment.

It was going to take some getting used to. And the fact that there could be a succession of strangers wandering in and out was somewhat disconcerting. She was used to a more sedate life.

Then she paused – how *old* was she? At her age, a sedate life should be the furthest thing from her mind. She was young and free, and she should be enjoying herself, partying and stuff. She wasn't entirely sure what 'stuff' might entail, but she definitely should be doing it.

New country, new place to live, new job (hopefully), new life.

New Sophie.

There was one more thing she needed to do and she held off doing it until she was back at the villa and alone in her room.

'Aunty Anne?'

'Hello, love, how are you?' Her aunt's warm tones caused tears to gather in the corners of her eyes. She was her last link to her mum, and it was going to be hard to let go.

'I'm good, thanks. You?'

Sophie listened as Anne shared details of the babies, how Denise was planning to return to work, and that Anne would be looking after the little ones three days a week. Then there were the two boys to discuss – the eldest was already fretting over his exams in the summer, and the whole family were feeling the effects.

'They're thinking of moving, you know,' Anne said. 'To a bigger place with a granny flat for me.' She sounded so excited Sophie had to smile. The twins had given her aunt a new lease of life, and Sophie guessed that being needed and feeling useful was part of it.

'I'm thinking of moving too,' she said.

'That's nice. Have you got yourself sorted with somewhere to live? It's amazing what you can do on the internet.' Anne had a smartphone and used it for Facebook and WhatsApp, but the rest of the technology it contained was an endless source of amazement to her.

'I'm staying in Tenerife for the foreseeable future. I've got a place to live and I'm looking for a more permanent job.'

There was silence for a while, then, 'If that's what you want, then you should do it.'

'You think?' She knew she sounded hesitant, but her aunt's support meant the world to her. She needed someone to tell her she wasn't being silly, or overambitious, that she was capable of taking this huge step and not falling flat on her face.

'Definitely. I'm not getting any younger, and one thing age has taught me is that life is over far too quickly. Take the opportunities when you can, because you may not get them again.'

'But what about you?'

'Is that what's bothering you? I'll be fine. I've got Denise and the grandchildren. Of course I'll miss you, but you've got to do what's right for you. And if this is it, then you've got to go for it.'

Sophie heard the hitch in her aunt's voice and she blinked away threatening tears. 'It won't be forever,' she said, 'and I'll be back for visits.'

'I know you will, my lovely. And we'll keep in touch by phone and Facebook and whatnot.'

Sophie didn't trust herself to speak.

'Your mum would have been so proud of you,' Anne said, and then the tears did fall, and the pair of them were laughing and crying, and promising to take care.

And when she finally got off the phone Sophie felt as though she was turning the page on a whole new chapter of her life, and the thought both scared her and excited her. But at least she had her aunt's blessing.

She had the strangest feeling that she had her mum's too...

Chapter 30

Sophie was having second thoughts. She wasn't sure if she wanted to be a new person. She was quite happy with the old Sophie, and the thought of moving in with Dominic worried her. The thought of not having a job worried her. The thought of having to look for one scared her to death.

But she didn't intend to live in Dominic's flat forever. Eventually she'd get her own place. She knew it wasn't going to be cheap to rent an apartment on her own, but she'd be happy with somewhere inland where the prices weren't as high; and she didn't expect it to be in a posh complex with a pool either. A flat above a shop would do just fine. As long as it was somewhere she could call her own, that was all she wanted. And as for a job, she'd get one eventually. All she had to do was believe in herself. She was capable of this; she'd cope.

'I am going to play *zanga* with friends later in Tamaimo,' Hugo announced, breaking into her thoughts.

Tamaimo was a village in the mountains above Los Gigantes. She'd passed through it a couple of times on the way to somewhere else, and it struck her as being far less touristy than its showier neighbours on the coast; sleepy and lived in mostly by locals, with hardly a tourist in sight, apart from those driving through it.

'What's *zanga*?' she asked, hoping it wasn't too energetic. Hugo wasn't up to much in the way of exercise yet, and she imagined him bending and stretching trying to play boules or something similar.

'It is a card game,' he said. 'And I am very good at it. It is for old men with nothing better to do than sit outside a café drinking strong coffee and smoking strong cigarettes,' he told her.

'What time do you want to leave?' She'd have to drive him because he wasn't quite ready to drive himself yet.

'An hour?'

'OK.' They were out in the garden again, Hugo watching Sophie plant little courgette seedlings. In a few months, he should have a decent crop of the vegetables; as long as he remembered to water them every evening, she thought.

It gave her a pang to know she wouldn't be there to see them mature. She was really going to miss the garden, almost as much as she'd miss Hugo. Surprised at how much she enjoyed grubbing around in the dirt and watching things grow, she wondered if Dominic would mind if she put a couple of pots on his balcony and grew some tomato plants. There was nothing quite like the satisfaction of eating something you'd grown yourself, and they tasted so much more flavoursome than the ones you bought from the supermarket.

It was something to ask him, the next time she saw him.

After a shower and a quick spot of lunch, Sophie drove Hugo to see his friends. They were already there, four elderly gentlemen with lined faces and ready smiles, with a bottle of something alcoholic in the middle of the table, along with several tiny cups of black coffee. A pack of cards sat next to the bottle and one of the men patted it when he saw Hugo get out of the car.

He was greeted by what sounded like friendly teasing and she left him to it, arranging to collect him later. She hoped he wouldn't get up to any mischief between now and then because, despite their advanced years, those men seemed a rowdy lot. With a warning to Hugo to behave himself, and feeling more like his mother than an employee half his age, she drove back to the villa for another spot of gardening.

Chickens, she mused as she drove. They could keep chickens and have fresh eggs every morning. They didn't need to have a flock of them – three would be enough. Not that she knew anything about chickens, or how to care for them, but she— Wouldn't get the chance to find out, that's what.

Will you stop this silliness, she told herself. All these ridiculous thoughts about what she could do with the villa were fruitless. It wasn't hers. And it mightn't be Hugo's for much longer either. Which brought her back to thinking about Alex and whether he was doing anything to sort out Hugo's problem. Or was it a case of out of sight, out of mind? Somehow she didn't think so, and she dearly wished she could pick up the phone and speak to him. Just hearing his voice would be wonderful.

It would also be rash and silly, and would do little to help her forget him.

She simply had to trust that he was doing what he could and let him get on with it. Besides, she didn't have his number. Which was a good thing really.

It was almost time to put her tools away and take Paco for a stroll, she noticed, feeling the beginnings of a blister on one of her palms and a pleasant ache in her back and shoulders. As she stretched out the kinks, she realised that physically she felt better than she had done for months. She was toned and tanned and felt incredibly healthy from the mixture of good diet, warm sunshine and plenty of exercise. Her mind and her heart would catch up with her body eventually, she knew. Grief didn't come with a time frame, and it affected everyone differently. But she could tell she was slowly healing from the pain of her mother's passing and the sorrow was no longer as sharp or as debilitating. She would always carry it with her, the same as she would always carry her mother's memory in her heart, but it was manageable.

She deliberately ignored the other ache, the Alex-shaped one.

A noise at the gates alerted her that someone was outside. She was used to people passing by, either dawdling along the coastal path with their dogs, or joggers with their harsh breathing and buds jammed in their ears. There were cyclists too, and lots of casual walkers out to stretch their legs. Some slowed down when they reached the villa, peering in through the gates at the pretty garden (just as she had done – it seemed such a long time ago now), and occasionally someone would actually stop and press their face against the wrought-iron for a proper gawp (she'd done that too).

She usually tried to ignore them, but whoever was standing there – she could see a figure out of the corner of her eye – was taking his or her sweet time about moving on. It was more than idle curiosity. How would they like it if she wandered past their garden and stopped for a good long stare?

Feeling a little cross, she turned around slowly, hoping the fact that she had noticed their unwelcome scrutiny would shame them into moving on.

It didn't.

The figure was a man and he continued to stare, rather rudely she thought, especially when she put her hands on her hips and gave him a questioning look, raising her eyebrows meaningfully.

When he still failed to move, or even to speak, she said, 'Can I help you?' in a tone clearly meant to convey that no help would be forthcoming whatsoever.

'Is Señor Santana at home?'

She realised she'd spoken in English and that the man had answered in kind. His accent was Spanish, and his tone formal. He was dressed formally too, in a suit and tie, with shoes that might have once been shiny but were now covered in a fine layer of dust from the track leading to the villa from the road.

She squinted, seeing a black car in the distance and guessing it was his. 'Sorry, he's not. Can I help?'

'You are...?'

'Sophie Lakeland.' She didn't want to volunteer any further information until she knew who she was dealing with.

'You live here?'

'Yes.'

'With Señor Santana?'

'That's right.'

He studied her for a moment, then seemed to come to a decision. 'You have heard of The Zykov Corporation, yes?'

Sophie hesitated. Wasn't that the name of the company who'd sent the letter to Hugo upping their offer? It was, she was sure of it.

'Yes, I have,' she replied confidently, thinking that this guy was definitely not Russian.

'He has not replied to the letter we sent him.'

'He's been... unwell. An operation.'

The gleam in the man's eye unnerved her. 'He is better now?'

'Getting there.'

The gleam faded and he nodded slowly. 'Is he considering our offer? We will not offer any more than this.'

'He is considering it,' she said, uncertain whether Hugo was or wasn't, but not wanting to jeopardise any plans he might have. If he did in fact intend to sell up, then it wasn't her place to alienate the buyer. Although this man's attitude was making her cross and there was something rather creepy and slimy about him.

'Tell him Zykov will not wait for ever. Tell him, we have other... er...' He hunted for the right word. 'Options. You should also tell him to take care.'

What the hell did he mean by that? 'Excuse me?'

'He is no longer a young man. He should be careful with his health.'

Sophie blinked. She hadn't really heard what she thought she'd heard, had she? No, he couldn't have threatened Hugo. She'd taken it the wrong way; his accent *was* quite strong, and although his English was good, there had clearly been something lost between his mouth and her ears.

'I'll be sure to pass the message on,' she said.

'And make sure you tell him we wish him to soon be well. *Adiós*.'

'*Adiós*,' she repeated numbly, and watched him pick his way back along the track.

She continued to watch him until he got in his car and drove away.

Slowly she put her tools away, had another swift shower, and called to Paco to go for a walk. She needed to think. She needed to clear the man's skin-crawling presence from her mind.

She also needed to speak to Alex. Urgently.

'Sorry, Paco,' she said as she went into the living room, and the dog's ears drooped in disappointment when he realised he wouldn't be going for a walk after all.

Hating herself for snooping again, but this time doing it deliberately and for a good reason, Sophie opened one of the drawers in the ornate sideboard. She'd not had any reason to look in here, or the cupboard underneath, but now she embarked on a methodical search. She hoped Hugo would have made a note of Alex's number somewhere, and she knew he must have it on his phone, but she didn't want to ask him for it.

It took her a while, but eventually she found what seemed to be an old address book. It was battered and well-thumbed, with curling pages. Many of the entries looked like they'd been made some time ago and several were crossed out.

Sophie went straight to the A page, her disappointment keen when she didn't see Alex's name. She flicked through the rest of the pages, not really sure what she was looking for, but hoping that something would jump out at her. She suddenly realised she didn't even know Alex's surname. It wouldn't be Santana Negrin because Hugo's sister was married and—

Actually, come to think of it, didn't Spanish surnames differ to English ones in the way they were passed down? She could have sworn she'd read that somewhere…

Fetching her phone from the table in the hall, she typed a question into the search engine and read a couple of answers. Yes, she was right. Spanish women didn't normally change their surnames when they married, and Spanish children took their father's first surname and added it to their mother's first surname. Alex's mother would have the same surname as Hugo – Santana Negrin – therefore Alex's name should be Alejandro something Santana.

All she needed to do was to look through the address book until she found a 'something Santana', and she'd have his number. If, that is, Hugo had actually written it down. And if there wasn't more than one 'something Santana'.

She found it under the Ms and didn't bother looking any further. 'Marrero Santana' – 'Alejandro' in brackets next to it.

She closed her eyes briefly and swallowed.

In a minute or so she'd be speaking to Alex, and her heart sang with joy.

Oh dear, she really did have it bad, didn't she? And it was much, much worse than she'd been letting herself believe.

If she didn't know any better, she'd think she must be in love.

Chapter 31

In the end, Sophie chickened out of phoning Alex. Time was getting on and she had to fetch Hugo soon. Besides, she had to prepare what she wanted to say. She didn't want to make it sound as if the visitor had rattled her (although he had) or that she was worried for Hugo's safety (although she was). The man – and she wished she'd thought to ask his name; she'd call him Slimy Guy for now – hadn't actually *said* anything untoward. It had been implied. Or she'd imagined it and had taken an innocent remark the wrong way. But she still felt she ought to tell Alex that Slimy Guy had paid Hugo a visit. He needed to know. And she was desperate to hear if Alex had any ideas on how to help Hugo.

Oh, don't kid yourself, her subconscious piped up; the only thing she was desperate for was to hear Alex's voice again, and calling him about Slimy Guy was just an excuse to do exactly that. But she'd do it later. He was probably at work now anyway. It might be better if she called him after dinner. She'd take Paco out for his walk and phone Alex then.

Heart thudding at the thought of speaking to him, she typed the number into her phone, carefully put the address book back where she'd found it, locked up and went to collect Hugo.

Hugo, bless him, was happier than she'd seen him for a while, and she hated to put a dampener on his buoyant mood. She suspected the bottle on the table might have had something to do with his high spirits, and she seriously debated whether she should mention Slimy Guy's visit; but if she didn't and Hugo found out, then she'd have a devil of a job explaining why she didn't tell him. After all, she wasn't supposed to know about the offer or Hugo's financial problems.

'Someone popped by the villa while you were out,' she said, trying to make light of it. 'A man. I didn't catch his name, but he said he was from a company called The Zykov Corporation. He asked whether you were considering their offer and wanted to tell you they won't offer any more. He also sent you his best wishes after your operation.'

She concentrated hard on looking at the road ahead and not at Hugo, but at the mention of TZC she saw him stiffen out of the corner of her eye, and when she eventually glanced across at him she noticed how pale he'd become.

'Did this man say anything more?'

'No, that was it.' She continued to keep her tone light, but it was getting to be a bit of a strain and she was worried her expression might give the game away.

Hugo said nothing further and the journey continued in silence.

He seemed older suddenly, as he got stiffly and carefully out of the car, and she worried that the news had set his recovery back. But she didn't mention her concerns. Instead she set about making dinner, leaving him sitting in his favourite chair and staring out of the window.

'Right, I'm taking Paco for a walk,' she said, calling the dog to her and picking up her phone.

'It'll be dark soon,' Hugo said.

'Yes…?' She often took the dog for a quick walk at night. This was nothing new. So why the concern?

She guessed he might be feeling vulnerable, that maybe he'd pushed his problems to the back of his mind to concentrate on getting better, and her news had brought them to the surface once more.

'I'll be fine,' she assured him. 'We've done this loads of times before. I can hardly get lost, can I?' The coastal path was linear, and as long as she stuck to it there wouldn't be a problem. She had no intention of clambering over any rocks in the dark, and to the other side of the path was either a wall shielding the banana plants from the wind, or rubble where the wall had collapsed. 'Besides, if I do, Paco will lead me home.'

'Keep him close,' Hugo said, and she nodded thoughtfully.

Maybe she hadn't misheard or misunderstood Slimy Guy after all, she mused. Hugo did seem genuinely concerned, so perhaps the threat she thought she must have imagined had been real?

On second thoughts, this wasn't a thriller. This was real life. TZC was an international company, with rules and regulations. They weren't the Mafia; they were an organisation with a business proposition and a profit to make. She was being silly, and Hugo was worrying over nothing.

She went over to him and gave him a kiss on his whiskery cheek. 'I'll be careful,' she promised, 'and I won't be long.'

However, once she was out of the garden with its high stone walls and formidable iron gates, she couldn't help glancing around cautiously.

There was no moon this evening, so the night was a dark one, and cloudless too, she judged, from the number of stars glittering overhead.

She breathed deeply, peace washing over her. No one was anywhere near, and although on other nights she sometimes heard people passing the villa heading for a night out or going home after one, tonight she heard nothing. The only indication of other people was the distant rumble of traffic from the road, the twinkling lights from Playa de la Arena behind her and the dot of light from the farmhouse. Alcalá wasn't visible from here, but the glow from the village could be seen, and she made her way towards it, aiming for the headland. That was as far as she went on her nightly walks, and when she reached it, she found her favourite rock and sat on it, Paco by her side.

Steeling herself, she took out her phone and stared at it for a moment before she plucked up the courage to call the man she thought she had inadvertently fallen in love with and missed so much it hurt.

It was daft really, since she hardly knew him, and they'd only met a short while ago. How was it possible to fall in love under those circumstances, she wondered? But she had, and now she was paying the price for it.

Her heart thudding, she pressed the green icon and listened to the phone ring, realising she was trembling as Paco whined in her ear and shuffled closer.

About to give up and end the call (she wasn't sure whether she was relieved or disappointed), she inhaled sharply when she heard it connect and a voice said, 'Hello?'

It was him, Alex, and she blinked back a sudden rush of tears when he spoke.

'It's Sophie,' she replied hesitantly.

There was a pause, then, 'Is everything OK? Is Hugo all right?'

She could hear music in the background and the sound of laughter. A woman.

'Hugo's fine,' she said, wishing she'd never called. She should have sent him a text instead…

'What is it?'

Clearly it didn't occur to him that she'd call him just for a chat or to hear his voice – but then why would it? And he was correct, that wasn't why she'd phoned him.

'A man came to the villa this afternoon. Said he was from The Zykov Corporation. He asked if Hugo was considering the offer and said that they had no intention of raising it higher.'

'Oh, I see. What did Hugo say?'

'He wasn't there. I told him later.'

'Does that mean Tío is aware you know?'

'No, he doesn't know I know.'

'Did this man say anything else?'

Sophie hesitated, debating whether to share her concerns. Deciding against it, she said, 'No, that was it.'

'What did Hugo say when you told him?'

'Nothing. He went very quiet and withdrawn. And he'd been having such a good time with his friends. I'd taken him to Tamaimo to play cards.'

'And drink lots of *vino tinto*, I expect.'

'Yes, I did spot a bottle of wine on the table when I dropped him off.'

'Just the one?' Alex's laugh sent tingles down the back of her neck, and she shivered.

Getting back to business, she asked, 'Do you have any news?'

A pause. 'I might, but I don't want to share it with anyone until I am certain.'

Anyone – he'd referred to her as 'anyone'. The ache in her chest made her cough, and she cleared her throat.

'Right. Good. I'll… um… leave you to it,' she said. 'I just thought you should know.' She listened to more female laughter in the background and she felt like crying.

'I'm glad you did,' he replied. Then he lowered his voice to add softly, his words clearly meant for her ears only, 'I'm really glad you did. How are you? How have you been?'

'Good, I'm good. Getting on with things. Hugo's good. Recovering nicely. Becoming stronger every day.' This was awkward and painful, and she might as well be talking to a stranger.

'I mean, how are *you*, *pequeña*?'

'Great. Fine. I've… um… got to go. I don't like leaving Hugo for too long – he worries about me being out here on my own at night, you see.'

Neither of them mentioned the obvious fact that the beauty of a mobile phone was that it was *mobile*. She could just as easily have walked and talked at the same time.

Instead, Alex said, 'Where are you?'

'The headland where the surfers – sorry, bodyboarders – usually are.'

'It's not safe,' he said, 'especially at night. You might fall and break a leg, or—'

'I'm fine. I come here a lot. To think and stuff.' She very nearly told him that she'd sat in this same spot on the day he'd left the island, watching planes pass overhead and wondering which one of them was taking her heart away.

'You'd better get back. You don't want Hugo to worry,' he said, and she took the hint.

He was done talking with her. He probably wanted to get back to his lady friend, the one with the tinkling laugh. And she wondered whether he was at a party, or was it a party just for two?

'I'll speak to you soon,' he promised. 'When I have more news.'

'OK. Bye.'

'*Hasta la vista, pequeña,*' was his soft reply, before the phone went dead.

She looked at the screen for a while, then she stood up and walked slowly back to the villa, and with every despondent step she couldn't help wondering why he'd called her 'little one'.

Chapter 32

'I am going shopping,' Hugo announced one morning a couple of weeks later. 'I need to buy food for our special dinner. I will get the best fish, the freshest. *Es magnífico.*' He kissed his fingers. 'You will enjoy and ask for more, like your Oliver Twist, yes?'

She smiled at him indulgently. He was trying so hard to be upbeat, but she could tell from the deepened lines around his eyes and the permanent frown on his brow that he was worried.

'You will come with me?' he asked, and she nodded. She loved shopping for food and seeing all the weird and wonderful things that weren't to be found in her local branch of Asda. And the abundance and variety of fresh meat and fish was quite astounding.

'*Bueno.*'

Following his progress across the living room and into the hall with narrowed eyes, she wondered how much time he had left before TZC's offer was withdrawn. The company wouldn't wait forever, and as Slimy Guy had said, they had other options. Hugo's villa and land probably weren't the only locations they were considering.

She was still torn about the whole thing. On the one hand, she knew Hugo couldn't survive financially for much longer the way things were. On the other, she hated the thought of the villa being demolished to make way for a soulless hotel. But what else was he supposed to do?

She wished she was in a position to buy it off him, Maybe if she found a job, she could suggest that she'd continue to live at the villa and pay rent. Would that help? It might, she mused, but it wouldn't solve the problem of those fields going to ruin, would it?

She was having increasingly frequent conversations with herself like this one, but despite all her pondering and planning, she wasn't getting anywhere.

'Do you want me to drive?' she offered, when he emerged from his bedroom having changed into a pair of trousers and a clean white shirt.

'No, I shall drive.' Hugo had driven for the first time since his operation only a couple of days earlier, and now that he'd got his independence back, he seemed determined to enjoy it to the full.

'Where are we going?' she asked as she slid into the passenger seat.

'Playa San Juan. There is a *pescadería*, a fish shop, at the marina, and I need mussels and clams, *vieiras*, *gambones*, shrimp and lobster.'

'*Vieiras?*'

'*Sí*, er… like the shell.' He made a fan shape with his hands and Sophie took a guess.

'Scallops?'

'Yes, and *gambones* are prawns. We will have all this for the fish stew I will cook for you.'

Playa San Juan was a bustling town with a working harbour and Hugo found a parking spot within view of it. It was a gorgeous day, with the sun sparkling off the sea and small boats bobbing in the marina. It would be a nice place to live, she mused, wondering how far away Dominic's apartment was. It couldn't be far, because she remembered seeing the sea from his balcony.

She could see a stretch of sand and people sprawled out on towels, while others paddled and swam near the shore. Seeing them reminded her of the last beach she'd visited. It had been with Dominic and she wondered what he was doing this afternoon. She'd not spotted anyone in the water off the headland, because the waves were too small, and she hoped he might be in Mrs Tiggywinkle's. She'd not seen him for a few days, so she'd pop in later – it was good to keep in touch since she'd be sharing a kitchen with him in the not too distant future.

Hugo drove into the parking space, and Sophie dashed around to the driver's side as he carefully levered himself out of the seat, in case he needed a bit of extra support. He brushed her off with an impatient wave of his hand, using the other to hold onto the roof of the car until he was steady and sure of his footing on the rough paving.

'It is there,' he said, pointing to a row of wooden huts lining the side of the harbour wall.

Wrinkling her nose when she detected the unmistakable aroma of fish in the air, she eyed the shop with concern. It was a far cry from the sterile cleanliness of a supermarket, and thoughts of salmonella flitted through her mind.

'All the restaurants come to Alonso for their fish,' Hugo said. 'So if I want fish, good fish, then I come here too.'

She smiled a hello when Hugo introduced her to Alonso, then left them to it, finding the fishy stench too overpowering. Instead, she dawdled along the wide harbour walkway and admired the boats moored there.

Some of them were huge and must have cost a fortune. She strolled to the far end and took in the view of the now familiar banana fields which dotted the southern part of the island, interspersed with villages and hamlets and the occasional hotel. Her attention was drawn to an enormous red-brick complex in the distance, and she wondered if TZC's proposed hotel would look similar. The thought of the rugged beauty of the coast being marred by such a monstrosity (although the hotel she was looking at was probably really nice to stay in) made her feel incredibly sad.

To take her mind off it, she turned to look at Teide instead, just visible beyond a ridge of closer mountains. The sky was incredibly clear, with not a cloud in sight, the volcano appearing much closer without its customary haze. She couldn't imagine being in the UK right now, with the long, dark nights, damp chill in the air, and the grey of winter bleeding all the colour and joy out of life. She had no urge at all to return, no longing for the place of her birth, no homesickness. This was home now, and impulsively she opened her arms wide, closed her eyes, held her face up to the sky and did a twirl.

'Are you dancing?'

Sophie squeaked in alarm. 'Hugo, you made me jump.'

'You look happy.'

'I take it from the tone of your voice that it doesn't happen very often?' She slipped her arm through his and they headed slowly back the way they'd come.

'Not so often,' Hugo said, 'but I see how hard it has been for you.'

'Yeah, losing someone you love takes its toll.'

Hugo gave her a sharp look before saying, 'You will be fine. Look.' He held up an ancient cool box. 'I have our fish. Alonso has lent me this and packed it with ice. He is a good man, a kind man. He also knows his fish.'

'Fancy a coffee before we head back? My treat?' With the fish safely stored in ice, they didn't need to rush back to the villa.

'That would be nice.' Hugo grinned at her. 'And cake?'

'And cake,' she confirmed, so they found a café facing the sea and placed their order.

Sophie let out a contented sigh, a smile on her lips.

'Your mother, would she have liked it here, on Tenerife?' Hugo asked. When she didn't answer straight away, he added, 'I am sorry if talking of her makes you sad.'

'That's OK, I like talking about her. I don't do it nearly often enough.' She didn't really have anyone she could talk to, so it was nice that Hugo had brought it up. 'I think she would have loved it, the weather especially. It's such a perfect day – I can't believe it's nearly the middle of winter.'

'Ah, that is about to change, so Alonso said. We are going to have a storm.'

Sophie's eyebrows rose. 'Really?' She let her gaze wander over the calm sea and clear blue sky, the sun hot on her exposed skin.

'Yes. He is not wrong. It comes tomorrow, I think. The waves will be very big, very strong.'

'Dominic will be pleased.'

Hugo shook his head. 'Too big for surfing. Too dangerous.'

Although she knew that the Canary Islands were out in the Atlantic, she'd not really thought about it except to compare the temperature of the sea here to that of the Med, where it was considerably warmer, and she wondered just how big those waves would get. It was quite exciting to think there would be a storm, and worrying too, considering the villa was so exposed. Still, she reasoned, it had been standing for a good few years and had probably seen its fair share of bad weather.

'Do you get many storms on the island?' she asked.

'A few every year, just like we have rain sometimes in the south. The car is parked next to the Barranco de San Juan, where sometimes a river comes if there is much rain in the mountains.'

'Wow. Does *barranco* mean river, or stream?' she wanted to know, but when Hugo wasn't able to translate for her, she looked it up on her phone and saw that the word meant ravine.

'*Sí*, ravine. There are hundreds of them on the island. Tenerife has water under the rocks, and when that water becomes too great because of the rain, the *barrancas* are like rivers. Small rivers,' he laughed, 'little, not like your English rivers.' He'd watched the BBC news with her the other evening, when flooding had been reported because of all the rain, and he'd marvelled at how green her native land was.

'There is a *barranca*, Barranca de la Punta Blanca, which comes from the mountain and ends where you watch the surfers.'

'There is? I hadn't noticed it.'

'It is small, just a little…' He made a V shape with his hands. 'It comes down behind Luis's farm. You do not see it because you are too busy watching the surfers,' he said with a smile.

'Yes, you're probably right,' she admitted, 'and even when they're not there, I'm always looking at the sea.'

'You will miss it when you go back home.' It was a statement, not a question, and she decided that now was the right time to tell him about Dominic's apartment.

'I don't think I will be going back to England. Not yet, anyway. When my time with you is up, Dominic has suggested I move in with him.'

Hugo was reaching for his coffee, but his hand stilled and he gave her a sharp look. 'Dominic Brockman? He wants you to live with him?'

'Yes.'

'I see.' He picked up his coffee, then put it down again before he'd taken a sip. 'I wish... but no. It is impossible.'

'What is?'

'For you to stay at the villa. No, it is better that you accept Dominic's offer. But please make sure that this is what you want. For a while, I thought... ah, never mind.'

'Oh, you think—? It's not like that. He said I could live with him until I get another job and can afford a place of my own.'

'It might not be like that now, but Dominic is hand-some and *encantador*, and soon you will be in love with him.'

She made a mental note to look up the word 'encan-tador' later. 'I doubt it. I don't feel that way about him, not like—' She stopped herself just in time. Hugo didn't need to know that she was pining after his nephew – it might make things awkward between them. Maybe it was for the best if he did think that she and Dominic had something going on, despite her protests to the contrary.

Anything would be better than seeing the pity on his face when he realised that she had fallen in love with a man who lived several thousand miles away and was already taken.

Chapter 33

'Encantador' meant charming, she discovered later, after they'd returned to the villa and she'd completed her chores for the day. Hugo was certainly right about that – Dominic was charming, but she didn't hold that against him, and she desperately tried not to compare his sunny, outgoing personality with Alex's more introverted and serious ways. The two men were polar opposites and each of them invoked different feelings in her. The one was more like a brother, the other…? The least said about that the better, she thought.

Giving herself a mental shake, she took her coffee out onto the terrace and was surprised to see how angry the ocean had become. This afternoon it had been almost millpond calm, but now it was a mass of white-crested waves, and the boom of them hitting the shore was louder than she'd ever heard it. She pitied anyone out in a boat in these conditions; although she expected most of the tourist vessels would be safely moored, there was still the occasional fishing boat braving the sea.

'The storm, she is coming,' Hugo said, taking the mug she held out to him.

'So I see. I can't decide whether I'm excited or scared.'

'Both, perhaps. There is nothing like the mountains or the sea to make you feel small. You cannot fight nature; all you can do is accept it.'

That sounded like good advice for her personal life too. There was no point in bemoaning her lot – she needed to accept it and learn to live with it. Eventually her feelings for Alex would fade until they became bittersweet memories, but until then all she could do was to ride it out, the same way she was still riding out the loss of her mother.

Grief reared its head again and stared her in the eye, and she knew it was going to be one of those nights where sleep would refuse to come. Oh, well, she reasoned resolutely, the noise of the approaching storm would probably have kept her awake anyway.

She decided she'd better take Paco for his evening walk before things got any worse, and needing to stretch her legs and hoping that the freshening air would blow away her swirling emotions, she called to the dog.

'I'll be about an hour,' she said to Hugo.

'Be careful. It is dark and the sea is rough. I do not like you going out alone at night.'

'I always take Paco for a walk in the evening,' she replied. 'I'll be careful. It's not like I'm about to go clambering over the rocks or anything.'

'I worry about you.' He beckoned her over to him and indicated that she should bend down. Planting a kiss on her cheek, he said, 'I have become very... er... I don't have the English word for it, but you are like a daughter to me.'

'Aw...' Sophie's eyes filled with tears and she blinked them away. 'I am very fond of you too, and I promise I'll be careful.' She kissed his cheek and gave him a hug.

Although she'd miss not living at the villa with Hugo, at least she'd still be able to visit him (wherever he might be). They had become friends rather than employer and employee, and she was so pleased she didn't have to leave the island, because she knew she'd do nothing but worry about him if she did.

The wind was up, buffeting her so that her hair whipped about her face in wild tangles. Paco's ears flapped and his thick fur rippled as the wind caught it. And that was before they'd even left the protection of the villa's garden walls. It wasn't cold, although the temperature was a little lower than usual, and she decided against going back and fetching a coat. The sky was still relatively clear, so the likelihood of rain in the next hour or so was minimal. Anyway, she was British – this was nothing but a stiff breeze!

The sea was impressive, though, and even in the darkness she could see the foam churned up by a mixture of wave and wind action. It had become worse in the short amount of time between taking her coffee onto the terrace and venturing onto the coastal path.

Movement caught her eye, and she glanced around to see the remnants of Hugo's banana plants being blown this way and that. A shadow on the track made her pause, and she could have sworn there was a person standing there, some way along it. But when she pulled her hair away from her face, it was gone, so she must have imagined it. No one else would be daft enough to venture out on a night like this, and if anyone else had a mind to walk their dog or go for a jog, then they'd most likely stick to the more sheltered streets of Alcalá or La Arena. She had the path to herself, just how she liked it.

Paco, lower to the ground and with four paws anchoring him rather than her two slightly unsteady ones (crikey, but that wind really was strong), fared better than she was doing, and seemed to be enjoying himself, lifting his muzzle into the wind and snuffling.

She had to laugh at him; there was nothing quite so joyous as a happy dog. Even in the dark, she could see his flopping tongue and the ecstatic expression on his face. The headland was calling, and although she had no intention of sitting on her favourite bit of rock, she was determined to make it that far. She had a feeling that the waves hitting the shore there would be spectacular indeed, even at night, when all she could see at the moment was surging blackness and the pale grey of the spray in the distance.

'Wow,' she muttered, seeing a plume of airborne water surge into the air. It was certainly exhilarating and—

She halted as Paco let out a low growl, barely audible above the wind blowing in her ears and the mighty boom of the sea. He brushed against her leg, leaning into her slightly, and she turned to face the way they'd come, and peered into the night.

'What is it, boy?' she asked, knowing he'd understand her meaning, even if the words themselves were incomprehensible to him.

He growled again and this time she felt, as well as heard, his warning, as his chest rumbled against her legs. She reached out and stroked his head, feeling his body's stiffness through his fur. There was no doubt that he was on high alert, and a frisson of unease travelled down her spine.

Should she turn back and confront whoever (*whatever* – because her mind was going into overdrive and she was imagining all kinds of things) lurked in the deep shadows? Or should she keep going towards the headland (in the opposite direction to whatever was out there) and hope that Paco was hearing things and would calm down?

She kept going. After all, it might well be someone as daft as her, braving the wind to walk their dog, and Paco was simply growling at the other pooch. He didn't usually react much to other dogs, but sometimes one would get his back up for no apparent reason, and he'd let it know in no uncertain terms that it wasn't welcome and that he wasn't to be trifled with.

If the person was a jogger, then they should be near enough for her to see them by now; unless they were really, really slow. That was also assuming it was a person and not some weird creature native to Tenerife that had claws and fangs big enough to make Paco growl...

It must be a dog walker, she concluded, and began walking along the path once more, Paco keeping pace at her side. Nevertheless, she couldn't help looking over her shoulder every so often. Once, she was certain she saw a shape moving on the path, but it could just as easily have been a shadow caused by the wind gusting through one of the low scrubby bushes.

As she drew closer to the headland any thoughts of being followed (*stalked? hunted?*) vanished from her mind at the sight before her. The waves were enormous, smacking into the rocks with a slow, inevitable majesty, breaking in huge plumes of spray high in the air. The smell of salt and seaweed stung her nose, not unpleasantly, and a fine mist of windborne water coated her from her hair to her trainers. It was thrilling and breathtaking, and more than a little awe-inspiring. Never had she witnessed such raw power in nature, and she felt humbled, her own problems fading into insignificance at the spectacle. The sound of the sea was a continuous roar, filling her ears and her mind until there was no room for anything else. A wild excitement coursed through her, making her heart sing at the sheer beauty of it all. The island had so many faces, and she was thankful that she was able to see this one. No wonder people lost their hearts to it...

But that wasn't all she'd lost her heart to, was it, and she remembered sitting almost in this very spot, watching the man she loved (yes, *loved*, she might as well admit it to herself), be whisked away in a giant tin can thousands of feet above her.

A deep ache settled in her heart to join the other emotions whirling through it.

But at least she felt alive, incredibly alive. Gone was the all-consuming numbness of the last few months of her mother's life, the denial, the soul-crushing grief. Now she felt everything, both good and bad, and she rejoiced in it, even as the sorrow of losing her mum and the pain of loving a man who'd never love her back gouged deep cracks in her heart and soul. She'd survive. Somehow.

Paco growled, the sound vibrating through the air, and she whirled around, fear pumping adrenaline to her fingers and toes. They tingled and throbbed in response, and she fought the urge to run. Which way should she go? She squinted at the path, wondering where the danger was, but there was nothing obvious.

Something had certainly spooked Paco, though, because the growls grew louder, more menacing, a clear warning to whoever it was to back off. She was thoroughly scared now, and her fear intensified as the dog took a couple of stiff-legged steps forward, putting himself between her and whoever was out there.

Slimy Guy's face sprung into her mind, and she swallowed convulsively. What if it was him? She *knew* he'd made a threat; she *knew* it. It hadn't been her imagination. And now he, or someone sent by him, was making good on it.

Maybe they just meant to scare her? If so, they were doing a damned good job of it, because she'd never been so frightened in all her life.

With the angry sea at her back and a person or persons in front who might wish her harm, her only defence was the dog. And although he looked formidable with his raised hackles and alert stance, she wasn't prepared to risk endangering him. What if they had a knife? Or worse?

Maybe she could edge around the rocks and double back that way? Right now, she was standing on a relatively flat piece of ground between the path and the rocks proper. But if she crept forward a bit, she could pick her way over the rugged boulders and head for the pebbles which formed the precarious and not very comfortable beach to one side of the villa. It would involve a lot of clambering and would take a great deal of effort, not to mention be rather dangerous, but it was preferable to meeting whoever was waiting for her on the path.

Paco made her mind up for her. Abruptly his growls turned to outright snarls, and the fine hairs at the back of her neck rose in response. The snarling turned into fierce barking, and she caught a glimpse of gleaming fangs and the whites of the dog's eyes. He meant business.

'Come, boy,' she said quietly, 'let's go.'

The dog looked at her, wagged his tail once, then turned back to face the threat.

'Paco!' she hissed. There was no way on earth she was going to leave him here while she fled to safety. This was nothing to do with him; he was an innocent animal, doing his best to protect her, and she'd never forgive herself if anything happened to him.

The sooner she got him away from here the better, and the villa was their only real hope. She briefly debated trying to reach Luis's house, but there wasn't a single light on. Besides, the person or persons unknown were between her and the farmhouse, and she doubted she'd be able to make it in time.

The villa it would have to be. And the only way to reach it was to clamber over the rocks, risking a broken ankle and a drenching. The soaking was a sure thing. As for the ankle, she'd just have to be really, really careful.

'Paco, *ven aca*, come here,' she commanded, and moved closer to the rocks and the spuming, frothing sea.

To her relief, the dog ceased barking and followed, still growling his warning, hackles still raised, his movements stiff and threatening. But at least he was going with her and not staying to see off the danger. She put a hand on his fluffy head, and he stopped growling long enough to nudge her with his nose. 'It's going to be OK, boy,' she muttered. 'Everything's going to be OK. Argh!'

A wave broke, larger than most, spray rising high into the air and falling back down, drenching her in the process. She spluttered as seawater cascaded over her face, making her eyes sting. Blimmin' heck, that was *cold*!

Using her hands to grip the rocks as she scrambled over them, and wincing at the scrape of her skin against them, she picked her way slowly and carefully closer to the water. Paco whined uneasily, hanging back.

'Come on, boy, it's OK. See?' She straightened and turned to him, and—

The wave was colossal and as it slammed into the shore, a wall of water shot skywards and cascaded down on her. Instinctively she grabbed for a handhold, her fingers grasping a sharp, jagged boulder. Her skin tore, and she jerked her hand back with a cry of pain, and lost her grip.

Unbalanced, she felt the wave pick her up and drag her back, pulling her into the boiling, churning sea.

Letting out a scream of terror, she took one last desperate breath before her head was underwater and the sea claimed her.

Chapter 34

Her mind was screaming but her mouth was firmly shut, as she desperately held that one final breath inside and fought to reach the surface. Not knowing which way was up, the water turning her over and over, she struck out, her arms flailing, her legs kicking frantically.

She didn't know how much longer she could hold out. Her lungs were burning with an agony greater than she'd ever known, and the need to breathe was overwhelming. *Just another second*, she pleaded. *Please, just another second and I'll—*

Something grabbed the collar of her jacket and she felt herself being dragged through the water. Terrified, she thrashed wildly, bubbles streaming from her mouth as she lost the last bit of precious air, then her head broke the surface and she sucked in a huge lungful, spluttering and coughing. Her head went under again, but she kicked with all her might, the pressure on her collar tightening, pulling her back up.

Something struck her on the back, once, twice, three times, and she had the impression she was being towed…

Paco! It was Paco who had hold of her, his jaws on her collar, his sturdy webbed paws powering rhythmically through the roiling surf. She twisted in his grasp, the better to keep her face from being submerged, and she heard his laboured breathing, loud and harsh in her ear.

In the darkness she was unable to tell if he was winning the fight, but she spluttered another snatched breath and swam with him, using her arms and legs to help him drive through the waves, until exhaustion claimed her and she just hung there, her only thought being to keep her head above water.

Once, faintly, she thought she heard someone shout her name, but it might have been the wind or the sea calling to her, urging her to let go, to cease her fruitless struggle and let peace claim her. She was so tired, so desperately, utterly tired…

Paco whuffed through his nose, his breath hot on her neck, and one of his claws raked her back, the pain jolting her out of her stupor. If she didn't try to help the dog again then both of them would surely die. And there was no way she was prepared to let Paco drown.

A fresh surge of energy filled her, and with one final desperate lunge, she struck out in the direction Paco was heading.

Pebbles shifted beneath her, and sharp rocks battered her feet as she kicked.

Waves broke over her head, again and again. Then Paco's paws were biting on solid ground, his weight and strength carrying them both forward until she was on her knees and crawling up the slope, each wave threatening to drag her back into the watery depths. Paco shook violently beside her and snorted to clear his nose. Then hands grabbed her roughly underneath her arms and hauled her clear of the sea.

A man's voice called her name, panic-filled and terrified. A dog's soft breath was on her cheek. A hand on her
face. A kiss, hot on her cold lips.

Darkness.

Nothing.

Chapter 35

Sunbeams were shining behind her eyelids, flashing pink, green and orange as Sophie slowly came to. She lay there for a while, not wanting to wake up just yet, but there was something not quite right...

Strange noises assaulted her ears, and her nose was filled with an odd antiseptic smell. Together they brought a flood of memories rushing back to haunt her, of the days and weeks spent at her mother's bedside as she underwent various treatments.

Her eyes flew open and she tried to sit up, before falling back into the pillows with a groan of pain.

She knew exactly where she was and the reason why.

'Paco?' Her voice sounded thin and weak, the word lost amidst the bustle beyond her room.

But someone heard her.

Alex, sitting near the door, got slowly to his feet. Sophie stared at him, unable to take in what she was seeing. Was that really him?

'*Gracias a Dios*,' he breathed.

He didn't move, just kept staring at her. His dark eyes were strained, his clothes rumpled and creased, his expression serious.

'Paco?' she repeated.

'He's fine. Do you remember what happened?'

'Yes. Some of it.'

'Good.'

'I don't remember being brought here.'

'You kept slipping in and out of consciousness. The doctors suspected you might have had water in your lungs.'

'That's not good.'

'No.' He swallowed and looked up at the ceiling, blinking hard. 'You could have died. You nearly did. If it wasn't for Paco...'

'How did I get here?'

'I brought you in the car.'

She gingerly eased her body up the bed until she was reclining rather than lying flat on her back. 'There's a lot more to it than that,' she guessed, her voice growing a little stronger to her immense relief. 'Tell me.'

'I heard you scream,' Alex said. 'I didn't see you go into the sea, but I saw Paco leap in after you. He dragged you to the beach, or what was left of it with the sea being so high. I took over from there.'

'I remember you calling my name. I thought I was dreaming.' She brought her hand up to her face and touched her lips. 'You kissed me.'

'CPR.'

'I didn't stop breathing.'

'How do you know you didn't?'

'I just know. You kissed me.'

'I did CPR,' he insisted.

She shrugged, wincing as the movement sent aches and pains around her body. 'Did I break anything?' She wiggled one foot, then the other.

'No, you were lucky.'

'There was a man. At least, I think it was a man. He might have been following me, I'm not sure.'

'I didn't see anyone, but I heard Paco barking when I arrived at the villa. It didn't sound like him – I've never heard him bark like that before – but Hugo knew it was him and that something was wrong. He thought you'd been swept away.'

'I almost was.' She shivered, the memory of the dark, dark sea still too fresh and raw. It would be a long time before she did more than dip her toe in it again. If ever.

'I think I already have been.' Alex's teeth caught his bottom lip, and he reddened and glanced down at the floor.

'Why are you here?' she asked.

'I brought you here, remember? I wasn't going to leave you in hospital all alone.'

'No, I mean, why are you back on Tenerife?'

'Ah, you are awake, no?' The voice belonged to a man in a white coat with a pen in his pocket, a pair of glasses perched on his nose, and a stethoscope around his neck.

He checked her over, asking her questions, shining a light in her eyes, listening to her chest, front and back. Alex had slipped out into the corridor at the start of the doctor's examination, and she heard him talking to someone in Spanish just outside the door when the doctor left.

Alex returned, and the weariness and worry in his face had been replaced by smiles.

'The doctor said I can go home,' she told him, studying his expression, waiting for a reaction, good or bad.

His smile grew wider. 'I know. That is the best news. Speaking of news, I have some too.'

She froze, hoping he wasn't about to tell her he was getting married.

'It's about Hugo,' he added.

Oh, yes, of course. Hugo. How could she have forgotten?

'He does not have to sell the villa,' Alex said.

Sophie took a deep breath and let it out in a rush. 'That's wonderful news! How did you manage that?'

'Do you know Luis?'

'He owns the fields next to Hugo's.'

'That's right. He also now owns most of Hugo's fields. Or he will do when the *abogado*, the solicitor, has drawn up the contract.'

'Will it be enough so that he doesn't have to worry about money for a while?' Not that she had any idea how much farmland cost over here, but she was pretty certain the money from the sale wouldn't last indefinitely.

'I will be helping Hugo with the bills, and everything else, so he will be fine.'

What did he mean by *everything else*? Did he mean that it was time for her to go? Nooo, she wasn't ready. Not yet.

'I don't understand,' she said in a small voice, wishing someone would fetch her clothes so she could dress and get out of here. 'Does Hugo want me to leave?'

Alex chuckled, the sound sending shivers down her back and making her stomach do an odd little flip. 'He says you can stay at the villa for as long as you want.'

'*I can?*'

'Apparently he likes having you around.' Alex cleared his throat, his attention on the less than inspiring view through the window. 'So do I.'

Now she really didn't understand. It was all too much to take in.

She shook her head slowly, thinking hard. 'I can get a job and help pay the bills and—'

Alex held up a hand. 'As I said, he will not need any help from you. I'm to pay the bills. It will save me renting, and I love the villa.'

She shook her head. 'Now I'm really confused.'

Alex took a step closer, then another, until he was standing right next to her bed. 'I'm sorry, I'm not making myself clear; I am going to live at the villa.'

'You are?'

'With Hugo – and with you, if you would like to stay.' The smile faded from his face to be replaced by uncertainty. 'Unless, of course, you still intend to move in with Dominic Brockman?'

'But what about Iceland? And your girlfriend?'

'I don't have a girlfriend.' His brows drew together as he frowned. 'I don't have a job in Iceland any more either.' He took hold of her hand. 'I have just accepted a position at INVOLCAN. My home will now be on Tenerife and I will live at the villa.'

Sophie was speechless, the words sticking in her chest, which seemed to be swelling to unmanageable proportions as joy swept through her.

'You're not happy about this?' he asked, all trace of brooding Darcy-ness gone. How on earth could she have thought he was grumpy? He looked uncertain and worried, and rather vulnerable.

'I am very happy,' she said.

He squeezed her hand and she squeezed his back.

'Good. I was worried that you might not want me at Villa Delfin. Or that you would still want to move in with Dominic.'

'You don't like him much, do you?'

'I was jealous of him because I thought you liked him. And he's a bit of a player too. From what I've heard, he doesn't believe in commitment.'

'And you do?'

'Most definitely.'

They were still holding hands, and Sophie pulled him down to her, his face inches from hers.

'And I was jealous because I thought you had someone special in Iceland. When I phoned you I heard a woman laughing.'

Alex frowned then his brow cleared as she realised what she was referring to. 'That was Angetta, a colleague. There was a group of us out that night. I do not have a girlfriend,' he repeated.

'I'm so glad. You do realise we'll be living in the same house?' she murmured.

'I do. It will be wonderful.'

'Not in the same bedroom,' she warned.

He gave her a hurtful look. 'I think we need to get to know one another better before that happens, don't you?'

'Good. I don't want you getting the wrong idea. Now kiss me, then go and ask someone where my clothes are so I can get dressed.'

The kiss took far, far longer than either of them had anticipated... But neither of them were complaining at the end of it.

Chapter 36

Last night seemed like a lifetime ago. When Sophie got out of the car – the back seat still damp from Alex's mad dash to the hospital, with her semi-conscious – the sea was its usual relatively calm self, the storm having blown over during the night and the early part of the morning. Apart from a few palm fronds scattered on the path and her tomato plants looking the worse for wear, no one would ever guess anything untoward had happened last night.

Hugo and Paco were waiting anxiously by the door for her, and Hugo enveloped her in a big hug the moment she stepped through it. Paco leaned against her leg, and she nudged him gently with her thigh in acknowledgement.

Hugo buried his nose in her hair and muttered, 'I thought I had lost you…' He trailed off, and sniffed again, and when she pulled back to kiss his cheek, his eyes were wet with unshed tears.

'I'm fine,' she assured him. 'A little bruised and I've got aches in places I didn't know could ache, but that's all.'

'I told you not to go too near the sea. It is dangerous when it is rough.' He threaded his arm through hers and led her into the living room, settling her on the sofa and sitting down next to her, holding her hand. Paco followed, so closely that his nose kept bumping into her leg.

'Bring tea,' Hugo called to Alex. 'With sugar.' He lowered his voice a little and said to her, 'It is good for the shock.'

'I'm not in shock. Can I have coffee instead, without the sugar?' She ruffled Paco's ears and the big dog landed a sloppy wet tongue on her cheek. She laughed and gave him a one-armed cuddle, because Hugo was still gripping her other hand, refusing to let go.

Hugo narrowed his eyes, searching her face. 'Are you sure you are OK?'

'They wouldn't have sent me home if I wasn't.'

'Alejandro, coffee not tea, and no sugar,' Hugo yelled.

Home, she'd said *home*. 'Can I really stay here with you?'

'Do you want to? Or would you prefer to live with Dominic?'

'I want to stay here,' she replied firmly and without hesitation.

'It won't just be me…'

'I know, Alex told me.' It was her turn to scrutinise Hugo. She hadn't noticed it when she'd seen him at the door because she'd been too busy being hugged by him, but now that she had a chance to examine him properly, she realised there was something different; he looked younger, less fraught, less worried.

'It is good news, yes?' he said, beaming.

'Yes, it most certainly is.'

'I knew he liked you from the start.'

'Excuse me?'

'Alejandro. And you like him. I can tell.'

That wasn't what she'd meant, but perhaps Hugo didn't know that she knew about TZC, the Russian offer, or his financial problems, so she decided not to mention anything. Changing the subject, she said, 'About last night – someone was following me. Paco heard them, and when he began snarling and barking, I thought the only thing to do was to skirt around the rocks and try to get back to the villa that way. Then a wave hit and I—' She gulped back sudden tears, her eyes stinging and her throat burning. 'Paco saved my life. He jumped in after me and pulled me to the shore.'

'I know,' Hugo said, looking up at Alex as he entered the room holding a couple of cups of coffee. 'Alejandro came to the villa, and when I opened the door to him, I heard Paco barking. He never barks, so I knew something was wrong. Alejandro went looking for you and found you and Paco on the beach. He took you to hospital.' Hugo's expression had grown solemn. 'We did not know whether you would survive.' He hugged her again, his voice breaking.

'I'm fine,' she said, tears wetting her cheeks. 'More importantly, how's Paco? He looks OK, but…?'

'He's good. Tired, worried about you, but he is not hurt.'

'He's one very brave dog, aren't you, boy?' She leaned forward to put both arms around his neck and he snuggled into her, whuffing softly in her ear. 'Thank you,' she whispered in his.

She'd buy him the biggest steak she could find, she vowed, because without his bravery and total disregard for his own life, she wouldn't be here. Tears threatened again, and she blinked them back. She'd done enough crying in recent months. Now was the time for rejoicing. She had a place to live, with two people (three if you counted the dog) she had come to care for deeply, and Hugo's problems were solved. All she needed to do now was to find herself a job so she could contribute to the upkeep of the villa. She had no intention of scrounging off either Hugo or Alex. Besides, now that Hugo was almost back to normal (another couple of weeks should see to that), she'd be bored. She had to do something with her life, otherwise it would be like she was on a perpetual holiday, and as nice as that was, it would grow stale eventually.

'Shall I start lunch?' she asked, wanting to get back to normal. Her stomach was rumbling and although it was getting on for mid-afternoon, she needed to eat. Alex too, because she guessed he'd been sitting by her bedside ever since he'd taken her to the hospital last night.

Alex. Just the thought of him sent little tremors through her.

She glanced up to find him watching her, a small smile playing about his lips, his dark eyes full of love.

Could she hope that…?

It was too early, too soon for anything like that. They barely knew each other. They'd have to share many more kisses before the L word was mentioned, if indeed it ever would be.

'You are not doing anything, *pequeña*. I shall make us a snack. You're to rest for a couple of days, at least.'

'But—'

'No.' He held up a hand to stop her. 'I insist. Hugo insists. You are not to do anything, not today, not tomorrow.'

She bit her lip, trying to look as though she was going to comply. She probably would for today, because she had to admit she felt washed out and was still sore and achy, but as for tomorrow…? She'd wait for Alex to go to work, then she'd—

'I know what you're thinking, and it's not going to happen. I don't start my new job for a week. I will be here to keep an eye on you and make sure you don't overdo it tomorrow, and the next day, and the one after that. Then we shall see. In the meantime, tell me what needs doing and I shall do it.'

Sophie screwed up her face, thinking. OK, if that's the way he wanted to play it, then she'd see what jobs she could find. She'd certainly enjoy bossing him around and giving him a taste of his own medicine.

'All the beds need changing for a start, and the windows could do with a clean. Then Paco could probably do with a bath after his dip last night, and you'll have to check all the plants to see which ones can be saved, plus they'll need to be watered thoroughly to make sure all the salt spray is washed off them, otherwise you'll lose them. After that, the villa should be swept and—'

'OK, OK, I get the message. You're going to keep me busy as a punishment for not letting you do anything.'

She smiled innocently up at him. 'Would I do such a thing?'

'Yes.' He said something in Spanish to Hugo and Hugo saluted.

'What did you just say? You do know it's rude to speak Spanish when you know I don't understand.'

'Which is exactly why I did it. I told Hugo to make sure you don't move off the sofa while I make us a meal, even if he has to make Paco sit on you to keep you there.'

Paco whined, his tongue drooping comically out of the side of his mouth, and Sophie could have sworn he

281

understood what was expected of him, because he placed one heavy paw on her lap as if to hold her down.

'I'll get bored,' she warned, as Alex, clearly thinking he'd won the argument, turned to leave.

He stopped and looked at her, a wicked expression on his face and a twinkle in those gorgeous dark eyes. 'I'll just have to find something to keep you occupied, then, won't I?' And with that he gave her a wide smile which sent her heart racing and a pulse leaping at her throat.

Kissing him for hours on end would certainly keep her occupied, all right.

Chapter 37

'Sophie, there's someone here to see you,' Hugo called from inside the house.

She was supposed to be relaxing on the terrace while Alex walked Paco (she was actually covertly giving it a good going over with a broom, and she could see the pair of them in the distance, sauntering along the path towards the headland. The thought that she could have so easily died there sent a shudder through her, and she was glad of the distraction of a visitor.

'Dominic!' she exclaimed, when she walked into the living room and saw him standing in the doorway. 'What a nice surprise. What are you doing here? Please, take a seat. Would you like a coffee?'

'No, thanks, I'm not staying,' he said, making no move to sit down. 'I just stopped by to see how you are. I heard about what happened. Are you all right?'

'I'm fine, although Alex and Hugo haven't stopped fussing over me. Between you and me, they're driving me mad.'

Bless him, Dominic was looking serious and concerned for once. 'The sea is dangerous,' he said. 'Especially where we surf.'

Yeah, she'd found that out for herself...

'News travels fast,' she said. 'How do you know about my little escapade?' She was doing her best to make light of it, but her voice broke on the final word.

'My mother was told by one of the shopkeepers along the promenade, who'd heard it from someone he was having an early morning coffee with, who'd been told by...' He waved his hand in the air. 'Despite all the tourists, La Arena is a small place. We look after our own, and you're one of us now.'

'Er, um, about that. I'm sorry, but I'm not going to need your spare room after all.' She chewed at her lip, hating to let him down.

Dominic shrugged. 'No worries. Are you returning to the UK? I hope what you've been through isn't driving you away.'

'No, I'm staying here, at the villa. Hugo has said I can stay for as long as I want. I do need to get a job, though...'

'I could ask around for you, if you like. Do you have anything in mind? Bar work? Shop? Office?'

Sophie glanced at Hugo, who widened his eyes at her. 'I've no idea. I'm not really qualified for much, especially over here where I can't speak anything except English.'

'That shouldn't be a problem – most people have a smattering of English, regardless of their nationality, and as there are so many Brits over here, both expats and tourists, you should be fine. Leave it with me. I promise I'll ask around.' He took a step towards the door, then paused. 'I nearly forgot.' He handed her a bag. 'It's a bone, for Paco. My mum got it from the butcher for him.'

'Oh, that's so kind of her. Thank her for me, will you?'

'You can thank her yourself next time you're in the shop,' he said. 'Come here.'

He beckoned her closer and gave her a hug.

Just at that moment, Alex arrived back with Paco. The dog wagged his tail at Dominic. Alex's reaction wasn't quite as friendly; in fact, he positively scowled.

'Dominic came by with a bone for Paco,' she said. 'I've told him I'm not taking him up on the offer of his spare room.'

Alex nodded curtly but didn't say a word, and after she'd seen Dominic to the door, she rounded on him angrily.

'You didn't need to be so rude.'

'I'm sorry.' His reply was short and he didn't appear to be the least bit remorseful.

'What's got into you?'

'I don't like him.'

'Why ever not?'

'Because he suggested you move in with him.'

Sophie shook her head. 'It's not like that. He was just being kind.'

'Hmm.'

She rolled her eyes. 'Think what you want, but Dominic sees me as a friend, the same way I see him. Nothing more.'

He gave her a long, level look, before nodding again, this time in acceptance. 'I'm sorry. It's just…' He sighed. 'It doesn't matter.' With a visible effort, he changed the subject. 'I have news. A man *was* following you last night; you didn't imagine it. It was a drunk on his way home. I met him a few minutes ago. Paco must have recognised him and barked at him, and the man said that the dog had scared the life out of him last night. He thought Paco was going to attack him.'

Sophie sagged against the arm of the chair. Thank God for that! She hadn't really wanted to believe that someone was out to do her harm, but Slimy Guy had unnerved her a bit, and she honestly wouldn't have been surprised if he really had threatened her and then made good on it.

'That's a relief,' she said. 'I was a little concerned, to say the least. Now that I can sleep at night, the final thing to sort out is a job. Dominic said he'd keep an ear open for me.'

Hugo grunted. 'You do not have to worry about a job.'

'Yes, I do,' she insisted. 'I don't intend to live at the villa without pulling my weight.'

'Tell her,' Hugo said, and Sophie looked at Alex.

'I told you that Tío didn't sell all his land; he kept two fields back – the ones either side of the track. He wants you to have them, for vegetables and… chickens?' Alex's voice rose on the last word. 'You want to keep chickens?'

'Well, yes, but that's not a proper job, is it?' she objected.

'Maybe not, but you will be able to produce enough fruit, vegetables and eggs for the villa, and when Hugo begins to fish again, that will contribute to the food on our table. You can sell the excess to local restaurants, which will give you some income too.'

'Give *us* some income,' she pointed out. 'Considering the land actually belongs to Hugo, then it's only fair that anything grown on it is his too.'

'Have it your way, but it won't be an easy ride for you. Clearing those fields will take a great deal of hard work.'

Sophie wasn't bothered – she didn't mind hard work – and she was thrilled that she'd have the opportunity to do more of what she'd begun to find so satisfying and enjoyable. Of course, she'd still have to get a proper job, but suddenly the future was looking very rosy indeed.

She flung her arms around Hugo and rained kisses on his lined face, full of gratitude for his kindness. He was such a sweetheart, and she had grown to think of him as family.

'When you've finished, do I get a turn?' Alex asked. 'I think I deserve a kiss too.'

He most certainly did, and Sophie made a point of giving him several until Hugo reminded them that he was still there by coughing loudly, and even Paco whined until Alex released her with a final kiss on her nose and a look that told her there was more where that came from.

As she looked at the two men who had entered her life, her heart was filled with love and gratitude, and she finally felt she had found somewhere she could call home in this little Spanish villa by the sea.

Chapter 38

Sightseeing wasn't quite what Sophie had envisaged when Alex had promised to keep her occupied, as he drove them through the pretty town of Santiago del Teide with its quaint square and lovely old church with a bell on the top, and out the other side of the town. As they passed through, she stared wistfully at the restaurant where they'd shared their first meal; it felt like such a long time ago. So much had happened since then.

'Where are we going?' she wanted to know.

'A town called Garachico, on the other side of the island. I know a lovely little place that does the best paella, right on the seafront.' He hesitated and shot her a quick look. 'If you don't mind being near the sea again. I didn't think—'

'Don't be silly. If I had a problem with the sea, I wouldn't be able to live in the villa, would I?' she teased.

She still couldn't believe it; it was too good to be true. There was a little nagging doubt regarding what would happen if her and Alex's very young and very tentative relationship fell apart, but she tried to ignore it. She honestly didn't want to consider the possibility. It might just break her heart…

Beyond Santiago del Teide, the road rose sharply, twisting and winding through the mountains. They passed a couple of places to pull in and admire the view of the surprisingly green valley below and the majestic Teide in the distance. It was picture-postcard beautiful, and showed her yet another face of this remarkable island.

What was even more beautiful was the view from the other side of the mountains as they began the descent down to the coast once more. They had driven over the ridged spine of the island and in front of them the land dropped steeply down to the sea. She could see the road hairpinning below them, and she swallowed a little nervously, thankful that it was Alex behind the wheel and not her.

The ocean looked huge, a vast expanse of blue, navy and turquoise glittering and sparkling in the sun, and the towns and villages strung out along the coast seemed very small and far away indeed.

Without warning, they pulled over into a lay-by and Alex indicated that they should get out of the car. They walked towards the wooden barrier which was all that separated them from a precipitous drop, and he pointed to a small town below.

'Garachico, said to be the prettiest town in Tenerife. But then, several others lay claim to the same title. We are spoilt for choice – there are so many beautiful places. You'll see how lovely this one is when we get there, and I have so many others to show you.' He turned to her, a soft smile lighting his face, his eyes liquid chocolate as she gazed into them. 'I'll make you fall in love with the island, so you will never leave.'

'I don't think I ever want to leave here,' she murmured as he came closer.

His arms wrapped around her, pulling her to him, and she sank into his embrace. As his mouth descended on hers, she parted her lips and closed her eyes, losing herself in the delight of the passionate kiss.

When they eventually parted, she found that her legs were trembling, and a soaring excitement made her heart fizz and her senses reel with longing. She could stay here forever, she thought, content to be in his arms, her own coiled around his neck, holding him close.

He bumped noses with her, then kissed the tip. 'Hungry?'

She nodded, but it wasn't food she was hungry for. She wanted another kiss, then another, and maybe (definitely) several more after that. But he had other ideas and stepped away to take her hand and walk back to the car.

Garachico was every bit as lovely as he'd promised. From above, the glimpse she'd had of the town had suggested it was on the level, but as they came closer, she realised it was built on an incline. From the wide road which separated the sea from the buildings, the town rose above them in a series of whitewashed houses and cobbled streets.

She was dying to explore, but first they had lunch at an open-air restaurant surrounded by natural seawater pools in which children played and people swam.

'I've ordered paella for two,' Alex told her. 'I hope you don't mind.'

She didn't mind at all, and when it arrived in a huge, sizzling black skillet, her mouth watered. If it tasted as good as it looked, she was in for a treat indeed. Chunks of white fish, which Alex told her was monkfish, nestled in a bed of saffron rice, alongside mussels, king prawns, calamari, and the vibrant colours of green beans and red peppers. The dish was served with a simple basket of chunky cut bread and a drizzle of fragrant olive oil.

Alex poured them both a glass of crisp, chilled white wine, and he raised his in a toast. 'To us.'

'Is there an "us"?' she asked, her glass poised ready to clink against his.

'I really hope so. You are the reason I came back to Tenerife.'

'I am?' Her breath caught in her throat and her mouth was suddenly dry.

He nodded slowly. 'When I had a phone call from INVOLCAN asking me to view some data, I thought, I *assumed* that it would be a quick visit and I would see my uncle at the same time. What I saw was you, sitting up in bed, fists raised, ready to punch me. I think I fell in love with you right there and then.'

'Wait, *what*?' Had she heard him correctly? Did he just say he loved her? Oh, my Lord…

'Yes, I love you,' he said, somewhat defensively. 'Is that so bad?'

'No, it's… it's… wonderful!' she blurted, and the look of relief in his eyes made her want to cry.

'I understand we've only known each other for a short while, but this feels right. I've never felt like this about any woman before,' he said, reaching across the table with his free hand and placing it over hers, his fingers curling around her own. 'I also understand if you don't feel the same way, but please give it time. Time to get to know me properly. Time to fall in love with me, maybe? *Mierda!* I didn't mean to say all this, not yet.' A frown marred his handsome features, and she wanted nothing more than to kiss it away. 'I wanted you to have a good time today; not to declare my undying love.'

He actually looked rather cross with himself, and Sophie couldn't help giggling. 'You goose, I feel the same way about you too. I don't need time to fall in love with you, because I already am.'

'Thank God,' he whispered, and as he stared into her eyes she saw the love brimming in their depths, and her heart sang with sheer joy.

He loved her! And what a romantic place to declare it. How she'd ever thought him brooding and distant was beyond her.

'I love you,' she said. 'With all my heart. And I know we've not known each other long, but does it matter? We have all the time in the world and our whole lives before us, and I don't want to waste a single second of it.'

'I love you too, *mi amor*, more than you will ever know.'

He squeezed her hand and her heart was full to bursting. And as she sat there in the warm sunshine, the sea sparkling and a gentle breeze lifting her hair, she'd never felt so happy in her life. There was just one thing to cast a shadow on her bliss – she wished she could share her happiness and joy with her mum.

Raising her glass, she gazed at the azure sky, imagining her mother looking down at her. I love you, Mum, she thought. I'll always love you, and I'll carry you in my heart forever. Please be happy for me.

And when she felt the breeze brush across her face like the stroke of feather-light fingertips, she knew her mum approved.

Acknowledgements

Books like mine don't get written by themselves; actually they do – the first draft or three – but then a whole bunch of other people get involved. People like my editor, Emily Bedford, who deserves a mention and my heartfelt thanks for her steady guidance and support. Thanks, Emily.

I have to thank my husband for putting up with this writing obsession of mine, although he does have a cycling obsession of his own, so I suppose we can call it quits. Thanks also to my mum for reading my stuff, even though she prefers whodunnits; my daughter for being proud of her poor old mum; and you, my readers, for, well... everything else. You make the whole thing worthwhile. Thank you.